Addyson Elizabeth

TROUBLED SUMMERS

ADDISON ELIZABETH

ADDISON ELIZABETH

To the brightest lights in my world, my daughters,

I may have given life to you,

but you give me a reason to live.

Thank you for pushing me

to make my dreams come true.

TRIGGER WARNING

Please note that while this is a piece of fiction, there are scenes or conversations that may trigger adverse emotional reaction for some readers. While the author cannot identify all potential triggers for all readers, these are some that may affect readers:

- Recollection of police violence.

- Reference to drug and alcohol abuse.

- Reference to sexual abuse against a child, this does not include any depiction or description of the abuse.

- On page use of a firearm.

1

He watched her from afar, knowing if she saw him, everything would be over. He was a man obsessed. Driven by pain, by anger, by hatred, by vengeance, he wouldn't allow himself to fail.

Every time he saw her smile or laugh, he imagined her begging for her life. He imagined her apologizing for everything she had taken from him. He would stare into her eyes when he killed her, getting everything he dreamed of in return.

A slow smile pulled at the corners of his mouth, his fingers tracing the knife he kept at his side. "Soon," he whispered to himself, "Soon."

After a long flight, Eric Grayson walked out of the terminal where a loud whoop and a voice shouting, "Welcome home asshole!" greeted him. A grin spread over his face as he strode towards his friend and they embraced each other. "How was your flight, Eric?"

"Not bad," he replied. "The movie sucked, though."

His friend chuckled and cuffed him on the back as they skipped baggage claim and walked out into the sunlight. Eric was in his early thirties, broad shouldered and muscular, but still slim, with bright blue eyes thanks to his mother, and a head full of dark brown hair thanks to his father. He was 6'2" and was what most people considered handsome. And for better or worse, he was aware of that fact.

His buddy Mark looked like marriage suited him well. His once trim physique had developed into a softer one with the slight paunch of a man who enjoyed home-cooked meals with second helpings and a beer.

They had met in college when they were freshman dorm roommates. They had stayed close ever since, even after Mark moved to Podunksville, Nowhere, otherwise known as Spring Hills, Nebraska. Which Eric would now call home, too.

They strode through the parking lot, towards Mark's dirt covered pickup, and Eric's stomach tangled in knots. He had flipped between doubt and certainty for weeks now. Life in Los Angeles had gotten complicated, so with no safety net, he was starting over again.

As Mark drove, they made some small talk about nothing of importance and relaxed into comfortable silence. Eric pressed his forehead against the window beside him and the thoughts floating around in his head moved to what had brought him out to this no man's land.

A Los Angeles native, he attended UCLA and barely got a degree in criminal justice. After graduating, he joined the LAPD. At 28, he married a gorgeous, vivacious woman. It had been a whirlwind romance. A classic tale of the beauty and the boy in blue. It took 6 short months from that first, drunken night to "I do."

Unfortunately, the honeymoon period was short-lived. Two years after they were married, they split. Things were amicable, and by his thirty-first birthday, he was a divorced man.

His career was going well until a single moment changed all that. After finding the bottom of bottle after bottle for too many nights in a row, he stood in front of the mirror, hating himself. The reflection he saw reminded him too much of his father. Lost and unsure of what to do next, he called his brother, who didn't want to help, and then his friend Mark, who did.

Mark was the one who had told him about the opening at his local sheriff's department. A couple of Zoom interviews later and Eric got an offer. Without giving it much thought, he left his life in LA for a fresh start.

Mark's pickup struck a large pothole, knocking Eric's head against the window and snapping him out of his thoughts. He looked around and saw flat, tan nothingness for miles. "Thought you dozed off back there," Mark said, smiling.

"Yeah, kinda," Eric replied, shifting in his seat. "So, tell me more about Spring Hills." Eric had gotten the general overview from Mark before, but hadn't thought the details were too important until now.

"Well, it's a small, classic Midwestern town. We've got one bar, one restaurant and one grocery store. We've got about seventeen churches, though. Three of the towns in the area send their kids to one school. Which is where I teach.

"It's a great place to raise kids. They can ride their bikes and play without a parent hovering over them or fear of them getting abducted. But we have our problems too. Drinking and alcohol abuse are common. Kids have too much time on their hands. Throw in the availability of farm equipment and animals, and you get the picture. But I don't think I'd want to be anywhere else since Margie is pregnant."

The realization of what Mark said hit him, and Eric's jaw dropped. "Holy shit! Are you serious? Congratulations, man! You're gonna be a dad!" He cuffed Mark on the shoulder.

"Yeah, she's 14 weeks along now. I wasn't trying to keep it from you. I wanted to tell you face to face." Mark was smiling from ear to ear. Eric had seen him look this happy once before, when he was watching Margie walk down the aisle. Mark continued to ramble on about Margie's pregnancy, and while Eric felt happy for his friend, he also felt a pang of jealousy.

Although they were the same age, Mark was a happy, married, soon to be dad with an on-track career. Eric was divorced, couldn't keep a plant alive, and had uprooted his whole life to start over. His looks and his family money had made all of their college friends think Eric was the lucky one. How wrong they turned out to be.

After what seemed like an eternity, with the sun dipping below the horizon, Mark turned into a driveway long enough to have been a road. "Home sweet home!" he said.

He parked the truck in front of a modest house with a big front porch. A woman with copper colored hair and wide hips stood in the door. She smiled at the pair as they walked up. "Well, look what the cat dragged in!" She said, giving Eric a big hug and a kiss on the cheek. "We are both so excited you're here. Go on, dinner's almost ready!"

Eric put a hand on her arm. "Congratulations Margie, Mark told me on the way over. You're going to be the most amazing mom." Margie's cheeks flushed with color. She swatted at him and gestured for them to go inside.

Margie was a hell of a cook. The smell wafting from the kitchen hit Eric in the face like a ton of heavenly bricks. They spent the next hour eating more food than Eric thought possible, including apple pie Margie made using her grandma's recipe. They talked and laughed and caught up on the time they had been apart. All too soon, Mark was looking at the clock on the wall and saying, "Well, Eric, it's getting late. I guess I should show you your place."

Mark and Margie had helped Eric find a little apartment to rent. All Eric knew was that it was above a shop downtown. Eric hugged Margie, congratulating her again, and then he was back in the pickup with Mark.

After a short drive, Mark pulled into an angled parking spot in front of a building with a sign that read, "Country Ribbons," which he explained was a quilting shop. Eric looked around and saw a few blocks of buildings between nothingness.

After leading Eric up a set of stairs on the side of the building, Mark unlocked the door at the top and switched on the light. It was a small space, but it was bright and clean. Light hardwood floors lay before them and a small kitchen and living area ran together. Two doors led to the bathroom and bedroom.

To Eric's surprise, everything he had sent ahead had been unpacked. The bed was assembled and made. The couch and chair were facing a TV that was hung on the wall. Mark must have noticed Eric's puzzled expression. "Margie said we couldn't let you move in to a mess."

"I can't tell you how thankful I am for you guys," Eric said, pulling Mark in for another hug. The weight of the day fell upon Eric and tears welled in his eyes.

"Hey man," Mark replied, patting Eric's back. "Don't mention it for a second."

They said their goodbyes, and Mark was gone. He wasn't sure how he had gotten so lucky to have Mark fall into his life over a decade ago, but he knew he was grateful to have him and Margie.

Outside, he heard the slamming of a car door. Out of habit, or curiosity, he peeked through the blinds. The only person on the street was someone with a thin build, a black hooded sweatshirt pulled up over their head.

As Eric watched, he noticed the person had a strange gait, something between a normal walk and a limp. The person turned their head and Eric swore they looked straight up at his window. The figure turned and continued down the street. He had witnessed nothing, but he couldn't ignore the tingling in his stomach that made him feel as though he had.

2

Eric woke up the next morning to the sounds of a bell tinkling. It took him a moment to orient himself and realize the noise was coming from the shop under his apartment. His phone screen showed it was 7:30.

After getting out of bed, he threw on a pair of shorts and a t-shirt that had been folded and tucked into his dresser. He found his running shoes and a pair of socks also stowed away. Within minutes, he was out the door with his keys in hand. He hoped a morning run would help clear his mind and orient himself with his new environment.

The people he ran past on the street watched him with intrigued expressions. Eric surmised they rarely had newcomers. After running past a handful of buildings, he found himself beside a field of cows mooing at him.

He stopped, looking up and down the empty road. This new life of his was going to take more adjusting to than he thought. The sounds of taxis honking and street vendors shouting as he ran past were familiar to him, not the bellows of livestock. Although, by the time he reached his apartment again, he had to admit that the air was a little sweeter and a lot fresher here in Spring Hills.

After entering the apartment, he glanced at his phone and saw that Mark had texted, asking if he wanted to get breakfast with him. He shot a quick confirmation back and jumped into the shower. Mark showed up at the door 15 minutes later, as planned.

"Hey man! I'm excited to introduce you to Dolly's! It's the best place to eat in town," Mark said with a smile. It seemed he was always happy and loving life. Eric thought he'd love life just as much if he were in Mark's shoes, and another wave of jealousy washed over him.

"I thought you said there was only one place to eat in town," Eric said, locking the door and bounding down the stairs behind Mark.

"I did."

Eric rolled his eyes while Mark chuckled to himself. They walked three buildings down the street, again having people they passed stop and stare in Eric's direction and whisper to one another. They came to a building with neon lights splashed across the big front windows and a sign over the door that read, "Dolly's." Eric swore there was so much neon on the building he could feel it buzzing.

The bell above the door jingled as they passed through. "Hey Mr. Deveraux!" a young server said as she rubbed the counter with a dishrag. Her eyes widened when she noticed Eric. Perhaps without realizing it, she tucked a stray piece of hair behind her ear and stood up a little straighter, pushing her chest out. "Grab a seat and I'll be right with you!"

She scrambled for the menus and smoothed the front of the apron tied around her waist. "Welcome to Dolly's!" she said with a little too much gusto once she made it over to their table and handed them their menus. "My name's Grace."

"Hi, I'm Eric," he replied with a smile.

"Oh!" she put a hand to her chest, "The new deputy!" It surprised Eric that she knew who he was, but he realized it shouldn't. He'd always heard that news traveled fast in a small town.

"That's me," he said.

"Grace was a student of mine," Mark mentioned and Eric nodded while Grace beamed.

There was an awkward silence, and Eric could see her eyes moving over him. "Can I get a cup of coffee, please?" he asked.

"Oh, of course, I'm sorry! I'll be right out with that!"

Mark chuckled when Grace walked away. "Some things never change. I bet I don't even get a cup."

Sure enough, when Grace starting back toward them, she had one steaming mug of coffee. She looked up and smiled, but when she realized she was one cup short, she scurried back for another. Mark took it in stride and laughed. "Damn. I should have put money on that."

"Cream or sugar?" Grace asked, putting a mug in front of each of them and leaning over farther than was necessary. Eric sucked in a deep breath. When he was younger, he relished this kind of attention. Now, he just wanted to drink his damn coffee.

"Nope, I'm good. Mark?" Eric asked and Mark shook his head. "Alright then, we're good with coffee. I'll also take an omelet, with mushrooms, green pepper and onion and hash browns and sausage, please."

Grace appeared taken aback by her advances going unnoticed, and she hurried to get her notepad from her apron. She scribbled down what Eric had said, asking if he wanted sausage links or patties. Mark asked for his 'usual' and she grinned while scribbling on the notepad. She said she'd put in the order and retreated to the counter.

"Ouch," Mark replied, still smiling. "She looks like that one stung. For my sake, I hope she just spits in your food and not mine. What's it like being Eric Grayson, hot bod diner?" Mark asked, drinking from his cup.

"It's not all it's cracked up to be," Eric replied, frowning. "What's it like being Mark Devereaux, happily married dad to be?"

Mark smiled. "It's pretty damn great, Eric."

They chatted about the diner, Mark's favorite things in town, the bar and lots of other little details about Spring Hills that Eric soaked in. Their food arrived in short order and Grace seemed to have licked her wounds and was taking another shot.

After setting their plates down in front of them, she reached across the table to bring the hot sauce and ketchup bottles closer. She leaned on the table and turned toward Eric. "If there's anything else you need, you let me know," she breathed. She winked before slinking away, sashaying her hips.

Eric tried to stop himself from rolling his eyes and Mark started stuffing food in his face to keep himself from laughing. Eric glanced out the window and noticed a big silver pickup pull in across the street.

It was a truck out of a country song, huge and lifted. Eric wondered what country stereotype was going to leap out of the front seat. He pictured a man with a sleeveless flannel, faded jeans, cowboy boots, and a mouth full of chew.

He almost choked on his eggs when, instead, a slim woman slipped from the front seat. She was wearing jeans and a tank top, so he got the sleeveless part right at least. A baseball cap was jammed on top of long, blond, braided hair that trailed down her back. Muddy work boots were on her feet. He saw her reach back in the cab, and there it was, a long-sleeved flannel shirt she pulled on over her shoulders.

"Who's that?" Eric asked Mark.

"Of course she'd catch your eye," said Mark, again smiling from ear to ear. "That's Andy Summers. She owns Summers Ranch."

Eric watched the woman he know knew as Andy dash across the road and into Dolly's. "Hiya Grace," Andy said with a raspy, husky voice that took Eric by surprise. He had expected a much softer, sweeter voice to match her slight frame. "Can I get a coffee to go, please?" Andy had already pulled a couple of bills from her pocket.

"Sure thing Andy. Coffee maker still broken?" Grace asked as she readied a foam cup and plastic lid.

"Yeah, it's dead, like my soul without caffeine," Andy replied, drumming her fingers on the countertop. Eric noticed the feminine shape of her body in her tight-fitting jeans as she propped a foot up on the bar that ran under the counter.

Grace handed Andy the cup and said something to her that Eric couldn't hear. Andy glanced over her shoulder in his direction. She turned back towards Grace and shrugged before heading toward the door. He watched as she hauled herself back into her truck with apparent grace and without spilling a drop of her coffee.

"I've seen that look before, Grayson," Mark said, wiping egg from the corners of his mouth. "Tread lightly with that one."

Eric smiled and lifted his coffee mug. "I don't have the slightest idea what you're talking about, Devereaux."

3

With Mark in tow, Eric spent the rest of the day driving out to the nearest car dealership. He found and purchased an older model, but still serviceable pickup truck. It had rust spots and the A/C didn't work, but it was within his small budget.

By the time they made it back to Spring Hills, the sun had set. Eric's cell rang. "Hey," he answered after seeing Mark's name on the screen.

"Margie called. We're going to meet her over at the bar. She's going to bring dinner," Mark said.

"God Mark, you hit the lotto with Margie. Does she have a sister?"

"No, she's got some brother's if you wanted to try that out though."

"While Margie's cooking is good, I'm not sure it's good enough to get me to like dick so, I'll pass. See you at the bar."

"It's next to Dolly's, called The Lodge."

Eric pulled into the parking spot reserved for him in the alley behind Country Ribbons. Then he strode down to the street. The Lodge was a definitive cowboy joint. Horns and antlers of various species of animals decorated the walls. It was dimly lit, with beer paraphernalia decorating any spot on the wall devoid of dead animal bits. They saw Margie sitting at a table with a large brown paper bag.

Mark sat down in the booth beside Margie and put his arm around her before planting a big, sloppy kiss on her cheek. Margie giggled and returned the gesture, then pulled out wrapped up sandwiches from the bag. "I used some leftovers from yesterday to whip up some chicken salad."

She barely had the sentence out and both of them had already tucked in. "Oh my God," Eric groaned. "Margie, if Mark hadn't already made an honest woman out of you, this chicken salad would make me propose."

Margie blushed and chuckled. Mark growled with his mouth full of food, "Good thing I found her first."

A tall woman with black hair that matched her leather bustier came to the table. "Hey there," she said with a wide smile, her teeth showing between bright red lips. "I'm Louisa. You must be the new deputy."

Eric wiped any trace of chicken salad from his face and said, "Yes, I'm Eric. Nice to meet you."

"The pleasure is all mine, or it could be," she purred. If Margie had rolled her eyes any harder, Eric thought they might pop out.

With a few exchanged pleasantries, they ordered drinks that Louisa returned with quickly. "Is there anything else you need, handsome?" she asked, resting her hand on Eric's shoulder.

Eric sensed she was the type of woman who had chewed up and spit out her fair share of guys. "I'm good, thanks," he replied. She winked and walked away to another table.

Eric's back was to the door, but he soon heard a familiar, distinct voice from behind him.

"No Romeo, you shouldn't have drafted him to your fantasy team! I told you he'd be injured by the second week," the voice said. Eric glanced behind him and saw Andy Summers walking in with her baseball hat on and a couple of tall, rugged looking men at her side. An unexpected wave of jealousy grew in his chest.

The three of them made their way to a table nearby. The two men were wearing cowboy hats, which they took off and set on the table. When he got a better look at them, Eric realized they were much older than her. Their skin was wrinkled and while one had a darker complexion, they both looked like people who spent a lot of time outside.

"Romeo and Carl are ranch hands. They worked for her dad and now they work for her," Mark said. It annoyed Eric that Mark could read his mind, but he also couldn't ignore that the tightness in his chest was receding.

Louisa approached Andy and the ranch hands' table carrying a rocks glass filled with an amber colored liquid and two bottles of beer. It surprised Eric when the rocks glass was set in front of Andy. He watched Andy as she took a sip and then licked her lips.

She looked up and caught Eric looking at her. A half-smirk spread across her face, and she cocked her head to the side. Then she stood up and walked over to where his group sat. When she reached them, she didn't acknowledge him, but turned to Margie.

"Margie! I heard the news today! Congratulations! And to you too, Mark. You're both going to be such wonderful parents," she said, smiling.

Margie got to her feet and wrapped Andy in a tight squeeze. With her arm still around her, Margie turned to Eric. "Have you met Eric Grayson? He's been Mark's best friend since college and he's the new deputy."

Andy stuck out her hand. "Hi Deputy, I'm Andy."

He stood, shook her hand, and smiled. "Please, it's Eric. Nice to meet you."

Andy looked at him, eyes squinting slightly. "Well, I better get back. We're arguing over football. They always make such terrible fantasy picks. I'm not sure why I even try to help. They dig their own graves every year and then bitch about it for months."

"You're into football?" Eric asked, desperately trying to continue the conversation.

"You could say that," she replied. "See you guys around. And again, congrats to both of you." Without another glance at Eric, she turned and walked back to her table.

Mark looked like he had swallowed a lemon and it was obvious he was trying very hard not to laugh. "Man, I don't get you. You can have pretty much any woman besides Margie in the tri-county area and you pick the one who is unaffected by your charms. And before you ask, she is NOT a lesbian. At least I don't think she is."

"No, she was engaged to that guy back in New York, remember?" Margie said.

"Oh, that's right," Mark added, taking a swig of his beer.

"Mark, I don't know what you're talking about," Eric interjected. "I was merely trying to make conversation."

"I saw your attempts to pick up women for four years during college. I know what it looks like, bro, so don't bullshit me."

"Are all women around here into football?" Eric asked, taking a swig of his beer.

"A lot of them are, but Andy grew up with brothers," Margie said over her water. "Two of them played football in high school.

One played in college, the other one would have. Andy's dad was a permanent installation at the high school field for years, Andy in tow. Theo, the younger one, played on the same team as my brother. We all thought he would go pro. He was a good guy."

"Was?" Eric asked.

"It was tragic, devastated the whole town. His senior year, he got drunk, got behind the wheel of his truck and ended up hitting a tree. He was in critical condition for a few days but didn't make it. It was awful," Margie said. "Mr. Summers was never the same after that. Then Andrea passed not too long after. That was a hard year for them."

"Andrea?" Mark asked.

"Andy's mom. She had breast cancer. Unfortunately, it took her pretty quickly after her diagnosis. Andrea was an exceptional woman, involved in pretty much everything she could be. It was a tremendous loss to the whole town when she died."

Eric glanced over at Andy, who was laughing with her ranch hands and working on her second whiskey. She looked up, and they locked eyes. Eric's skin tingled when she didn't break his gaze while she took a drink.

"Eric...Eric!" said Mark.

"Sorry Mark, I was...distracted," Eric replied, pulling his gaze from Andy. Mark glanced over his shoulder.

"Mmhmm," he laughed, then he struck up a conversation about college and soon he, Eric and Margie were swapping stories about "the good old days." Margie had gone to UCLA too, the only one of them with a scholarship.

The three of them were still chatting when Eric noticed a man in jeans at least two sizes too tight and a faded blue flannel shirt stalk over to Andy's table. Andy's posture went on the defensive, so did her ranch hands.

Andy's arms crossed over her chest. The darker complected man clenched his beer, his other formed a fist on the table. The other man stood up. Eric's body tensed and he was ready to break up a fight that seemed inevitable.

Too-tight jeans bent down into Andy's face, and apparently, she didn't respond the way he had hoped. She glanced at the man who had stood and he sunk back into his chair. Then she said something to Wranglers, and he slammed his hand on the table before storming off. As he walked away, she tossed back the rest of her drink, setting the glass back on the table with a thunk.

The sound of Mark's voice interrupted Eric's observations. "Margie and I have to get going. Growing a baby is tiring work."

He and Eric put their money on the table and the three of them went their separate ways. Turning toward his apartment, he got a strange feeling that he was being watched. Stopping dead in his tracks and looking around, he couldn't find the source of his unease. Shoving his hands deep down in his pockets, he stood there for a minute until he heard that raspy laugh again.

He swiveled around and saw Andy walking out of the building with the two men before they parted ways. She noticed Eric and nodded at him before jumping up into her truck and driving off. Eric watched her taillights disappear and thought to himself, "I am so fucked."

4

Anger flowed through Andy as she drove back to the ranch. Everything that was aggravating her was swirling in her mind like a tornado. Frank-fucking-Miller had again offered to "take that big old ranch off her pretty little hands." Repeating his old line that it was too much for a little thing like her. That arrogant prick. She would let the ranch go to him over her dead body.

And that Eric guy who kept staring at her. What the hell was that? Like he was God's gift to women. Fuck him. She'd heard about him. The new deputy coming all the way from LA. Yes, he was good looking, but he was also the kind of guy who knew it.

Her memories flitted to her ex-fiancé Jake. His British accent, handsome face, perfect hair, well-fitting clothes, expensive colognes, charming words. The way he'd played her like a fiddle. She shook her head as if removing the memories like cobwebs.

She pulled her truck between the large wooden posts that marked the driveway to her ranch. The ranch that had been in her family for four generations, the one she watched her father pour his blood, sweat and tears into. The ranch that she both loved and resented.

She parked the truck, but instead of going into her house, she walked over to the horse barn. She was too angry to sleep, anyway.

Mostly because of that shit-eating Frank Miller and some half-assed draft picks.

She entered the barn and let the smell of horse and hay wash over her. This had always been her happy place, even when she was younger. She walked over to one of her favorite horses, who came forward to greet her. Resting her hand on his flank and nestling her face against him, her heart rate slowed and calm consumed her.

After a while, she returned to the large, empty house. She pulled her boots off and hung her jacket up on the hook near the door before arming the security system again and padding into the kitchen.

After taking her dad's favorite glass down, she poured a shot of Jack Daniels and threw it back, enjoying the way it burned her throat. "Cheers, dad," she whispered and made her way up to her bed.

5

Eric was settling into his role as deputy for Florence County. He had finally met the Sheriff in person, and so far, he liked his commanders. Once he had completed orientation, he began riding solo, a thought he didn't relish after what had happened in LA.

He was learning the ropes and finding that patrolling such a vast and open area differed from the population dense, but small, beat he had in California. In his first week, he handled a lot of calls that he was used to, a loud party, a couple domestics, assisting paramedics. He had some new calls too, like a cow in the middle of the road and a broken down tractor blocking traffic.

He was so tired when he returned home that he would microwave a frozen meal, have a beer, and go to bed. He figured being a homebody in Spring Hills was okay when there was only one spot to go at night. The thought of trying to avoid Louisa's advances again and again was enough to make him not want to become a regular at The Lodge.

On Saturday, his first day off in a week, he went over to Dolly's. He didn't want to deal with Grace, but it would be worth it to get an omelet and hash browns.

He walked through the door, and the bell jingled. Grace wasn't behind the counter, instead an older woman with a large bust, wide hips and graying brown hair was. "Take a seat, be with you in a minute," she said, without so much as a passing glance. Relieved, he breathed out a big puff of air.

He turned to the booths and his pulse shot up a bit when he saw Andy sitting in one by herself. His mind flashed back to her steely stare at the bar last weekend, and he decided against asking if he could join her.

Instead, he sat at the booth in front of hers, but positioned himself so that if she looked up, she'd be able to see him. He looked at the menu even though he knew his order. In reality, he was using it as a poor excuse to steal glimpses of her. She was reading some paperwork while pushing the food on her plate around and sipping her coffee.

The server soon came over and took his order. After she brought him his coffee, she went to Andy's table and offered to refill her mug. Andy looked up at her to thank her and her eyes fell on Eric, who was trying to look oblivious to her presence.

When he looked up, she was glaring at him with the same squinty, suspicious stare he had seen at The Lodge. He smiled and said, "Hey Andy." Then he glanced down at his phone, like he was reading something very interesting.

"Deputy," she responded, like the word tasted bad in her mouth, and went back to her paperwork. Eric's food came quickly, and he devoured it. Just as he was shoveling the last bit of food into his mouth, Andy got up, threw some cash down on the table, and scooped up her paperwork before walking out the door.

He sighed at his empty plate, paid his bill and left too. When he walked outside, he saw Andy squared up with the too-tight Wranglers guy from the bar. She held her papers tight to her chest, pinning them there with one arm. Her other hand was clenched in a fist at her side. She said something to Wranglers, and a vein in his neck bulged. He bent down to within an inch of Andy's face.

Eric sensed this was a powder keg waiting to explode and sprung into action. He sprinted over to them. "Hey! What's going on here?" he shouted.

"Who the hell wants to know!" yelled Wranglers, turning around to face him, spit flying from his mouth as he hollered.

Eric remained calm, replying, "Deputy Grayson. And you are?"

The man's face was the same bright red as the flannel he wore. He puffed out a breath in a sort of chortle. "Frank Miller. You would know that if you were any good at your job, Deputy."

"I'm sorry Mr. Miller, I haven't had time to meet everyone here in Spring Hills," Eric responded, trying to sound polite and shooting him a smile. He figured he'd start with the old "kill them with kindness," technique. "So I'm going to ask again, what's going on?"

"You on duty Deputy?" Frank asked, sneering.

"Always," replied Eric, with a movie-star smile. "So Frank, I guess you're going to make me ask again. What's going on?"

"Just trying to get this bitch to realize that she shouldn't try to hang with the big dogs," Frank spat in Andy's direction. Surprisingly, she didn't move a muscle. She cut into Frank with an icy stare, and Eric noticed her jaw tick.

"I think it's time to walk away, Frank," Eric said, stepping between the two of them.

"Sure Deputy," Frank said, laughing, adding, "Whatever you say. See you around. You too Andy, I guarantee that. And maybe next time

Hollywood won't be here to interrupt us." Frank turned on his heel and walked away, still laughing.

Eric turned to face Andy. Her cheeks were flush, and he saw the same red color peeking out in splotches across her chest and neck. Inhaling, she closed her eyes. "You OK?" Eric asked, resting a hand on her arm.

"Yeah. I'm fine." Her eyes flew open, and she took a step back, just out of reach.

Eric's hand dropped to his side. He watched as she climbed into her truck, set the paperwork down on the passenger seat, and rested her head back against. Her hands clenched the steering wheel, and she squeezed her eyes shut again. He saw her exhale and then she opened her eyes, turned over the engine, and drove away.

———*ll*———

Eric shook his head. Then went to his truck and drove over to Margie and Mark's house since he had volunteered to help paint the nursery. Before long, he and Mark were up in the small room brushing a happy yellow color on the walls.

"What's up with Frank Miller?" Eric asked as he cut in around the baseboard.

"He's a dick," said Mark without a moment of hesitation.

Eric was a little shocked. Mark rarely spoke ill of anyone. "What's his deal with Andy?"

"He's got a ranch, big one. Real commercial. His dad made a couple good deals before he died, so Frank's got money. He's been after Andy's ranch since her dad died, probably before. Trying to undercut her, take deals out from under her...like I said, he's just a dick. Plain and simple."

"Frank's always been that way," Margie said, entering the room, passing each of them a glass of lemonade. "I was a freshman in high school when he was a senior. He was always just a cheating, dirty sneak.

"He cheated on his schoolwork, he cheated at football. When he got benched, the rumor is he gave the other guy something to make him super sick. Poor kid was out for a few weeks and Frank played his receiver spot for the rest of the season. Obviously, that's all silly high school rumor and speculation, but that it's believable tells you the kind of guy Frank is. Why do you ask?"

"When I left the diner this morning, he was up in Andy's face. It looked pretty heated, so I intervened. In the end, he walked away, but she seemed pretty shaken up by it," Eric answered.

"Ugh, poor Andy. Frank's been going after her for the last two years. That poor woman could use a break." Margie gave Mark a kiss on the cheek and left the room.

"Do not take that as an invitation to play hero, save her from the big bad Frank Miller and try to get in her pants, Grayson," Mark said, chuckling.

"I didn't get in the way to get in her pants, Mark. I am an officer of the law. It's my duty to keep the people of this county safe," Eric responded and emptied his glass.

"Right, Deputy Get-some." Eric threw a towel at him and continued painting.

After they finished making the nursery happy and yellow, Eric pitched in with some yardwork, since he had nothing better to do than sit in his apartment alone. Then Margie made dinner. He offered to help but she flat out refused any help. Instead, he and Mark grabbed a beer and watched Sports Center. Eric felt he could get used to this feeling of family. It was a new thing for him, but he liked it.

6

After Margie had fed him and packed him leftovers, Eric took off to give Mark and Margie some time alone. He wasn't ready to sit in his empty apartment, so he drove around for a while. He was enjoying his joyride, taking in the clean air through his open window and listening to his tires on the gravel, when he heard the truck's engine sputter.

"Oh come on baby," he said, stroking the steering wheel. But his encouragement wasn't enough to overcome mechanical failure, and the engine sputtered some more. He pulled over to the side of the road before it died.

"Shit, shit, shit," he chanted as he got out of the truck and opened the hood. Steam hissed out, but he did not know what the hell he was looking at. He knew nothing about cars. He pulled his cell phone out and saw he had no signal. "Well, that's just great."

He was about to walk to town when he heard the crunching of tires on the road. An enormous truck pulled up to a stop beside him. The window rolled down, and sitting behind the wheel was none other than Andy Summers. "Having some trouble with your truck, Deputy?" she asked without a smile, dark circles under her eyes.

"Yes, but I would be lying if I said I knew what the trouble was," he said, throwing a smile at her. It didn't have the same effect it had

on other women. In fact, it seemed to have the opposite one on
Andy, and she looked annoyed. She sighed and pushed her head
back into the headrest like he'd seen her do earlier that day.

"You need a ride home?"

"If you don't mind, I would appreciate it. I don't have any signal
out here to call anyone."

"Get in before I forget my manners and change my mind,"
she replied. Eric slammed the hood of his truck shut, grabbed
the leftovers from the passenger seat, and climbed up into Andy's
vehicle. "I need to run my groceries to my house. We're just a couple
of minutes away. Then I'll take you back downtown, OK?"

"Yeah, sure thing," Eric said, fastening his seatbelt.

They drove in near silence. The radio was the only thing in the
cab making any noise. She pulled into a long driveway. When the
headlights illuminated the property, he noticed a couple of vast
barns and a mammoth old farmhouse.

"Nice place," Eric said, thinking it looked like something out of
a country-western movie.

"Yeah, thanks. Wait here. I'll run these in," Andy said as she slid
out of the car.

"Actually," Eric interjected, "Can I use your bathroom?
Please?" He brought his hands up with the palms pressed together
to seal his plea.

Andy sighed, her growing annoyance apparent. "Fine, but make
it quick, Deputy."

"You know you can call me Eric," he said, taking the grocery
bags from her without asking and following her up to the house.

"Deputy is fine," she replied, not looking back and not thanking him for carrying the bags. She punched some numbers on a keypad lock and he heard the bolt move. He followed her inside and saw they were in a large country kitchen. He put the bags on the table and imagined the magic Margie could work in a place like this.

"Down the hall, first door on the left. And if you can make it quick so I can get into bed soon, I'd appreciate it. I've had a long day." Andy turned her back and put away her groceries.

He tried his hardest to push the image of her in her bed out of his head. He knew if this was another woman, he might make a haughty quip about how he could just stay. But as he felt like he was on thin ice with Andy anyway, although he wasn't sure why, he nodded and headed toward the bathroom.

When he was done, he walked back into the kitchen, noticing the hallway was full of family photos on the way. He wanted to stop and look at them, but he saw Andy waiting by the door, arms folded across her chest. "All set," he said with a smile.

Silently, she punched the numbers in on the alarm keypad and opened the door. He followed her out into the cool air before she closed the door and locked the deadbolt again. They walked toward the truck, hearing only the crunching of the stones in the driveway beneath their feet and crickets chirping in the fields.

They pulled out of the driveway and began the trek back to town. Again the truck was silent except for a crooner with a southern accent on the radio singing about the love he'd lost. The palpable tension was driving Eric crazy. "Why do I get the sense you dislike me?" Eric asked, feeling like this was as good a time as any to get throat punched.

"I don't dislike you. I just don't care to know you," Andy replied without looking at him.

"I'm not sensing a distinction between the two."

"Look, I know your type. You're attractive and you know it. Guys like you are cocky and you think that you're a blessing to whatever woman you choose. You're used to breaking hearts and getting notches in your belt; am I right?"

"You think I'm attractive?"

A soft laugh escaped from Andy's lips, surprising Eric. "Of course that's the take away. You know you're attractive. You don't need me telling you that."

"Maybe, but it's still nice to hear you say it."

"Did you hear me say the other parts, though, the cocky part in particular?" she quipped back.

"Yes, but in life, I choose to focus on the positive," he said, wiggling his eyebrows at her. "For the record, I think you're stereotyping me."

"Am I? Can you say that nothing I said was true? I'm familiar with the mentality guys like you have."

"Guys like me?" Eric scoffed, feeling himself getting irritated. "You know nothing about me. And how do you know about 'guys like me' anyway? I didn't think there were many transplants to Spring Hills."

"There's not."

"Well, how do you have any idea about 'guys like me'?"

He heard the puff of air pass her lips and knew he'd cornered her into telling him more than she wanted to. "I left Spring Hills after high school and went to NYU on a scholarship. I lived in New York for four years for my bachelors, and two years for my masters."

"What'd you major in?" Eric asked, happy to get the illusive Andy Summers talking.

"Art history."

Eric looked at her, his mouth parted and eyes wide. A rancher with a master's degree in art history had to be one in a million. "Art history?" he repeated, stunned.

"Yes, and conservation," she replied matter-of-factly. "So, I lived in a big city long enough to meet assholes who were born with good genetics or enough money that they think they can use or manipulate anyone they want to."

He realized whatever issue she had was personal and not something he could talk through with her. He tried navigating the conversation into more amicable territory. "What do you miss most about New York?"

She seemed taken aback by the quick change of topic. She exhaled a sigh, and he saw a small smile turn up the corners of her lips. "What do I miss? Everything. The noise, lights, food, people. There's so much to experience.

"Spring Hills is a bubble and people here don't realize there's so much more out there." Then she thought for a second. "But what do I miss the most out of all? Hands down, fantastic sushi."

Eric laughed, "Really...sushi? That's it? The thing you miss above all else?"

"Oh yes," she replied with a genuine smile that made his heart flutter out of nowhere. "Nigiri, sashimi, poke. I love it, all of it. And eel sauce...ugh I could die a happy woman in a bathtub of eel sauce."

For the second time that night, Eric had to do his best not to imagine her in a state of undress. Here was a woman who raised horses and cattle in the middle of a landlocked state, and the thing she missed most about the city was raw fish.

"Are you liking Spring Hills Deputy?" she asked. It shocked Eric that she was trying to make conversation with him.

"It's different, a lot different. Adjusting has been interesting, but there are a lot of good parts," he replied.

"What's your favorite thing about this one stoplight town?"

"The quiet. LA is full of honking and yelling and cursing. Here, you can hear yourself think. What about you? What do you like most about Spring Hills, Andy?"

She had pulled into a parking spot in front of Country Ribbons. "We're here," she said without answering his question.

"How did you know where I was staying?"

"Only rental available in town." Andy closed her eyes and rested her head against the window beside her. He sensed the exhaustion rolling off of her.

"Oh, that would do it, huh? Well, thanks for the ride." He opened the door to step out.

"Deputy, call Sam Granger tomorrow. Best mechanic in town. He can figure out what's wrong with your truck, which you left on the corner of Polk and Hunter's Ridge."

"Thanks Andy." He shut the door, making a mental note of what she had said and she drove away without a backwards glance.

7

It was early morning, and Eric was wrapping up his night shift when he got a call. "Hey Mark, what's up?" he answered.

"Margie wants to know if you're coming out tonight."

Eric sighed. "I hadn't planned on it."

Margie's voice came on the line. "Come on, Eric! It's your first Harvest Festival! It's a Spring Hills tradition, you have to come!"

"Oh, do I?"

"Yes, you most absolutely do. These are the people you've sworn to protect. And, it'd be a great way to get to know everyone a little better. More people than just the Spring Hills folks will be there. You might even meet someone! You haven't been on a single date since you've been in town."

"Margie, I've only been here a few weeks! Give me a break. And the pool of eligible women around here seems pretty shallow. Wait, are you trying to set me up with someone?"

"No, no, no. I'm saying it'd be nice to see you happy, to have some of what Mark and I do," she said, her voice trailing off. The comment made Eric's stomach sink, but only because he'd thought the same thing every time he left Margie and Mark's place.

He exhaled. "What do you want me to wear Margie?" he asked, having already realized that resistance was futile.

"Yay, I knew you'd come around! Just your usual jeans and a nice shirt. With that face you don't have to do too much to get attention. I'm so happy you're coming, Eric! We'll see you there around seven?"

"Your wish is my command, Queen Margie." He heard her giggle, and the call disconnected.

He knew Margie meant well, but he'd seen what Spring Hills had to offer, and, besides Andy, who had made it clear she was not interested, Louisa was the best option in his age bracket. However, she scared him shitless. Every time he stepped foot in the bar, she made some innuendo or comment, finding any excuse to touch him. He had a gut feeling that she was more than he could handle.

After he'd slept a while, went for a run and ate, he showered and changed. He chose jeans and a light blue button up that played off the color of his icy blue eyes. He had opted to not shave off his stubble. Everyone else in this town had a beard or a 'stache, why not be on trend?

He took one last look in the mirror, grabbed his jacket, and walked the block down to the center of town. Hundreds of string lights illuminated the roped off area. A stage had been set up, and a dance floor had appeared, as well as wooden booths with a variety of offerings. Eric almost laughed at the thought of all the square dancing that he expected to witness.

He saw a pretty sizable crowd had formed, some milled about with drinks from the small makeshift bar. A band, complete with fiddle player, was getting ready to take the stage.

"Eric!" Margie shouted, as she rushed over and enveloped him in a hug. Her belly was getting more pronounced, but that didn't stop her from giving everyone the tightest embraces she could muster. He squeezed her back.

"Hey man," Mark said, smiling and handing Eric a beer, "I tried to talk her out of calling this morning."

"Nah," Eric said, accepting the beer with a nod, "It's alright. Probably better than being home, relaxing in peace and falling asleep early in my nice, warm bed." He winked at Margie for good measure.

"Oh hush," she said, swatting his arm before linking one elbow through his and the other with Mark's. She led them toward the middle of the square where all the action was. They found a table and set down their drinks. Eric leaned against it as they talked about their days. Mark and Margie always liked to hear about the crazy things he saw during his shifts.

As they talked, Eric scanned the crowd. His training was entrenched, and he liked to be aware of what was going on in his surroundings, especially in crowds. He saw nothing remarkable until his eyes settled on the other side of the square where Andy stood.

He wasn't sure why he still hadn't given up on her. She'd already formed an opinion about him, albeit unfairly if you asked him. She made it clear she wasn't interested in even getting to know him casually, much less intimately. He wouldn't mind knowing her, though, especially with how she looked tonight.

She was wearing her usual tight jeans, but instead of a t-shirt or flannel, she was wearing a v-neck, wine colored sweater that showed a tiny, tempting bit of cleavage. She had a black leather jacket over it. This was the first time he'd ever seen her with her hair down. It tumbled down her shoulders in soft waves that he longed to touch. The cowboy boots on her feet were the only thing that made it look like she belonged here and not at a bar in New York. Staring at her, his mind was filled with another fantasy that she starred in, just like the ones that had been playing on repeat in his head for the last few days.

The band began to play, and Margie let out a squeal that broke Eric from his trance. Mark laughed and took her hand. "Excuse me, Eric, my wife needs to dance." The two of them strode off, claimed a spot on the dance floor, and swayed together.

Eric took this opportunity to visit the bar made from a long folding table. He paid for another overpriced beer and while he waited for the woman behind the "bar" to grab it from a cooler, he overheard the conversation of the men standing near him. "Go ask her, man!" one said.

"You don't go ask Andy Summers to dance," the one in the middle of the group replied.

"Why not? When's the last time you talked to her? Last Harvest Fest?"

"Probably," he hissed.

"Well, go get it, man. She's probably lonely, livin' in that big house all by herself. Buy her a drink. Hell, buy her a few. If you get her drunk enough, she might go home with you. I haven't heard that she's dated anybody since she moved back home. She's got to be missing dick by now," the guy said.

Eric wanted to punch him in the face, both of them for good measure. Instead, he took a long swig of his beer, for courage and because he didn't want it to go to waste, and put the rest of the can back on the bar. After he wiped his mouth with the back of his hand, he took a deep breath.

Trying to pump himself up for the interaction to come, he ran a hand through his hair as he approached her. "Andy," he said, and she looked up.

"Deputy," she replied. Both her voice and face were blank.

"I know you hate me, or don't want to like me, or however you want to phrase it. But I'm here to help you."

"How do you figure?" she asked, confused.

"See that guy by the bar in the red flannel, the one surrounded by a bunch of country boy assholes? Well, right now, he is trying to work up the nerve to talk to you."

Andy looked past Eric toward the group he had pointed out. "Oh?"

"Yes," Eric replied. "I can assure you it's not to shoot the shit."

Andy caught his drift. "Ahhh. I see. And how are you going to help with that situation?"

"Well, I figured I could ask you to dance, then maybe he wouldn't, and it'd save you the effort of shooting him down publicly."

"I'm well versed in shooting someone down. It's no effort at all actually," she said, cracking a smile. He smiled back despite himself.

"Oh, I believe you are very well versed. However, he's been standing at that bar for at least half an hour and that's a pretty large stack of empty's behind him. I'm not sure that a simple, 'No thanks,' is going to cut it for our friend there. Then the shooting him down gets long and drawn out and maybe there's a scene, and wouldn't you like to enjoy yourself without being the cold-hearted bitch that shot down poor what's-his-name, when all he wanted was a dance?"

Andy sucked air through her teeth and said, "Cold-hearted bitch is very on brand for me, though." He couldn't help but let out a low laugh at her blunt statement.

The man in red flannel sidled up beside them. "Hey Andy. You look real good tonight," he said. The smell of stale alcohol and cigarette smoke rolled off of him. His eyes traveled her body. "How ya been?" he asked after far too long.

Her eyes flicked between the man in flannel, and Eric as she seemed to weigh her options. "Hey Jerry. I'm great," she replied, then set her beer on the table nearby. She wiped her palms on her jeans and held her hand out to Eric.

He smiled and led her to the dance floor. Several eyes watched them and there was a quiet stirring of conversation as he put one hand on her waist and took her hand with the other. "I think we might be a sensation," he said as they danced.

"Well, you know, the charming new deputy cracking the hard exterior of the town's resident ice queen nearing spinsterhood would be quite a sensation for Spring Hills," she replied.

"Charming?" he said, raising his eyebrow.

"Well, I mean, you think you are."

"And you don't?"

"Not at all," she replied, smirking.

"Damn, I've got to try harder," he chuckled. She rolled her eyes despite the hint of a smile spreading across her face.

As they danced, Mark caught Eric's eyes and made a shocked expression. The song concluded and Andy took a step backwards. "Flannel is still watching you," Eric said.

"Ugh," Andy replied. "You dance with a guy once and they never leave you alone."

Eric caught her message, but maneuvered around it. "You can come over and have a drink with me, Mark, and Margie. Then you and Margie can talk. You can pretend I don't exist, and Flannel may still leave you alone."

"You're going to have to come up with a better nickname for him because ninety-nine percent of the men here are wearing flannel," she paused for a moment, then sighed, "But that doesn't sound half bad."

He walked beside her, wishing he could touch her, but didn't dare to. They made their way over to the table where Mark and Margie were sitting. "Margie's feet were hurting," Mark said, gesturing to the stool they had gotten for her. "Hey Andy."

"Hey Mark, hey Margie," she said, smiling. Eric knew he would do a lot to get a smile like that from her.

"Can I go get you a beer?" Eric asked.

"Sure," she replied, pulling a five-dollar bill from her pocket and handing it to him.

"Would you let me buy you a beer?" he asked.

"No," she replied.

He nodded and pocketed the bill. When he asked, both Mark and Margie said they would love another round, water for the latter, and Eric made his way back to the bar. He finished ordering when he felt a tap on his shoulder.

Turning around, Eric found himself face to face with Flannel, who had clearly had another adult beverage while Eric had danced with Andy.

"What the hell?" the guy asked Eric.

"I'm sorry?" Eric replied, raising his eyebrows.

"What the hell is going on between you and Andy?"

"Well, we danced, as I'm sure you saw. I'm getting her a beer. And now, you're all caught up," Eric said, his words dripping with sarcasm.

"You stay away from her," Flannel said, taking another step towards Eric.

"Or what?" Eric asked, mirroring Flannel and taking a step forward so he was only inches from the man's face. He knew what he was doing. He knew he was baiting this overgrown child, and he wasn't sure why, but he was enjoying it.

"Or I'll kick your ass is what!" The guy shouted. One of his friends hissed something.

"No, I will not calm down. I don't give two shits if this guy is a deputy," Flannel sneered back, slurring his words. Eric knew this guy had already had a few too many, and didn't want to have to kick a drunk guy's ass, but he would if he had to.

Andy appeared at Eric's side. "Hey, what's taking so long?" she asked, acting as though she was unaware of the situation that was developing.

The bartender put three cans of beer and a Styrofoam cup of water on the bar and shifted her gaze between Eric and Andy, and Flannel and his buddy.

"Thanks Renee!" Andy said and picked up a can. "You coming?" she asked Eric and took his hand in hers. The spots her fingers touched tingled, and he felt his heart rate jump. The look in her eyes made him feel like his there was no other choice.

"Yeah, sure thing," Eric said, smiling back. Andy dropped his hand, grabbed the water cup, and handed it and the beer in her hand to him, then picked up the other two beers.

"Have a good night Jerry," she said, before leading Eric back to Mark and Margie. Jerry said nothing back, but started muttering to his friends as soon as they were out of earshot.

When they got back to their table, Mark gave a low whistle. "Andy, that was some good stuff there. Stopped two meat heads from making a spectacle of themselves."

Andy chuckled, "Growing up with three brothers teaches you a lot of skills about fighting, including how to avoid them." She took a pull of her beer and made a face. "Ugh, Bud in a can. It's...Bud in a can."

Eric laughed. She had echoed his sentiments. Andy talked with Mark and Margie about the ranch. They asked her questions, and she answered. A lot of what they said went over Eric's head. He was glad he was within a few feet of her, and she wasn't glaring at him or telling him how much she disliked him.

After she took the last sip of her beer, Andy told them she had to be going, and said her goodbyes. As he watched her leave, Eric heard Mark say, "Eric, my man, you are going to crash and burn."

He had watched them from afar. The overwhelming rage that had flooded through his veins when he first saw her almost consumed him. He watched as the deputy approached her and he had almost laughed. Did that guy have any idea what he was getting himself into with her?

He had watched her walk to her truck alone, his fingers almost itching to wrap around her throat. "Patience", he thought to himself.

8

The day after the festival, Andy pulled her truck into a space in front of the tack shop in town. She was picking up some things she was having repaired.

She hopped out of the pickup and entered the shop, sucking in the intoxicating scent of clean leather. Walking past the racks of saddles and bridles and bits, she dragged her fingertips against the items on the wall. She wound her way through the narrow store to the counter where she waited to be helped.

"Heya, Andy," the shop owner said as he came up to the counter. He had a belly that showed his affinity for beer and cured meats, and a kind, cheerful smile that lit up the room. "You here to pick up your stuff, or is there something else I can help you with, hun?"

"Well Buck, while I would love to buy about ten new saddles and that pair of chaps I saw over there, just the stuff I brought in, please," she said, returning his smile.

He nodded. "Lemme go grab them for you. I think they were finishing up on that saddle," he replied and headed back through the door he'd emerged from.

She was leaning up against the counter when she felt a tap on her shoulder. When she turned, she saw Joyce Newcome, a box-dye redhead who'd graduated the same year as Andy's mother and had a propensity for gossip. "Hey Annnndy," she said with a sly grin and a sing-song voice.

"Hi Mrs. Newcome, nice seeing you here today," Andy said, smiling through her lie.

"Oh, I'm sure sweety," Joyce said, waving her hand in front of her. "Anywho, dear, you caused quite a stir at the festival last night. But I'm sure you know all about that."

"I'm sorry Mrs. Newcome. I don't know what you're talking about," Andy said.

"Well," Joyce said with an exasperated sigh, "Obviously I am referring to you and that handsome new deputy holding each other close on the dance floor, dear!" She batted a hand at Andy's arm to appear playful.

"Ohhh," Andy replied, chastising herself for not realizing sooner how the gossips of the town would have already spread that information like wildfire. She'd thought their brief interlude would have looked much like an awkward middle school dance, with the distance she had ensured they'd maintained between one another. "It was just a dance, Mrs. Newcome, nothing more."

"Oh, pish posh! I heard it was quite a spectacle, that young, handsome, hard bodied deputy twirling around with our little ranching beauty. Surely more than just a dance, huh?" Joyce replied, raising her brows up and down, and tapping a bright red fingernail on her lip while a grin spread across her face. Andy almost rolled her eyes, but caught herself.

With impeccable timing, Buck came back through the door and hefted the saddle up on to the counter in front of Andy. "Here ya are

Andy, good as new," he said. Then he draped the rest of the repaired items over the top of it.

"Thanks Buck, you're the best," she said. She handed him her card and went to say goodbye to Joyce, but saw she had already disappeared. No doubt she was headed to some other old crow to twist everything Andy had said and invent entire portions of their conversation to make it seem like Andy was a lovesick puppy dog lusting away over the new deputy.

Andy had to admit that it had been sweet of him to step in and "save" her from Jerry, if not opportunistic. She had caught him glancing up at her more than a couple times, at The Lodge and at Dolly's. She figured that to him she was some intriguing new plaything that he hoped to add to the long list of women he'd made succumb to his charms.

Although, if she were honest, she had felt the tiniest something when he had placed his hand on her waist last night. But she had convinced herself it was because of the amount of time that had lapsed since she'd last been touched by a man and not because of the man doing the touching.

After Andy's transaction with Buck was done, she heaved the saddle back outside, refusing the offer of help from him. She had lifted it into the bed of the truck when she heard another vehicle pull in near her. When she turned, she saw old Jim Bishop, whom she had known in childhood as Young Jim, ambling toward the store, looking downcast.

"Heya Jim," she said, hoping the cheer in her voice would trigger at least a grin. Jim nodded and waved, but he seemed far away. She walked up to him and put a hand on his arm.

"Jim, what's wrong?" she asked, concerned about this man who always had an amiable smile for everyone. He looked up at her and sucked in a deep breath.

"Why don't we go sit in your truck...I'll tell you all about it, Andy," he said, his voice matching his countenance. They sat in the cab of her truck and she listened to Jim. As he spoke, her stomach twisted itself in knots.

⸺ele⸺

Andy had popped into the small grocery store in town. She had worked hard on the ranch all day and her whole body felt stiff. Leaning on the little grocery cart that contained the haul she'd collected from the aisles thus far, she was looking at bread when she heard a song she recognized over the speakers. Without thinking, she sang along quietly and after she had thrown a loaf in her cart, she heard a voice from behind her whisper, "You think The Lodge would ever consider adding karaoke?"

She spun around and standing there, close enough to hear her singing, was Eric. He was leaning against his cart, smiling at her. The little flutter that she felt in her stomach and the way her breath hitched in her throat at the sight of him alarmed her. "Not sure the crowd at The Lodge are the karaoke type," she replied, adding with a smirk, "Although I'm sure you could run it by Louisa."

He smiled and inhaled. "Yeah, I dunno about all that," he said as he pushed his cart so he was beside Andy in the aisle. "What's up with her, anyway?"

"Girl's a go getter. She sees something she wants, she goes, she gets it," Andy replied.

"Does she ever take no for an answer?" he asked. He was close enough she could smell his cologne or body wash, or whatever he wore that was causing something in her to stir. If someone asked her right now, she would have had a hard time telling anyone he wasn't desirable. He wore a half smirk, and she thought about how soft his lips might be. She blinked quickly, wiping the distraction from her mind.

"Not that I know of Deputy." She hoped the sense of formality would deter him. She half hoped he would move along and create some space between them she felt was needed. But part of her wanted him to stay close to her.

"Shit," he replied, still smiling.

"Oh, come on, you can't be sad that you're growing a little collection of groupies," she replied. "I've heard Grace has quite the crush, too."

"What?" his eyes were wide. "Where'd you hear that?"

"Nothing in this town stays quiet for long. For instance, a couple days ago, one of the town gossips interrogated me about our dance at the Harvest Fest."

A big smile spread across his face. "You're serious? We caused a commotion, huh? People must think we look good together." He winked, and she felt that flutter in her stomach again, but shoved it back down.

"People can think what they want," she said, crossing her arms. She noticed his smile dulled a bit, but didn't leave his face.

"You cook?" he asked, nodding to Andy's cart full of raw ingredients. She looked at his cart and saw a stack of freezer meals, some lunch meat, and other easy to eat items.

"Rarely, but more than it appears you do," she said. She was torn between the voice in her head telling her to wrap up the conversation, and that feeling in her stomach that was drawing her to him.

"Yeah, not my forte. There were a lot more take out joints in LA. Now I might have to learn how. I could use a teacher."

She heard the opening but refused to take the bait. "Margie is a splendid cook," she said with a grin. "I'm sure she'd be happy to teach you the basics."

"Hmmm," he said nodding, then reached past her and grabbed a loaf of bread, coming so close to her she felt his breath on her face. The butterflies in her stomach went haywire at his proximity.

He withdrew, tossed the bread into his cart and said, "Well, Andy, I'll let you get back to it. See you around." Then he continued on in the opposite direction. She watched him walk away and noticed how his jeans hugged his body just right. Even she had to admit she enjoyed the view from this angle.

She finished up her shopping and checked out, hoping not to have another run in with the deputy. She wasn't sure if her resolve would hold up with him that close to her for much longer.

When she was tossing her groceries into the truck, she got the sensation that she was being watched. Although the hair on the back of her neck stood up, she didn't see anyone watching her.

9

A week has passed since his run in with Andy at the grocery store, and Eric was patrolling. He'd seen Andy at The Lodge when he was with Mark and she was with the men he now knew as Carl and Romeo. She'd watched, not hiding her smirk, as Louisa had made another aggressive advance on him. When he'd made eye contact with her afterwards, she seemed to laugh a little and had waved, so he considered that progress.

While taking a long pull of his mediocre, lukewarm coffee, he heard a call come over the radio. "Intruder alarm, 100 Summers Lane, Spring Hills." A flash of recognition of the address flipped in his head. There was only one house on Summers Lane, Andy's house. Eric pointed his patrol car toward the ranch.

"Unit 338 responding, I'm in the area," he flicked on the lights and sirens and smashed the gas pedal to the ground. Minutes later, he turned into the drive and gravel flew up in his wake.

He turned off the siren, threw the cruiser into park and rushed toward the door, drawing his weapon as he radioed to dispatch that he was on scene. When he reached the door, he saw the lights inside were off. Muscle memory took over, and he raised his gun and flashlight in tandem. Blood was pumping through his veins and he heard his heart beating in his ears. It was the first time since he'd been in Spring Hills he'd felt this rush of danger that he had felt so often in LA. "Police!" he shouted.

His training kicked in as he swept the room. Loud footsteps, heavy boots, stomped on the scraped wood floor. They were running toward him. He swung his weapon toward the steps when someone slammed into him. He lost his balance and fell against the countertop. The person who'd hockey checked him stumbled but ran past. He pushed himself up and was about to give chase when he heard a woman screaming.

He heard sirens coming up the drive and queued up his radio. "Suspect running on foot heading west!"

There was a squelch from his radio followed by, "I saw him, deputies in pursuit, west toward Dixon." Knowing that the suspect was being pursued, he ran to where the screams had come from.

He made it to the top of the stairs when Andy crashed into him as she ran down the hallway. She panicked at first, arms flailing, trying to push herself away from him. "It's me, it's Eric. Deputy Grayson!" The words tumbled out of his mouth so quickly it almost sounded like one word.

He saw recognition wash over her, and she collapsed against him, sobbing. "Is anyone else up there?" he asked. She shook her head no, still sobbing, and he holstered his weapon. His heart fell to his stomach as he wrapped his arm around her shoulders and led her down the stairs.

He hadn't heard the deputies calling out their locations over the radio, but he had noticed the radio crackling, so he knew they were. When he got Andy downstairs and into a chair in the living room, he heard a pop of the radio static, then breathless shouting, "We lost him!"

Eric bent his knees and lowered himself in front of Andy so they were face to face. "Are you hurt?"

She looked up at him, tears still streaming down her face, "No."

He exhaled in relief and handed her a tissue from the table beside her. She wiped her face and blew her nose. Another deputy and a sergeant entered the room. "Can you tell me what happened?" Eric asked Andy and nodded to the other officers, who fanned out to search the house.

"I was asleep in my bed upstairs," Andy took a deep breath and wiped her nose on the tissue again before she continued. "Then I heard the alarm. I didn't know what to do. I heard them, so I got out of bed and, as quietly as I could, went to the next room and hid.

"I figured if they saw the empty bed, they'd think I wasn't here. Maybe they'd take whatever the hell they were trying to find and leave." She blew her nose into a new tissue. "They moved like they had all the time in the world. The alarm was going crazy, and they didn't care.

"They came upstairs, and I didn't move. I don't have a gun, don't like them. I don't even like to hunt. They went into my room and I heard the blankets move. Maybe the bed was still warm, I don't know, but they didn't leave."

Her tears had stopped, and she was tearing the tissue in her hands to shreds. Her eyes flicked to Eric and back to the floor. "I heard them come through the door where I was hiding and I thought, 'I am about to be raped, or killed, or something.' I was so scared...then I heard someone downstairs. It must have been you...

"I heard you shout, and the footsteps stopped. I heard them mumble something, then they ran." She looked back up at Eric, the green irises of her eyes contrasting with her bloodshot corneas. "You saved me."

The other officers walked back into the room. "It's clear."

"Yeah," Eric replied, tearing his eyes away from her for the first time since she had spoken. "She said she only heard one person."

"Good thing you've got an alarm," said the deputy. Andy nodded.

"It was lucky you were close too, Grayson," the sergeant said. "Sounds like you spooked him. Just pissed we didn't catch him."

Over the next hour, they completed paperwork. It looked as though the intruder had picked the part of Andy's lock that used a key instead of the code. Andy signed her statement and the deputies and the sergeant got ready to leave. Eric watched as she clutched her arms against her body. The strong, brash woman seemed to disappear, replaced by this small, scared version he yearned to pull into his arms.

"Wait," Andy said, "You're going to leave me here alone again? What if he comes back? He was looking for me...me. I swear!"

"Andy," the sergeant said. "We don't have the resources to have someone sit here all night. Chances are he won't come back, but if he does, we'll be back too."

"And what if you're not quick enough? You just said that I was lucky Deputy Grayson was close! What if no one is close next time?"

The Sergeant took a deep breath and said, "I understand you are scared. Perhaps there's somewhere else you can go tonight?"

Andy huffed. "Yeah...sure."

Eric felt himself being overwhelmed with the desire to protect her, to make her feel secure. He wanted to say that he would stay, but knew crossing his sergeant was the wrong idea.

He nodded to Andy and walked out with the others. They had parked their cruisers behind him, so he waited for them to leave and then he walked back up to the house. He knocked, and the door whipped open.

Andy stood in the doorway, looking at him with eyes rimmed with tears that were trying to be angry but still looked scared. "I can come back if you want me to," Eric mumbled. "This is an overtime shift for me, so they're gonna cut me in about an hour. I can come back and check on you."

Andy looked like she was fighting a battle within herself. Struggling to choose between wanting to keep him at arm's length and her desire to feel safe in her own home. She looked away, and he figured she was running through every other option she had.

"You aren't giving in if you say yes. I promise to be a gentleman. I can check on you and go, or I can sit in the driveway if you want me to. No funny business, I won't try anything. Regardless of what you think of me, I'm not that big a dirtbag," Eric said.

"OK," she said, almost in a whisper. Her eyes flicked up to his before she closed the door.

10

Eric was turning his pickup, that the mechanic had repaired, and charged him an arm and a leg for, back into her driveway. He wanted to tear up the drive like he had earlier, but focused on driving slowly. He closed the door loudly on purpose, hoping that he wouldn't startle her when he knocked if she heard him now. When he reached the door, he took a deep breath before he tapped his knuckles against it.

Bloodshot eyes stared at him when the door swung open. Andy looked like all of her bluster and anger had dissolved. A big blanket enveloped her body. She wore slippers on her feet and her hair was pulled back into a knot on top of her head.

She looked at him and it felt like her green eyes were trying to peer through him, seeking his intentions. Then she stepped aside to let him through the threshold. He took off his jacket and shoes and stood, waiting for her to say something.

Since he had come in, she hadn't moved. "How are you doing?" he asked, desperate to break whatever thickness this was that hung in the air.

She pulled the blanket tighter around her. "I feel violated. I'm in my home, and I'm scared...and I don't like it," she said with a shake in her voice. She shuffled behind the island and pulled down two rocks glasses. "You want anything to drink? If you need food, you're free to whatever is in the fridge."

"I'd love a drink. It was a long day," he said, stopping at the opposite side of the island, making it a physical barrier between them. He sensed she was uncomfortable with him being there and wanted to do what he could to make his presence a little more bearable.

"What would you like?" she asked.

"Depends on what you have," he replied.

"My dad was a whiskey connoisseur, but there's scotch, rum and gin in there, too."

"That's quite a collection."

"It sure is. Every night he would take his shower, sit, watch TV and have a glass of something that I used to think smelled awful. My oldest brother even got him a couple of fancy bottles for holidays and birthdays over the years. He never got to try most of them." Her voice trailed off.

"I don't know much about whiskey. More of a craft brew drinker, so I'll take a recommendation." He replied. She nodded and took down a bottle and poured them each a glass. Then she shuffled to the sink and put a tiny splash of water and a couple of ice cubes into one of them and swirled it.

"If you're not used to it, the water and the cold help make it tolerable," she said, handing him the glass. "It's an acquired taste." Then she led him to the living room and curled up in a chair.

After he had left earlier, she made a fire that was roaring now. He sat on the couch across from it and next to her chair. She lifted her glass to her lips and took a sip. He did the same. The liquid slid down his throat with a unique burn, and he realized she was right. This would take some time to enjoy.

She stared into the distance and he could tell she was lost in the night's earlier events. "Art history," he said, breaking the silence. "What was your plan with that?"

She looked it him with a bewildered expression. A smile flashed across her face, like she realized what he was trying to do and was grateful for the distraction.

"Studying great art, cleaning and restoring masterpieces. I used to imagine my brush tracing the same strokes of the masters. I figured I would work in a museum and be happy but broke. I would teach or clean paintings by day, paint at night."

A far-off look crossed her face. "My ultimate pipe-dream was to work for the Louvre. Thinking about all those amazing pieces I would see every day. At night I would go drink French wine, eat French pastries, fall in love with a French man, have half French babies." She seemed to realize who was listening to her, "I'm sorry, I got carried away for a second."

He chuckled, "Don't worry about me. Sounds nice. Especially the pastry part."

A genuine smile crossed her face. "What about you? Did you always want to be a cop?"

"Yeah," he replied, "For as long as I can remember."

"Why Spring Hills?" she asked, taking another drink.

He took a long drink of the liquid in his glass and experienced that burn in his throat again. "My life was good, and then it wasn't. I was looking for something new. A fresh start. Mark and I have been best friends since college. He heard of an opening, knew what I was going through, and here I am."

"I get that," she said, draining the glass and setting it on the coffee table. He felt relief wash over him when she didn't ask for clarification. "That's why I went to NYU. I ran away from this place. Away from here, I wasn't a rancher's daughter or a football star's sister. I was Andrea Summers, that chick who paints, occasionally smokes weed and drinks a lot of coffee."

Eric mulled over what she said before asking, "Andrea?"

"Yeah," she replied. "That's my actual name, after my mom, who was also Andrea. Obviously, two Andrea's under one roof can be confusing, so I became Andy here. Honestly, I don't think my dad ever wanted a daughter, so that played a part, too. So, Andy, I was, and Andy, I still am...at least here."

"Which do you want to be?" Eric asked, sipping his drink.

She stared into the fire before turning back to him. "It doesn't matter what I want anymore."

"So, why'd you leave NYU? Why aren't you still painting and smoking weed while drinking wine and eating sushi?"

A smile bloomed on her face before disappearing. "Because dad got sick," she said, "He called, and I came home. I was the only one who came home. My brothers stayed far away."

"Couldn't you have gone back?"

"Ahhh, you know how it goes. Those damn death bed promises. He begged me to keep this ranch in our family as long as I could, and I told him I would. As a result, I got everything, which ruined my relationships with my brothers and tied me to this place until I either lose it, or I die."

"Wow," Eric replied. "That's pretty heavy."

"Yup," Andy whispered. They sat in silence until he shifted on the couch.

"You must be tired. You can go. I'll manage," she said.

"Andy, if you're OK with me staying and sleeping down here on the couch, I'm happy to do that for you. Maybe if I did, you might get some sleep," he said, careful not to sound overeager. He was honest when he'd told her earlier that he wouldn't try anything. But he couldn't ignore this overwhelming desire to take care of her.

She seemed to consider this. Then she nodded, went to a small closet and pulled out a pillow and some blankets, and tossed them on the couch.

"Thank you," Eric said. "I'm not on again tonight, so I can stay up if you need to talk more."

"I don't know what I need," Andy said, rubbing one of her temples. "Someone broke into my home and I don't know who, or why. I keep thinking about everything that might have happened, what he could have done to me..."

Quiet tears were streaming down her face as she slumped back in the chair. "How do I feel safe again? How do I sleep knowing that next time I might not be lucky enough to have you come rushing in?"

Eric sat, not knowing what to do or say to take this away from her. "Eric, you saved my life, you know that, right?" she said, choking on a sob.

Eric sat for a second, "You called me Eric." He said, smiling. She looked at him and smiled through her tears when she realized what he said was true.

"I guess I did. But I'm serious. If you hadn't—" Her voice shook and a sob interrupted her.

"I know. I'm glad I was close."

As her body shook with quiet sobs, she pulled her knees to her chest. He was fighting with himself. Struggling with wanting nothing more than to reach out to her, but wanting to respect her boundaries. There was a physical pain in his chest as he watched her cry.

"Andy," Eric said, standing up and moving closer to her chair. He knelt down in front of her, still surprised by this usually frigid woman's display of vulnerability. The only thing he wanted was to make it better, to have her smile and say something biting again. "Andy, tell me what I can do."

"I don't know," she whispered between sobs.

"There's one thing I can think of that might make you feel safe. Can I try? Even for a minute?" he asked.

"How?" she whispered.

"Nothing untoward, I promise, but I still need your permission before I'll touch you," he said, not moving from his place. She looked at him and then nodded.

He rose to his feet and slid an arm under her bent knees. When she didn't protest, he put another behind her shoulders and lifted her up. He took the few steps back to the couch and sat down, wrapping his arms around her and pulling her against him. She didn't resist or fight like he thought she might, instead she burrowed into his chest and cried.

He sat still and silent, his arms a cocoon around her. She seemed to fit this space perfectly. He rested his cheek against her head, smelling her shampoo, holding her, not moving, not speaking, until she too was still. He thought she was asleep until he heard her whisper, "I'm so tired, Eric."

He stood up, still holding her, and laid her back on the couch. She was still wrapped in her thick blanket, and he grabbed the pillow she had left for him and tucked it under her head. "I'll sit here until you wake up," he said, taking a seat in the chair she had been in.

He pulled the extra blanket up to his chest and watched as her breathing became rhythmic and his eyes grew heavy.

11

Eric woke up in the morning to the sound of a cupboard closing. He rubbed his eyes and stretched his back, aware that he would be sore all day from sleeping in the chair. Andy wasn't on the couch anymore, but the blanket she had used was. He stood up and cracked his neck before standing and making his way into the kitchen.

Andy was behind the counter, mixing something in a bowl, a pack of bacon sitting on the counter nearby. She looked up when he walked in. "Morning," she mumbled as her eyes darted away from him and a flash of pink spread over her cheeks.

"Good morning," he replied, settling onto a stool at the island. She stopped mixing and poured a cup of coffee from the fancy brewing contraption on the opposite counter and set it down in front of him, still avoiding eye contact.

"I'm making eggs," she said, "And bacon. I rarely get to make breakfast like this, but I called Romeo and told him about last night to explain your truck in the driveway. Which made him forbid me from touching a cow or horse today..." her voice trailed off as she pulled out a pan and turned on the stovetop.

"Are you hungry?" she asked, turning towards him. He nodded over his cup. "How do you take your eggs?"

"However, you'd like to cook them. I'm not picky about a free meal."

"Scrambled all right?" she asked. In the chaos of last night, he hadn't noticed the tight tank top she wore, but he noticed how it showed off her curves now.

"Uh," he started, trying to shake off the indecent thoughts running through his head. "Yup, scrambled is fine. You don't have to make me breakfast, ya know," he said.

"It's the least I could do after you saved my life, held me while I cried like a baby, and then babysat me while I slept," she said and in her voice he could hear the shame and awkwardness she felt.

"Don't mention it," he said, setting the coffee mug down on the counter.

"I'd like not to," she laughed, "But, it happened, and so here we are, me making breakfast in my pajamas in front of the guy who I embarrassed myself in front of last night."

He chuckled and ran his finger around the rim of the mug. "You didn't embarrass yourself. I think if you had reacted in any other way, I'd be more concerned."

She poured the eggs into the pan. "Bacon?" she asked.

"Is that even a question?" he responded. She tossed a few strips into another pan and grabbed her coffee, leaning back against the sink.

"What do I do now?"

He took a deep breath, watching her green eyes that were riddled with worry. "When I've had shit happen in my life, if I try to bury it down and ignore it, well, let's say it gets pretty ugly."

She nodded and moved to flip the bacon. He felt that familiar surge of protectiveness and wished he could take her into his arms again and hold her to give her some strength if she needed it. Even in her pajamas, sleep deprived with puffy eyes, he thought she was beautiful. He wasn't sure how she pulled that off. He wanted to tell her, but as it seemed like she could finally accept him being within a few feet of her without scathing remarks, he wouldn't push his luck.

She put a plate of food in front of him. "I can't promise it's any good. I spent more of my formative years with my hands up a cow's ass than in front of a stove, but scrambled eggs and bacon are pretty hard to screw up."

"Well, nothing makes me want to eat this more than thinking about you having your hands inside a cow." She laughed, a real, good laugh. He felt a surge of pride that he got that response out of her, considering all she had gone through in the last twenty-four hours.

"Oh, come on, I washed my hands." She smiled, sitting atop the stool beside him. "Eh, it's not Dolly's, but it won't kill ya," she said after taking a bite.

"You want it to taste like Dolly's? You're going to need more butter, way more."

She let out a small chuckle, and they ate the rest of their meal in silence. After eating, they sat quietly next to each other before Eric broke the silence. "I guess I should get going."

"OK," she whispered.

"You got something to write with?" She looked at him, cocking her head and then dug into a drawer, producing a pen and a pad of post-its. "This is my number," he said, scribbling it down on the top sheet. "I don't work tonight. If you need some company, or even someone to sit out in the driveway and monitor things, call me OK?" He ripped it off and handed it to her. She nodded, but said nothing in response.

He slid on his shoes and shrugged into his jacket. She turned off the alarm, and he stepped out into the brisk morning air. Before he could close the door, she said, "Thank you...Eric." His heart did somersaults in his chest, but he just shot her a small smile and shut the door behind him.

He had been so close. Rage and grief over his thwarted attempt had consumed him. Bottle after empty bottle had smashed against the wall until the ground glittered with shards of glass and still it had not felt like enough.

He had smelled how close he had been to her. His fingers had felt her warmth on the bed she had been in. If only he had found her before that damn deputy came crashing through the door. This would be over, and he could be at peace. He steeled himself and took a deep breath. "Soon," he whispered. "Soon..."

12

Andy checked the lock on the door about seven times. She made sure the red light on her alarm was shining just as often. It was only 9:00, but the quiet on the ranch and in her home was unsettling.

She tried watching TV, but was constantly turning down the volume to listen, trying to assess if she heard any unusual thumps or bumps. Three or four times she had picked up the bright pink post-it with Eric's number on it, but each time she put it down. She couldn't call him. She couldn't beg him to come and be her savior again. Showing any amount of vulnerability in front of anyone, much less the handsome, charming deputy who seemed to be chipping away at the wall she'd built up over the past few years, made her chest tight.

He had been so warm and had made her feel so small. Memories of the smell of him, the feel of his chest against her cheek, how secure she'd felt swirled inside her. She thought of how gently he laid her down on the couch and how much she had been wishing he would lie beside her and keep her in his arms. When she woke up, she had seen him sleeping in the chair, obviously uncomfortable. She hadn't been able to help but notice how handsome he looked as he slept.

He had done nothing to hurt her, or hint at hurting her. He could, though. She knew he looked at her. She knew he probably had a salacious thought or two about her, perhaps wondered a time or more about what she'd look like in less clothing.

She sighed deeply. She hadn't been with anyone since Jake. That cheating asshole she had said yes to. That cheating asshole that jumped into another woman's bed while she was here taking care of her dying father. She was in Spring Hills when she got a picture texted from a woman showing Jake in a rather compromising position.

Andy flew back to New York and barged into their shared apartment. She had confronted him, yelling that she knew the truth and throwing the ring at his feet before she gathered up a last bag of her things and flew back home. She hadn't heard from him again, nor did she care to.

Jake had been born and raised in London. He had taught her how to thrive in a city, taken her under his wing and then ushered her into his bed. He ticked all the boxes, or at least she thought he had.

Bile rose in her throat when she thought of him and how heartbroken she had been. Less than a week later, her dad begged her to promise to hang on to the ranch and then he was gone, too.

Her thoughts moved to Eric. His broad smile that seemed so easily given, his strong shoulders, his muscular thighs, his blue eyes that seemed to see right through her. She hadn't thought about anyone like this in years. It unsettled her she was picturing what he looked like without a shirt, wondering what his lips would feel like on hers. She shook herself clear of the image of him before her mind took things too far.

A loud bang from outside pulled her from her thoughts and nearly caused her to leap out of her skin. Before she knew what she was doing, she had dialed the number from the post-it and held the phone to her ear.

It rang once. "Grayson," the voice on the other end said. The background was loud. He must have been in The Lodge.

She hesitated. "Hello?" he said.

"Eric," she whispered.

"Andy? What's wrong?" he asked, sounding very serious all the sudden, the background noise fading as though he walked out into the street.

"I'm sorry, Eric, I shouldn't be calling you, but I think I heard something."

"What?" Eric said, alarm in his voice.

"I don't know. I'm here in the kitchen and I swear I heard something outside. It might be a dog, or a cat, or my damn imagination. I'm sorry, it's stupid, I'm being silly. I shouldn't have called. You're busy, I'll let you go..." she stopped talking when she realized she was rambling.

"Andy, I'll be right there."

"No, no, it's probably nothing. You don't have to come. I'm being stupid. I'm sorry," she muttered. Then she heard an engine turn over and she sighed. "You're on your way, aren't you?"

"Yes. Nothing you can say is going to make me turn this truck around. If you don't want me to come in, that's fine, but I'm going to walk around and make sure there's nobody there. When I get there, I'll knock on your door once so you know if you hear something, it's me. But don't open it until I knock twice."

"OK," she said, fear creeping into her voice.

"It'll be OK Andy, I'll be right there. Do you want me to stay on the phone?" The concern in his voice was genuine.

"No, I'll be alright."

"I'm on my way."

The call disconnected, and she paced the kitchen. What the actual shit was she doing? Why was she calling this man, this near stranger, to come rescue her again? She continued pacing, angry with herself. About ten minutes later, she heard the gravel in her driveway crunching under fast tires, then one loud, fast rap on the door.

She went still, wondering what he was encountering. Was it someone else who was trying to break in? She was straining to hear something, anything. It seemed like eons had passed when two loud knocks on the door made her jump.

She went to the door and flung it open, breathing fast, her heart racing. Eric stood on the step, a heavy flashlight in one hand.

"Opossum," he said, smiling, "By the first barn."

"Jesus," she said, rubbing her hand across her forehead. "Shit, I'm sorry Eric. I'm not usually this jumpy...I'm an idiot."

"No, I'd rather you call and it be a creepy opossum, then you not call and it be a creepy guy."

She smiled. "I interrupted you at The Lodge, didn't I? I'm so sorry." She pressed her palms to her cheeks to stop the red she had guessed was spreading across them.

"It's OK. I was watching the game by myself. Mark had already cut out to go home to Margie, so I was finishing my beer."

"Do I owe you a beer, then?" She asked before she could think about what she was doing. He shrugged, and she stepped aside and opened the door wider. "Come on in."

She walked over to the fridge and realized she was only wearing a pair of small gray shorts and a tank top. She crossed her arms across her chest, shielding herself from his eyes, and swore she noticed the corners of his lips curled up when she did.

"I've got a couple of craft beers from my last trip to the city," she said.

His eyes lit up like a kid on Christmas. "Hell yes," he replied as he set his shoes on the mat by the door.

She pulled out two bottles, popped the caps, and handed one to him before heading to the living room. He took the chair he had slept in the night before while she settled onto the far side of the couch. She sat cross-legged with her body facing the fire and pulled a blanket up to her armpits, covering her body the best she could. They both tried to break the awkward silence at the same time. He laughed, and said, "Go ahead."

"Thank you again for coming," she said, then ran a hand over her hair. "A freaking opossum. I feel so stupid."

"Don't. You had no way of knowing what it was." His blue eyes met hers and she felt like he was looking into her soul. Her eyes dropped to his lips, full, parted slightly. She wondered what kissing them was like. She imagined they would taste like the beer he was drinking. Shocked at herself and what she was thinking, she shut her eyes to stop the thoughts from continuing.

When she opened her eyes again, he was still looking at her. "Why are you looking at me like that? What are you thinking?"

He chuckled and said, "You don't want to know." Looking away from her, he took another pull from the beer in his hand.

His comment didn't make her feel as uncomfortable as she thought it should, and she could feel the heat rising into her chest. She pulled the blanket up higher, like it was some sort of shield. This evening was becoming more and more confusing by the second.

He stood up, shook his empty bottle, and walked into the kitchen. She heard the clink of glass on porcelain and assumed he placed it in the old sink. When he walked back into the room, he stood near the end of the couch. She saw his hands were in fists, but he'd pushed them into his front pockets. He chewed the inside of his cheek for a second before speaking.

"Do you want me to hangout in the drive for a bit, make sure nobody creeps around? I could crash on the couch too, if you'd like." He searched her face with his eyes. "What can I do for you Andy?" His voice was low and rich, like expensive scotch and it made her heart skip a beat.

She stared at him, a little taken aback that he was being so nice, asking what he could do for her. The moments where she'd treated him without as much consideration flashed in her mind and she felt embarrassed. She shook her head. "I'll be fine. Thank you for coming."

She wrapped her arms around her chest again and walked him to the door. She disarmed her security system, and they stood looking at each other. "Hey," he said, her heart pounding when his eyes fell on hers. She wished he would reach out and touch her. "I'm a call away."

She nodded, and he turned and left. After she rearmed her security system, she stood in the kitchen. She was tired, but she didn't want to crawl into her bed and listen for noises instead of sleeping.

Instead, she went over to her father's liquor cabinet. She reached out for the bottle that she and her father had opened the night before he died. She pulled it from the shelf and turned it over in her hands. The bottle made her think about her brother, Edward, who everyone called Eddie. He had given her father the bottle as a gift.

She hadn't spoken to Eddie (her father's namesake) or Braxton since the reading of their father's will. The three of them had gathered in this very room in front of their father's attorney. When the lawyer read she was to receive the ranch and all of her father's assets, Braxton had thrown his glass against a wall and stormed out.

Eddie, who had always been the more levelheaded of the two, said, "Well, that's that then," and shook the lawyer's hand before leaving. He hadn't cast so much as a fleeting glance at her before he walked out. Neither had understood, or tried to understand, that this wasn't what she wanted. They didn't take a moment to think that she was giving up everything for this, for a promise whispered to a dying man. She decided against pouring a shot of the amber liquid and placed the bottle back on the shelf.

She made sure every door and window were locked. After she double checked the window of what used to be her parents' bedroom, she stood in front of the wardrobe that sat against the wall. Staring at it, she took a deep breath before opening the doors.

The fragrance within hit her instantly. After all these years, the scent of her mom's perfume still lingered, as though the old wood had been soaked in it. She pulled out a big, gray cable-knit sweater, her mom's favorite. She put it to her nose and inhaled, wondering what her mom would say about everything that was going on.

Her mom had been her greatest supporter and had buoyed her up whenever she needed it. Without her, she had navigated some of the hardest years of her life alone. She'd had her dad, but it wasn't the same. She slid her arms into the sleeves of the sweater and pulled it tight around her body, like it would protect her against the world.

⁓ℓℓ⁓

He cursed at himself as he plodded through the tall grass in the field. If that damn opossum hadn't gotten spooked, he could have finished what he started the night before. He had gotten too close to the creature without seeing it and it had run and knocked over a metal can. His instinct had been to run fast and far, but he cursed himself again, wishing instead he had gone into the house and finished her.

His fingers went to the knife on his belt and he felt himself growing angrier at the thought of how close he had been. If it weren't for the deputy, he was sure he could have gotten to her last night, and now a rodent had deterred him. His hands shook, and he shoved them into his pockets. He took a deep breath. "Soon," he thought to himself again, trying to stay calm. "This will all be over soon."

13

Eric was surprised by how disappointed he had been when Andy hadn't asked him to stay the night again. He wasn't sure what he was expecting, though. She barely even knew him. But it meant so much to him when he felt like he protected her, like he gave her something she needed and he wanted to keep doing it. The breakfast and memories of her in that tank top didn't hurt, either.

It was a couple of days later when he pulled his truck into the spot near his apartment and glimpsed Andy's truck parked outside of Dolly's. He was supposed to meet Mark there for a late breakfast. He couldn't help feeling excited at the prospect of seeing her again.

He slid out of his truck, shut the door, and strode to the diner. Grace stood behind the counter and he let out a small groan of disappointment that he hoped only he heard. His eyes swept over the restaurant and saw Mark sitting at a booth sipping on his coffee. He saw Andy at a table with Romeo and Carl, the three of them looking at paperwork strewn across the table.

Andy looked up at him. She didn't smile or wave, but she also didn't look away. She watched as he walked to Mark's table and sat down. It was only when the darker skinned man at her table laughed she looked away.

Eric brought a hand to his face, which was covered in his now normal stubble. "Do I have something on my face?" he asked Mark as he slid into the booth.

"Yeah," Mark replied, with a look of grave concern on his face. "Too much handsome, ya big lug." Mark waggled his eyebrows, and they both laughed.

Before Eric could say anything more, Grace was beside the table. "Good morning, Eric," she said, trying to sound sultry, which didn't suit her at all.

"Hey Grace," he replied as she handed him a menu.

"Would you like to hear the specials?" She brought the end of her pen to her mouth. An obvious and desperate attempt to draw his attention to her lips.

"Uh, no thanks," Eric said. "I want waffles and bacon, please. Mark, you know what you want?"

Mark ordered, and Grace looked disappointed that Eric didn't seem to notice her more blatant advances, but giggled anyway and said, "All right, no problem. I'll get those orders in for you." She walked away, swaying her hips.

Eric looked up and caught Andy looking in their direction. One corner of her mouth rose in a smirk, and it was obvious she found his exchange with Grace entertaining. Again, he locked eyes with her, and the smile faded from her face. The men at her table drew Andy's attention again, and her gaze left his.

Mark and Eric chatted until Grace came out with their orders. "Here you go, gentlemen," she said, smiling. "Is there anything else I can get you? Eric, would you like some whipped cream? I love whipped cream. It's great on pancakes, waffles, ice cream. So many things."

She brought a finger to her mouth and traced her bottom lip, again a desperate attempt to appear seductive.

"I'm lactose intolerant," Eric replied.

"Oh," she said, her face dropping. "Well, enjoy anyway," she blurted out before she walked away again, a little less bounce in her step.

"You are not lactose intolerant," Mark hissed.

Eric shrugged and chomped on a piece of bacon. "She doesn't know that."

Then he heard Andy's raspy voice, "Hey Grace, can I get some more coffee, please?"

"Yeah, sure thing Andy, just a sec," Grace replied. But instead of getting the coffee, Grace stood behind the counter, tapping on her phone.

Eric saw Andy looking at Grace, her eyes wide, mouth agape. She cocked her head and waited a little longer, watching Grace's thumbs fly across the front of her cell phone. He saw Andy take a deep breath and run her tongue across her top row of teeth, then say something to the men at her table. They nodded, and she grabbed her mug and got up.

She walked over to Eric's table and sat in the booth beside him. She slid over on the bench seat until she was very close to him, so close he could feel the heat rolling off of her body and smelled her familiar scent. "Hey guys," she said with a smile. "How are you?"

Eric was confused, stunned, really. All his brain formulated was, "Uh...fine, you?"

"I want some more coffee," she said, sighing. "But it seems the service around here is, shall we say, lacking today. May I?" she asked, gesturing towards the mound of bacon on his plate. He was almost sure Grace had gotten him more than a normal portion of from the cooks.

"Help yourself," he said. She grabbed a piece and put it in her mouth. She succeeded at drawing his attention to her lips and stirring something within him unlike Grace had. "Everything good at the house?" he asked. Andy nodded and started to say something when they were interrupted.

"Here's your coffee, Andy," Grace said, appearing out of nowhere and pouring more steaming liquid into Andy's empty mug.

"Oh, hey thanks!" Andy replied, sounding sweet and staring up at Grace. Andy didn't drop eye contact with her as she finished the piece of bacon she had been eating. Grace's eyes flicked to Eric's plate, and she didn't move. She was glued to the spot, her face solemn.

Andy turned to Eric. "Yeah, everything's great at home. Thanks," she said, putting a hand on Eric's forearm and leaving it there. Grace's eyes bulged like they might pop out of her head before she scurried away.

Andy watched Grace tuck herself back in behind the counter, then turned back to Eric and Mark, smiling. She chuckled and said, "Next time, maybe she'll bring my coffee a little quicker instead of texting about the hot deputy she's lusting after, huh?" She winked and went back to her table.

Eric felt like his brain hadn't caught up with what had happened and sat, replaying the last few minutes in his head. Mark said, "That was Andy getting back at Grace for neglecting her needs to be caffeinated. That was not Andy making moves on you," and while Eric didn't want to believe it was true, he knew it was.

He was learning that Andy didn't like to be trifled with, and it appeared she didn't mind getting into a scrap with someone because of it. Then his memory flashed to the vulnerable, scared Andy he had held in his arms. He knew there were very few people in the world who had seen her that way, and that was likely how she preferred it.

Eric and Mark talked for a little longer before Eric announced he needed to get to bed. He and Mark exited the diner as Andy and her ranch hands were getting up from their table. Grace waved goodbye and told them to come back soon. He chatted with Mark for a minute before parting ways and was walking toward his apartment when he heard a shout from behind him, "Hey! Deputy!"

Andy was following him. "Can you come with me?" she asked. He noticed she looked on edge. Her cheeks were flushed, and she was chewing on her lower lip, so he nodded and followed her as she hurried toward her truck. When they reached the vehicle, she pointed to a piece of paper, torn on one edge, and stuck under her windshield wiper.

In red marker it said, "You'll get yours soon, bitch." She was biting her lip as she watched him read it.

"Grace?" Eric asked Andy.

"She never left the restaurant. She fawned over you, texted, got pissed at me, and then sulked behind the counter when you didn't take her into your arms and rip open her shirt like the cover of some romance novel," Andy crossed her arms over her chest as she glanced around the street. "It's got to be Frank Miller."

"I think you should call this in Andy," Eric said, digging his phone from his pocket. "We should report it." Eric pushed the button on the side of his phone and the screen lit up.

Andy put her hand on top of his, covering the phone. "Why? What good will that do? It's early. There's no one around who would have seen somebody do this. There are no witnesses, no evidence other than this note.

"A man broke into my house the other night, could have raped me and left me murdered in my bed, and the cops left me to deal with it. They won't do anything about a scrap of paper." Her voice rose at the end of her tirade as she grew angry.

"Maybe they'll take things more seriously now. The break in and the note, that's obvious someone wants to hurt you, Andy, or at least scare you," Eric said. "I'm sorry you don't feel like we did enough for you the other night and I agree with you, but we're stretched pretty thin, Andy."

Andy's face softened, and she opened her mouth to retort when someone called out, "Eric!" Both Eric and Andy turned to see Grace scurrying out of Dolly's with a bag in her hands. "I bagged up your leftovers, thought you might like them." She smiled. Eric looked at the bag, knowing he had nothing more than a strip of bacon or two and a corner of waffle on his plate when he left. Regardless, he thanked her.

When he glanced at Andy, she looked like she wanted to punch Grace in the face. Grace stood there for a moment, looking from Andy back to Eric, and when she realized they weren't parting ways, she breathed goodbye and scurried back into the diner.

"I swear, can you screw her and get this over with?" Andy said, exasperated.

"I'd rather not," Eric replied.

Andy stared at him and let out a deep breath. "The cops won't a damn thing about this note. You know that. I'm going to look an ass, or a crazy over worried woman and nothing will happen that will help me," she said, grabbing the note and jamming it in her pocket, "I shouldn't have gotten you. I freaked out for a second. It's fine. It's Frank Miller trying to scare me so I turn tail and run away and sell to him."

Before Eric could reply, she had opened her truck door and climbed in. She started the engine and rolled down the window. "Have a good one, Deputy." Then she left, leaving Eric standing in the street with his doggy bag and Grace's eyes boring holes into him from her spot behind the counter of the diner. Feeling exhausted, he went to his apartment, threw the bag in the trash, and climbed into bed.

14

Halloween was upon them. Eric didn't know how, as a new deputy with the department, he wasn't assigned to work that night. He was glad, though. Mark and Margie were having their annual Halloween party in the barn on their property and much of the town between the ages of 21 and 65 were supposed to be in attendance. No costumes though. Apparently, the farmers and ranchers of Spring Hills weren't keen on dressing up, but they enjoyed an excuse to get together, have a bonfire, and drink.

Eric spent most of the day helping Mark and Margie prepare their pole barn for the festivities. He and Mark cleaned, hung lights, put out decorations and set up tables while Margie told them what to do.

They were readying the final touches when Margie announced it was time that they should get changed. Eric had brought a change of clothes, per Margie's direction, and took a quick shower in the guest bathroom, also per Margie's direction.

The barn seemed to fill up quickly. Eric saw many of the people he knew from town, most of their names he had forgotten, but there were a few he remembered. He glimpsed Grace, but immersed himself in a conversation between a couple ranchers about the preferred temperature of bull semen for insemination.

He was getting a quick education on the art of impregnating a cow when he heard that familiar raspy voice coming near, "Paul, my daddy always taught me it's impolite to discuss getting a heifer pregnant when she's not here to defend herself."

Paul, an older rancher with a gut and a mustache that an eighties sitcom star would have been envious of, laughed and squeezed her against his side. "Little Andy," he said, "Your daddy is one hell of a proud man up there. You're doing magic on that ranch."

"Thank you," Andy said, and Eric thought he might see her blushing. "It's thanks to a lot of luck and a lot of great, loyal guys that I've always been able to call family."

"Aw hell," said the other man who had been talking about making baby cows, "You're one hell of a rancher Andy, it ain't luck, it's your blood." Andy smiled up at him and lifted her beer, he did the same and they both took a drink. Eric thought something in her eyes looked sad, despite the smile on her face.

Two women, one tall and thin, one short and plump, came over. "Andy, you look beautiful as always," the tall one said, bending down to give Andy a kiss on the cheek before turning to the man Eric now knew as Paul. "Now dear, if you don't come over and dance with me, I might have to ask this handsome young man to join me instead," she said, gesturing to Eric.

"Yeah, Chuck!" the short woman said to the other man.

"Aw come on," Chuck said. "Poor kid wouldn't last two minutes with you yapping his ear off." He winked at Eric and the men led the women to the middle of the barn and onto the makeshift dance floor, leaving Eric and Andy standing together.

"You will see some mighty fine square dancing this evening, deputy," Andy said, adding a little southern drawl to her speech as she stood beside him. He watched as she took a swig of her beer, her eyes scanning the room.

"Oh well," Eric said, "When I woke up this morning I said, 'Self, I've been in Nebraska for this long and I have seen no mighty fine square dancing yet. I must right this wrong.'"

Andy rolled her eyes. "I'm sure it won't stack up to the bumping and grinding of your LA club scene."

"Fine by me. Wasn't my scene."

"Grace will be disappointed to hear that."

He whipped his head in the direction Andy was looking. "Shit, is she coming? Where is she?" he said, almost panicked. Andy started laughing.

"You need to relax! You realize you're scared of a twenty-one-year-old girl, right? A girl who would be more than willing to show you the finer parts of Spring Hills...or at least her finer parts," she nudged him with her elbow at the last comment.

"I have zero interest in her finer parts. She's a kid."

"Hmmm..."

"Hmmm, what?"

"I didn't peg you for being the kind of guy to pass up on an easy score."

"Ouch. You don't know me well enough to peg me for anything, ma'am. You're basing all of your assumptions on a stereotype of 'guys like me.'" He finished his sentence, making air quotes with his fingers.

"Eric," Andy said as she looked over his shoulder, "Don't panic, but she is coming over here."

"Are you shitting me?" he asked under his breath.

"No, but don't worry. I owe you one, right?"

"Hey Eric!" Grace's saccharine voice called out behind him.

He sighed and then turned slowly. He smiled in an effort not to be rude. "Grace," he said.

"Having fun?" she asked, wiggling her brows at him and Eric wondered how much she'd had to drink before she'd even gotten to the party.

"Yeah, sure," he said. Wondering when Andy's "owe you one" was going to kick in.

"Me too, but I'm sure I could think of a few ways to have a lot more fun," Grace purred as she reached out and ran her fingers along his arm. He smelled the alcohol on her breath as she spoke.

Then he heard Andy say, "Hey Grace. How are you doing? I heard your brother was doing well on the football team this year."

"I'm fine. He's doing fine too, not sure why you care," Grace replied, trying to end whatever conversation, or diversion rather, Andy was attempting.

"Good," Andy replied with an edge to her voice. She drained her beer, set the empty on the table nearby, and without saying another word, grabbed Eric's hand and pulled him out onto the dance floor and away from Grace.

Eric was just as surprised as he imagined Grace was. Andy put her hand on Eric's shoulder and offered her the other to him. Still feeling a little surprised, he took her hand in his, then put his other hand on her waist.

The song that was playing was slow. The couples around them were holding each other close. Andy looked over Eric's shoulder and chuckled, "I'm not sure if Grace has processed what just happened, but she looks pissed."

"I can only imagine," Eric whispered. Andy took a step forward and brought both of her hands up around his neck. His breath hitched and his stomach felt like it was flip flopping as he settled his other hand on her waist. She looked up at him and winked. He knew this was all part of the show, but wished it weren't. "You're mean," he said, laughing.

"I tried to strike up a conversation instead. She wasn't having it. She brought this on herself. And I get called mean a lot. I also get bitch, ice queen, heartless, etcetera, etcetera. She should have brought me my damn coffee." Eric laughed again. Seeming to take her vengeance on Grace one step further, Andy slid her hand down onto his bicep and rested her head on his chest.

He wished her leaning against him like this wasn't only to save him from Grace and exact coffee-based revenge. He felt the heat of her body against his. They'd been this close once before, but that time she'd been sobbing. Standing like this, she seemed to fit under his chin, like a puzzle piece that was meant just for that spot.

The song ended, and they stopped swaying. Andy took half a step back and looked at him. Her mouth was open slightly. She looked troubled, maybe confused, as her eyes locked onto his. He couldn't put his finger on it. She shook her head and closed her eyes while inhaling.

Andy broke the uncomfortable silence, "If Grace could shoot bullets out of her eyes, I'm pretty sure I would look like swiss cheese." Eric glanced behind him and saw Grace standing with another woman about her age. Grace had her arms crossed tight over her chest and was glaring in their direction.

He shoved his hands into his pockets. "Might not want to eat at Dolly's when she's there. Could end up with a little extra something in your eggs," he said, miming spitting.

"Ugh, I would say we are even, but Jerry doesn't work at the only place to eat in town. So I may have one up on you."

At that moment, a plump Latina woman rushed to Andy and wrapped her in her arms. "Mija," the woman said, tears threatening to spill from her eyes, "You are an angel on this earth." He watched Andy's face soften.

Her lips curled into a slight smile as she leaned into the woman's hug. "Oh Rosa, it was nothing," Andy said softly. Rosa released Andy from her embrace, put her hands on Andy's biceps, and stared at her.

"It was everything," she said, still crying. "Romeo and I are so lucky to have you, Andy. We all are. Come, come, have a drink with us." She chuckled and slipped a thick arm around Andy's small waist. She nodded to Eric and ushered Andy towards a small group of her ranch hands and their wives.

Eric watched as Romeo swept Andy into an embrace, lifting her off the floor. When he set her down, two of her ranch hands took turns clapping her on the back, smiling. Romeo thrust a beer into her hand, and then they took turns clinking their bottles with hers.

"What the hell was that man?" Mark said, handing Eric a beer.

"I dunno. Her ranch hands seem pretty happy about something," Eric replied.

"No, you idiot. Whatever that was with Andy, you guys all smooshed up together!" Mark said, pushing his palms together as an example, exasperated that he had to elaborate.

"Oh, Grace was coming on pretty hard. I didn't want to deal with it, so Andy stepped in and saved me from her. Said she was paying me back for the Harvest Festival and that guy."

"You need to tell that poor girl you're not interested," Mark said, chuckling.

"Yeah, I know."

"But you're not upset that not telling her ended up with you and Andy so close."

"Yeah, I know." A Cheshire cat grin spread across Eric's face. He glanced over again and saw Andy with her ranch hands, smiles all around.

A while later, he and Mark had gone to find Margie to see what tasks she had for them, as the party was in full swing. They were dumping ice into coolers when Eric heard Andy tell her group she was going to go, so at least one of them would make it to the ranch on time in the morning. The men laughed, and the women assured her they would make sure their men weren't late.

Eric glanced up as he finished dumping the ice in the blue plastic cooler and saw Grace scowling at Andy. "Gimme a minute," he said to Mark as he handed him the empty bags from the ice.

He intercepted Andy as she headed for the door. "May I walk you to your truck?"

"Why?" Andy asked. "I promise, officer, my blood alcohol is well below the legal limit."

He smiled, "I'm sure it is, but Grace is still looking at you like a cheetah looks at her prey. Knowing that I'm the reason for that, I'd like to make sure she doesn't jump you on your way to your truck."

Andy leaned to look behind Eric and saw that he was telling the truth. Grace was still glaring at her over a red solo cup. "I'm pretty sure I can take her," she said, glancing back up at him, but Eric didn't budge. "Yeah, fine, OK," she agreed. She turned on her heel and headed out the door without another word. He followed behind and, once outside, picked up his pace to walk beside her.

She seemed distant, her hands were plunged deep into the pockets of her leather jacket, her shoulders hunched. He opted not to make any small talk. The moon was full, perfect for Halloween and for lighting their way. Had she been giving off anything other than, "if you touch me, I'll kill you," vibes, he would have even considered it romantic.

"This is me," she said, pulling her keys from her pocket and unlocking the doors. She stood beside the bed of the truck and turned to Eric. "Thanks for walking me out here, but it doesn't look like Grace is chasing me with a knife."

He chuckled. "I'll talk to her as soon as I can. Thanks for rescuing me from her." If he wasn't mistaken, he saw a flash of color flood her cheeks before she turned.

"Yeah," she said, opening the door to the truck, "No problem. Have a good one Eric." She closed the door and turned over the engine. He watched her pull away towards the road before realizing that even though she'd turned cold toward him, she hadn't called him "Deputy."

—ele—

He had felt all the air suck out of his lungs when he saw Andy exit the barn. His hand went to his knife, but that damn deputy was following her. He raged inside as he realized he had been thwarted again. He knew he wouldn't be able to see her limp body laying between the cars as he'd imagined for the last hour while he had waited in the shadows for her.

15

After she arrived home, Andy performed her security ritual and slid off her jacket. Her head felt fuzzy again. Not from the alcohol at the party, but from the emotions she was battling.

Her thoughts felt jumbled. She was so confused about what she was feeling about Eric. She thought she wanted to keep him at arm's length, but she was the one that pulled him closer to her as they danced. Worse than that, she had liked it a lot. Feeling his firm chest, the warmth of him, the savory smell of his cologne, the sound of his heart beating, the memories swelled up, and she felt desire stirring within her.

When they had parted for a split second, she'd wanted to grab his face and crash her lips against his, and it terrified her. She barely knew him, but in that moment, she couldn't deny that she wanted him, at least physically. She was so thankful that Rosa had come over when she did. Andy wasn't sure what she might have done otherwise.

Romeo and Rosa were like family to her. Romeo had mentioned that Rosa was missing her mother, who lived in Texas. Her guys worked so hard, and her ranch had been doing pretty well, so she shared some of what it had earned with them. Earlier that day, she had given each of them an unexpected, but well-deserved bonus, spurred by Rosa's wish that they had the means to go home to see her mom.

She knew she would give anything to see her mom again and felt like she needed to give that chance to Rosa. A lump welled up in her throat as she thought of her mom. She fought the tears she could feel in her eyes. Instead of giving in and sitting on the cold floor crying like she had the sudden and overwhelming desire to do, she trudged up the stairs and into the bathroom. She started filling up the old, claw-foot tub and then lowered herself into the hot, steaming water.

Her mother had taken a long, hot bath every Saturday night. The whole family knew that was her hour, the only one she got to herself all week. As Andy lay in the water with her head against the edge of the tub, the memories flooded back.

The day after they buried her brother, Theo, her mother got her diagnosis, stage four metastatic breast cancer. Her mother had only lasted a few months, and the treatments meant to extend her life had made her sick and weak. Andy would go to school, come right home, lay down in bed with her, and watch garbage TV. She would make her mother thin broth and spoon feed it to her when she was too weak to lift the spoon to her own mouth. Andy had been the one to hold her mother's hand as she took her last breaths, just like she had with her father.

As she lay in the water, she wondered what her mom would think about this situation with Eric. She wondered what she would say if they could sit on the porch swing and talk with steaming mugs of coffee in their hands. Her mom would smile when Andy told her when she had been dancing with him, pressed against him, she felt happy and safe. In his arms, she had felt a physical desire she hadn't experienced since Jake. She would tell her mom that it scared the shit out of her.

"Why him?" Andy said out loud. She could almost hear her mother's voice telling her that Eric wasn't Jake, that she would be cheating herself by not giving him a chance. Her mother would tell her it was OK to be scared, but she couldn't keep people out forever, as much as she wanted to. She imagined her mom telling her that being alone, albeit safer, wasn't how the Andy she knew would want to live.

Andy again thought back to the night of the break in and how safe she felt when he held her tight against him, his arms enveloping her. She thought about his smile, and as much as she hated to admit it, she thought of how ruggedly handsome he looked with the short, trim beard he'd adopted since his first few weeks here. She thought about the electric feeling she had whenever he touched her, and her mind went to how his blue eyes lit up when he smiled. He was handsome; he was charming and funny, and thus far, he had been kind.

Then her thoughts continued to wander, and she wondered what his skin would feel like against hers, then what it might be like to kiss him, to have his mouth on her body. She imagined how it would feel to wrap her legs around his waist as he pinned her against a wall and then carried her up the stairs to her bed.

"Shit." She groaned as the warmth growing from within her became more pronounced. Covering her face in her hands, she took a deep breath and sunk down into the water.

16

Eric headed to Dolly's early the next morning. He knew he had to face Grace and tell her he wasn't interested. Even though he'd never given her any ideas and had never led her on, he still felt deceitful by not shutting it down when he wasn't interested.

When he opened the door, he saw her behind the counter. A smile bloomed across her face, but before she said anything, he blurted out, "Grace, can we talk outside for a minute?" She smiled even bigger and nodded. He guessed that in that moment she was playing out scenarios involving him asking her out, or taking her in his arms and kissing her, confessing his desire for her. He inhaled, knowing this was going to be painful.

He held the door open for her and she stepped outside into the chilly morning air. "I'm sorry it's cold out here," he said. "I'll be quick."

"Oh, that's no problem at all, Eric," she said, smiling at him as she batted her eyelashes at him. She was tall, so unlike Andy, she didn't need to tilt her chin up to look him in the eyes. He noticed she took a step toward him to reduce the space between them. He fought the urge to take a step back, knowing he was about to hurt her.

"Grace," he started, "I've become aware that perhaps you have a romantic interest in me." He continued before she could respond, "I need to let you know that if that is the case, the feeling isn't mutual. From what I know, you are a great girl. But I don't see us ever being anything more than friends." Her face fell as he spoke.

"Uhm," she said, her eyes looking watery, "Thank you for letting me know." She brushed past him and hurried back into the restaurant.

Eric breathed out. A visible puff of white hovered in the cold air. "Shit," he muttered. He trudged back to his apartment, regretting that he hadn't gotten breakfast before having that chat.

He'd almost reached the store he lived above when he saw Andy's truck pull in to a spot in front of the hardware store. When she hopped out of the cab, she saw him. He thought her eyes got wide, and she dashed into the store.

He took another breath, wondering what in the world could have caused that reaction. He sighed and retreated up the stairs and into his apartment.

He cleaned, popped over to the grocery store and did his best to keep his mind off of Andy, but failed. He couldn't figure out what he had screwed up at Mark and Margie's party to deserve the reaction she'd had to him that morning. His thoughts drifted to the way she felt in his arms, the way her ass looked in those jeans, how her body felt against his, and how he wished he could have kissed her parted lips.

Video games were not cutting it as a distraction, so he pulled on sweats and a jacket, threw on a hat and went for a run. When he returned, his face was cold, but he was riding a high of endorphins from the physical activity. He hopped into the shower, changed into fresh clothes, and made himself some dinner.

After he ate, he settled down on the couch and tried to find something on TV worth watching. He'd settled on a basketball game when his phone buzzed. He figured it was Mark, but when he looked at the glowing screen, he saw a text from a number he didn't recognize.

"Hey, it's Andy. What's your opinion on s'mores?" The text read. His brain took a moment to reconcile that it was the same woman who had run away from him this morning.

"I am pro s'more," he tapped back.

"Well, I've got a pile of scrap wood I'm getting ready to burn and all the ingredients for them if you need a fix," she sent back.

His brain was running a million miles a minute. He could take or leave a s'more, but he'd take any opportunity to be around Andy. He couldn't believe she was inviting him to be near her.

"Yeah, sure, I'll be right there." He typed. Then he jumped up, threw on a heavy winter coat, shoved his feet into his boots and was out the door.

17

Andy had thought about him damn near all day, so when found an excuse to text him, she did. She hadn't allowed the functioning parts of her brain could tell her not to. Now that he was on his way, she was cursing herself. All day she had been hearing the voice of her mother telling her to give him a chance, give herself a chance at being happy. The words she imagined her mother saying were on repeat, telling her that even if it didn't work out well, it was a step in the right direction and that she couldn't keep punishing herself because Jake had been an asshole.

She was repeating these words in her head when she heard tires on the gravel in the driveway. He had gotten there quicker than she thought he would. Inhaling, she walked away from the fire.

"I'm glad to see you dressed warm," she yelled to him as he stepped out of the cab of his truck.

"It's freaking cold out here," he said as he walked toward her.

She wasn't sure what to say and the warmth of the fire was calling to her. Gesturing for him to follow, she headed back toward the flames. She heard his boots on the ground behind her and pointed to a camp chair when they'd gotten closer.

"Anyone else here?" he said, looking around as he took a seat.

"No," she replied, throwing another piece of wood on the fire. She could feel herself being awkward. Anyone would be though if they had, for some godforsaken reason, invited the guy they might have feelings for over to roast fucking marshmallows. Why had she invited him to come?

She handed him the bag of marshmallows and a long metal skewer and took a seat near him. She glanced at him. The firelight illuminated his face and her heart beat faster. "Get it together woman," she thought, scolding herself.

"So, how do you take yours?" he asked.

"What?" she said, snapping out of her self-deprecating internal monologue.

"Your marshmallows? I see you don't have one of these," he said, holding up the metal skewer. "So I was going to make one for you."

"Oh, thank you, but I'm very particular, so I can do it."

"OK, but that's still not an answer."

She laughed. "I like a perfect golden brown. Like if you were going to film a marshmallow commercial...that marshmallow. You?"

"Burnt. It's quick, and easy."

"You like things easy, and finished fast?" she said, raising her eyebrows. As soon as the words were out of her mouth, she regretted it. She saw Eric's eyes go wide.

"No, I-I didn't mean that how it sounded," he stammered. She could feel her cheeks flaming, but not from the heat of the fire. He laughed a low rumble and that now familiar flock of butterflies in her stomach took flight.

"For the record, I like things that are enjoyable and worth the effort, regardless of the time it takes to get there." His blue eyes danced, and she understood what he was referring to. "Marshmallows are the exception," he added as the one on the skewer caught fire. He looked at her after blowing out the flame and they both laughed.

"Rosa makes the best s'more cookies," Andy said as she watched Eric make his s'more with the blackened marshmallow.

"She seemed very nice."

"She's wonderful. After mom died, she really stepped up for me, did my hair for all my school dances, listened to my boy problems, ya know...mom stuff. They're great people. I couldn't do any of this without Romeo, Carl, or any of my guys."

"They worked for your dad, right, Romeo and Carl?" Eric asked as he handed the skewer to Andy. She noticed he'd already put a new marshmallow on it for her.

"Yeah, I've known Romeo for a long time. I think he came to the ranch when I was in elementary school. Carl has known me since I was born. Carl's like some cranky uncle, while Romeo's more like a way older brother to me, which is nice considering mine has disowned me."

"Well, that's something we have in common."

"Oh, yeah?" she said, raising her eyebrows as she twirled the marshmallow above the flames.

"Yeah..." The timber in Eric's voice changed as he spoke of his brother. "Will and I don't agree on much. He's cut me out. Which is OK I guess. When I needed him, he chose not to be there, so it is what it is. I guess I've kind of accepted that he didn't want to be a part of my life anymore. What happened to yours?"

"My brothers both cut me out. I'm not sure which one hurt more. Braxton's an addict. He started using in high school, maybe even earlier, pot and pills and god knows what else. It got worse and worse," she said. "After he graduated, I saw him once a year, usually at Christmas. One year, he and Dad got into it. It was ugly and Dad was going after Braxton, telling him he needed to get his shit together. Braxton told Dad he was a terrible father...it snowballed from there. He stopped showing up at Christmas after that.

"He didn't come see dad at all when he was dying. When he showed up at the funeral, he was strung out. He came to the reading of the will and then disappeared. I don't even know if he's alive."

He had been the one she was closest to. Eddie was the oldest, the revered namesake, and the one her parents poured their pride into. Theo was a joker and an athlete. It was easy to like Theo, but he was old enough to not have an enormous interest in his little sister, and he was taken from them all too soon. Braxton had always had a bit of a rebellious streak and hated everything about football and ranching, but he saw value in Andy's art when no one else did. As the only girl in the family, she was often on the outskirts of things like Braxton. They became allies until Braxton used.

"What about your other brother?" Eric asked.

"Eddie sounds a lot like Will. I feel like he made a conscious decision not to be involved in my life. I feel like with Braxton I can kind of understand. Addicts like that will pick the high every single time, over everything else. But with Eddie...he chose."

"Do you miss them?"

"I did. But after a while, after seeing Brax come home thinner, tweaking, him not being the brother I knew...I grieved him. I mourned him then. So, no, I don't miss him anymore. He made his choices, and I understand it's difficult to turn away from those choices...but, he never asked for help and he'd never accept the help we tried to give him either.

"Eddie...every once in a while, I miss Eddie. I never understood why he didn't come home for dad. He loved Eddie so, so much..." Her voice trailed off before she pulled her marshmallow from the fire and inspected it.

"Is it perfect?" Eric asked, smiling.

"Close, but not quite. Good things take time," she replied, and a smirk flickered on Eric's face.

They sat in silence for a while and she watched as Eric pulled out another graham cracker and piece of chocolate.

"No marshmallow? Am I taking too long?"

He flashed a smile back at her. "It's for you, silly," he said, and her heart did a somersault.

"It's a goddamn s'more woman!" She chastised herself again.

Finally, Andy pulled the marshmallow from the flames and added it to the parts Eric had prepared. When their fingers touched, she sucked in a breath and hoped Eric hadn't noticed.

Over the next forty-five minutes, they talked about nothing of substance, mostly the ins and outs of the people in Spring Hills. When Eric told her about the conversation he'd had with Grace, she cringed.

Andy felt a chill, and before she could stop herself, she asked, "Would you like to come in for a drink? Warm up a bit?"

"Absolutely," Eric said.

18

Eric woke up the next morning and rubbed his eyes. He had slept a little later than normal.

When they had gone into the house that night, Andy had dashed up for a shower, saying she couldn't stand smelling like smoke. She returned wearing sweats with her wet hair piled on top of her head. He realized he was smiling at the sight. She was so different from his ex-wife, who never in a million years would have let anyone see her like that. His ex always had to be made up and presentable. He guessed she went to sleep in at least some makeup.

They had shared a drink, talking only a little. Andy seemed far away, not distant, but like she had a lot on her mind. He hadn't stayed long, fearing if he did, he might cross a line.

After, he had tossed and turned in his bed, unable to sleep. He had replayed the end of their evening at least a dozen different times, fantasizing that it ended with her in his arms, him kissing her, but none of that had happened.

When he left, she had looked up at him from below her eyelashes and, for a split second, he thought he saw something there. Then she took a sharp inhale and thanked him for coming. He had gone out into the cold air and back to his empty apartment.

He was still contemplating the evening prior when his phone buzzed with a text. Glancing at it, he saw it was Mark who had what he considered good intel that Grace was not working that morning, so Eric agreed to meet him for breakfast. He walked in and his eyes swept over the diner. His shoulders relaxed when he saw no sign of Grace.

Mark sat in a booth, looking down at his phone. "Hey buddy," Eric said, sliding into the opposite side.

Mark put his phone in his pocket. "Hey!" he smiled at Eric. "Long night?" he said.

"You can tell, huh?" Eric replied, wiping a hand down his face. "I was making s'mores." Mark raised his eyebrows and opened his mouth to talk, but a surly looking server approached the table.

"Coffee?" she asked. They each nodded, and she plunked down a mug in front of them. "You know what you want?"

Both Eric and Mark told her their orders. She wrote nothing down and trudged back to the kitchen. Eric took a sip of his coffee, and Mark stared at him. "You sat out in the cold roasting marshmallows?"

"Yeah, Andy invited me."

"Damn, man, you've got it bad. Did anything else happen?" asked Mark as he sipped his coffee.

Eric chuckled. "No, we sat and talked, ate some s'mores, had a drink and I went home."

"Hmmm," Mark said, "Sounds like the friend zone to me, man." Out of the corner of his eye, Eric saw Andy slip into a chair on the other side of the room. He wanted to go talk to her, but he restrained himself and focused on Mark.

They were talking about Mark's students when Eric heard the bell at the front door chime. He heard boots stomping across the floor and saw the form of Frank Miller fly past him. Before he knew it, a chair scraped across the linoleum floor and Andy jumped to her feet.

Frank bent so that he was less than an inch from Andy's face, pointing a finger at her and screaming, "You bitch! He was days from selling to me and you meddled where you don't belong! I swear to you, I will make you pay for this!" Eric had leapt up and began moving toward them before Frank had spat out the last sentence.

"Hey!" Eric yelled, drawing Frank's attention.

"You stay the hell out of this, Deputy!" Frank yelled. Eric stepped between him and Andy, pushing Andy gently so she was behind him.

"I'm sorry Frank, I can't do that."

"Yeah, because you want to screw that whore!"

"Because I'm a deputy of this county and you are disturbing the peace here at Dolly's and threatening a patron. Here are your options. I can tell you to leave and you can turn and walk out the door, go back to your truck and drive away.

"Or you can put up a fight, and I can call another deputy to take you to jail after I kick your ass. It's your choice, Frank, but I hope you make the right one because I'd like to go finish my coffee before it gets cold." Eric stood unwavering as Frank flexed his fists, seeming to consider his options.

"Fuck you both," Frank said with a sneer and stormed out of the door.

Eric turned to Andy. She was trembling, and the desire to hold her almost overcame him. Instead, he crossed his arms to stop himself from doing it and asked, "Are you OK?"

Her face was red and the same color had sprung up in splotches on her chest. She was opening and closing her fists. "Yes, thank you," she replied, and he heard a shake in her voice. Without asking, he picked up her plate and mug and took them to the booth he shared with Mark. To keep himself from doing something stupid, he placed them on the side next to Mark. She followed without a fight and slid into the booth, putting her papers on the seat beside her.

Mark put a friendly arm around her, "You alright?" he asked. The other diners and staff who had stopped to watch the altercation went back to their business.

"I knew I'd piss him off," she said, pushing her almost full plate away and clutching her coffee in her shaking hands. "I talked to Jim Bishop a few weeks ago. Jim told me he was having a rough time, he was losing money hand over fist and he was considering selling to Frank.

"Jim and I came to an agreement. I need more land because my herd is growing. Jim's is stable. So we decided I would rent some of his land that was next to mine. It gives my herd more access to the river, and it gives him some money. Once he needs that land back, the agreement ends and the rent payments are done. We've even put up a temporary fence to keep the cattle from mixing. I also bought some from him to diversify the herd. We had planned that he could borrow one of my bulls to spruce his up, too.

"Jim told me Frank was still pestering him about selling, and he was going to tell him he wasn't interested anymore. Judging by Frank's reaction, he must have done that recently."

"All this," Eric said, "Over land and cows?"

Andy nodded, looking solemn. "Land and cows are our livelihood. If Frank can get ranchers to sell to him, he can get their land, their herds, and keep growing his own ranch. He's always been a cutthroat asshole. Instead of seeing a struggling rancher and trying to help, he sees his own gain. Dad didn't raise me that way. He taught me we help each other when we can, whatever it takes."

Andy took a long drink of her coffee, then she dug ten bucks out of her pocket and tossed it on the table. "Thanks for stepping in back there," Andy said, smiling. "I'm not sure who would have thrown the first punch if you hadn't." She stood up and collected her paperwork.

"You're welcome," was all Eric could muster. With that, Andy headed for the door and left Mark looking at Eric.

"That guy is a serious piece of shit," Mark said.

19

Shortly after breakfast, Eric and Mark parted ways. Eric wasn't sure what to do. He wanted to rush over to Andy's to make sure she was OK, but he didn't want to overstep. He wasn't even sure where he stood with her at this point. In the end, he decided he would drive over, but if he saw anyone there, he would leave.

He ran over his plan, or lack thereof, over and over in his head as he drove. This was stupid, but if there was someone there, he could explain that he had been at the diner and wanted to make sure Andy was okay. He was a deputy, after all, and it seemed plausible that an officer of the law would do something like that.

He pulled into the gravel driveway and immediately regretted his decision. A large blue pickup was parked next to Andy's. He threw his vehicle into reverse, but before he could back out even an inch, the man he recognized as Carl came out of the barn and peered at him.

"Shit," Eric muttered. He didn't have any choice other than parking the truck and explaining himself.

"Hey man," he said, sliding out of the cab. He was smiling even though he wanted to dissolve into the mud. He was sure Andy wouldn't appreciate it if anyone got the wrong idea about them.

"Hey yourself," Carl said, sticking out a hand for Eric to shake. Eric took it and pumped his hand twice. "What are you doing here?" Carl added, his eyes suspicious.

"Frank gave Andy a pretty rough time at Dolly's this morning. I got in the middle of things, but I wanted to see if she was okay," Eric said.

"That fucking asshole," Carl growled. He turned and stormed towards the barn, waving for Eric to follow.

"Andy!" Carl bellowed when he entered the barn. Andy, now wearing thick Carhart overalls, was digging through scrap boards in the corner.

"What?" she yelled back, climbing down from the stack of wood with a piece of timber in her hands.

"What the hell? Frank came at you this morning?" Carl yelled.

"How the hell do you know that?" Andy replied, then her eyes fell on Eric and she sighed.

"Eric told me. Said he was here to make sure you were alright because Miller gave you a rough time. What did he do?"

"Carl, he said some things. I refuse to tell you what. I will not have one of my best hands in jail because he went to exact revenge on my behalf.

"Yes, it was about Jim. Yes, I'm okay. No, the fence will not fix itself, and as it is a Sunday, I would like to not spend all day out here," Andy said, dragging the heavy board to the door.

Without thinking, Eric grabbed the other end and lifted it. She looked at him, but said nothing and continued walking toward a beat-up red pickup that looked like it was used for rough work. They lifted the lumber into the bed of the truck where other pieces of wood lay scattered, and Andy turned to look at him. "Well, since you're already here, getting involved in my business, are you gonna help us fix a fence or what?" she asked.

Eric was taken aback. "Uh...yeah, sure."

"Hmph," Carl muttered as he followed behind with a bag of tools. "Didn't know I signed up to teach a city kid how to fix a fence today."

"And I didn't know I signed up to get my ass chewed out by a grumpy old man. Looks like we're both surprised," she shot Carl a look. "You guys go up front. I'll sit back here." Before either could object, she had climbed over the tailgate and settled in the bed's corner nearest the cab. Carl shrugged and went to the driver's side, and Eric hurried to the passenger door.

They both climbed in, and Carl turned the key in the ignition. The engine rattled as it worked to turn over. "Heat doesn't work," Carl said. His eyes swept over Eric and then he gave the truck gas.

The old ranch hand drove slowly. Eric wasn't sure if it was for Andy's sake, or if it was as fast as the truck would move. "You came all the way out here to check on Andy out of the goodness of your heart, huh?" Carl said in a low voice.

Eric didn't quite know how to respond. "Yeah. Frank was pretty brutal. I would have been shaken up if I were her."

Carl's knuckles turned white as he gripped the wheel even tighter. "I could kill that asshole. Been after Andy since Ed died. Bad seed that one. He never would have gone after Ed like he is Andy.

"He hasn't gotten it through his thick skull that she isn't some chicken-shit, though. Miller thinks because she's a woman she's gonna be easy to railroad, but she's not. She's tough. She won't fold to him because he gets in her face and throws a tantrum. Her saving Bishop like that…that's something her daddy would have done. That man would be damn proud of the rancher she's turning out to be."

They rode silently for another minute. Eric peeked in the side mirror and saw Andy's head bobbing around in the truck bed.

"You screw her over and you better run back home to California as quick as you can, boy," Carl snarled. Eric tried to retort, but Carl raised a hand. "I don't wanna hear anything you've got to say. No excuses. You're both adults and you can do what you want.

"I've seen you eyein' her here and there, and I saw ya'll on Halloween. I'm not an idiot, I was young once. I would hazard a guess that you wouldn't have come to just anyone's house to check on 'em after a run in with Miller." A slight smile flashed on his face before it dissolved back into a scowl.

"I'm telling you, be careful. If you aren't ready for every ranch hand on this place to come after you, if you end up hurting her, you better not make any moves. Andy's got me as a dad and a bunch of men who are like her brothers, who would like nothing more than to keep her safe and happy after what she's been through."

Eric didn't know what to say, so he replied, "Yes, sir."

Carl came to a stop and turned off the truck in front of a piece of broken fence. Andy hopped out of the bed of the truck before Eric could shut his door. Carl put the tailgate down and he and Eric lifted out the enormous piece of wood. Andy grabbed the rest.

"Alright Eric. You're in Nebraska now, so you're gonna learn how to fix a fence," Carl said, rubbing his hands together.

"You'll be fine Deputy. You can handle a gun, so I'm sure you can handle a hammer. Or at least I hope you can," Andy said, smiling. Under Carl's tutelage, and with Andy handing him the proper tools,

Eric successfully completed the task. He took a step back, a smile on his face, his hands and ears numb from the cold.

"Good job Eric," Carl said. Then he looked over at Eric's huge smile. "Jesus Christ, you didn't perform brain surgery. You fixed a damn fence. Stop smiling like an idiot and get back in the truck before we freeze out here."

Andy laughed and headed back to the truck bed, where she hopped in and settled down. Carl and Eric climbed in and they headed back to the barn. Carl sang a song under his breath that Eric didn't recognize, but other than that, the ride back was silent.

When they reached the barn, Carl nodded to Eric, grabbed the bag of tools from the truck and took it inside, leaving Andy and Eric standing alone in the driveway. Andy turned to Eric.

"As you can see, I'm fine. I'm in good hands with Carl. He's very protective." She said, crossing her arms over her chest. "Frank Miller is a prick. Frank Miller has always been and will always be a prick, but he's also a lot of talk. I can handle it."

"He threatened you this morning, Andy," Eric said. "Whether he's always been a prick, someone broke into your house., it very well could have been Frank trying to scare you into leaving. It might be smart to take him serious." Andy stared back at him, unflinching. He saw something in her eyes, but couldn't quite place it. Then she glanced away.

"Thanks for coming by Eric." And without another look in his direction, she walked back to the barn, where Eric could see Carl watching them.

20

She was running. Her lungs were burning from the effort. Branches and brambles seemed to reach up and grab at her ankles. A branch whipped across her face, lashing her cheek. She looked behind her. The black figure was still close, chasing her. She could hear its breath, feel its fingers gripping for her shirt. She tripped and in an instant it was on top of her, clawing at her.

Andy woke up screaming, clutching the blanket to her chest. Her heart was pounding and tears rolled down her cheeks. The terror she felt in her dream had crossed over to the waking world.

This dream haunted her almost every night since the break in. Sleeping had been difficult since then, anyway. Every creak and bump made her jump, and there were plenty of those happening in this old house. Drawing her knees to her chest, she looked at the clock that showed "2:12" in bright red digits. Sighing, she laid back down, trying to fall back asleep, but the second her eyes snapped shut the faceless figure appeared in her mind and her heart rate climbed.

"Screw it," she said out loud and rolled out of bed. Throwing an old NYU sweatshirt on over her tank top and pulled a pair of socks onto her feet. She clambered down the stairs, pulling her hair up into a bun.

Minutes later, she was sitting in her truck, driving down the dirt road with no particular destination in mind, dust flying up behind her vehicle. It was better than sitting in her bed, willing herself to sleep when she couldn't even close her eyes without feeling terrified. Her mind drifted to Eric, the last person who'd made her feel safe at a time where she had been struggling to deal with her fear.

She thought back to the night they made s'mores. Afterwards, they sat in her kitchen on the barstools at the counter. She had thought about sliding down from hers, standing between his legs, taking his face in her hands and kissing him. She wondered what he tasted like, what it would feel like to have his tongue slide past her lips, but she chickened out.

Instead of giving in to her primal urges, she drew tiny circles on the counter. He asked her what was on her mind and she said she was thinking about what had led her home. She could have told him she was thinking about how much she wanted him; that she was wondering about what his mouth would feel like against hers. What would he have done if she revealed that she was thinking about if his hands wander her body, slowly traveling over her curves or would they be more fervent, hungry to experience every inch of her?

Stopping at the next intersection, and pressed her head back against the seat as these thoughts flew through her mind again. Why couldn't she jump? Why couldn't she admit she was into him and go for it? Why was she so scared? She was Andy Summers, dammit. She had always been a take no prisoners, act without thinking too much kind of woman, but maybe that was all behind her now.

She couldn't figure out why. Sure she'd been dealt a raw deal. She was stuck in Nebraska, running a ranch that she'd fought her entire life to get away from. She had gotten her heart run over by that unfaithful Londoner. All that stuff had been hard to swallow but, it was what it was. She had come to terms with that, and she needed to come to terms with this.

As much as she had tried to fight it in the beginning, she was willing to admit now that she felt things stirring inside her when Eric looked at her, even more when he touched her. Things she hadn't felt in years. Was she going to let those feelings flow through her and do nothing about it?

She rubbed her hands over her face and then noticed the red and blue lights flashing behind her. They came to a stop behind her truck and she heard the car door slam shut. "Seriously?" she said out loud.

She rolled down her window and waited. "Everything alright?" she heard someone say.

"Yes, I'm fine, I'm just..." she had been saying when she turned and saw who had approached. "Eric?"

"Hey Andy," he said as he leaned his arms against the door's window frame, "Everything OK? You've been sitting here a while."

"How do you know how long I've been sitting here?" she asked, her eyes narrowing.

"I was parked on the side of the road back there. There was a call a couple miles back, someone else responded, but I was already on my way, so I thought I'd hang out in case they needed some backup," he explained.

"I hadn't seen a car all night and then you drove past, but you've been at this stop sign for a few minutes. I didn't know if someone had stroked out or had a heart attack or something. You know as well as I do that lots of red meat and bacon get eaten around these parts, so

I figured I'd check it out. What are you doing out here, anyway? You OK?"

"Is that thing on?" she asked, pointing to the deputy's body cam. He nodded.

"Mmhmm, technically, this is a traffic stop." He winked and glanced at his watch. "I'm coming up on break soon. You gonna answer my question or make me late for my 'lunch'? Are you OK?"

She sat, looking at him for a minute. "I dunno," she responded, and drummed her fingers on the steering wheel for a minute. "You got plans for that lunch break of yours?"

"Oh yeah, big, big plans. Gonna sit in the cruiser, scarf down a sandwich and chips, drink some cold coffee. Ya know, living the high life," he smiled.

She couldn't stop herself from returning his smile. "Well, if you're interested, since I'm up...you could swing by the house and I could rustle up something a little more substantial for ya."

His eyes widened in surprise for a moment. "Would you tell me what's going on then?" he said in almost a whisper. She assumed it was so the body cam wouldn't pick up what he was saying. She considered it and then nodded.

"Fifteen minutes?" he asked, taking his arm off the door of the truck. She nodded again. He nodded back and walked to his cruiser. The red and blue lights stopped. The engine of his car started, and he drove past her. She turned the truck around in the intersection. As she drove, she wondered what in the hell she was planning on doing, but she kept hearing her mom's voice in her head repeating everything it had said over the past few days.

21

After Andy had returned to the house, she pulled out some leftover enchiladas that Rosa had brought by. Who didn't like enchiladas, especially Rosa's? She swore she gained at least fifteen pounds after she came home because of Rosa's cooking. More likely, though, it was muscle she had put back on from lifting hay bales, riding horses and scooping up cow manure, but she figured some of it could be attributed to fantastic, homemade meals. She was taking a pitcher of iced tea out of the fridge when she heard the knock at the door.

She peeped through the hole and saw Eric on the porch, and let him in. He took off his jacket, and she drank him in. She finally understood the whole man in uniform thing as she looked at him, the brown material tight in all the right places. His body cam wasn't just turned off; he hadn't even brought it in.

"So what's going on, Andy? Are you OK? I'm worried," he asked, looking her in the eyes, the concern oozing in his voice.

"It's stupid, really," she replied, walking back behind the island in the kitchen. "It was a nightmare. Like a literal one. You like enchiladas?" He nodded and took a seat on a stool at the island, still looking at her, so she continued.

"I've had this recurring nightmare since the break in. Every time I'm being chased by something, or someone, I'm not sure. I never see what it is. I always end up waking up, scared out of my mind. I tried to go back to sleep, but every time I shut my eyes, I saw the shape of whoever was chasing me."

The microwave beeped as she pushed the buttons on its front. "I have iced tea or water," she said as she turned back around to face him.

"Iced tea would be great," he responded.

"It's probably because of the break in, and the note, and Frank and all of it. So I thought I'd go out for a drive and try to clear my head. Then I started thinking again and then, well, you were there for the rest." She handed him the glass and his fingers grazed over hers. She fought back a shiver as a jolt of electricity shot through her. When the food had been reheated, she put it in front of him, handed him some silverware and leaned against the counter opposite of him. "Those are Rosa's enchiladas. They're pretty amazing."

"You hung out at a stop sign and thought about a bunch of stuff for long enough that I thought someone had died at the wheel. So, how are you feeling now?" he asked, before putting a bite of the saucy stuffed tortillas in his mouth. She shrugged and poured herself some iced tea.

"Like I've been slowly losing myself," she breathed, with her back to him. Her own honesty shocked her. "Shit, I'm sorry. Sleep deprivation must be taking its toll," she mumbled. When she turned around, he was wiping his mouth on the napkin she had given him.

"First, oh. My. God. You were right, these are amazing and if Rosa weren't married, I'd be on my way to confess my undying love to her right now. Second, why did you apologize? And last, but most importantly, what are you losing? If you talk to me, I might be able to help. I know a thing or two about losing things, and even if I can't help, I'm a damn good listener. I've been trained in it even." He stared at her, silent, not touching the food again until she spoke.

"High school Andy Summers was a take no shit, leave no prisoners, run the world bad ass with a dream and the drive to never give that up. NYU Andrea Summers was a classier, older version of that who could drink legally and was working toward that dream.

"Now I feel like I'm stuck. Stuck in this place, running this ranch, taking shit from Frank-fucking-Miller." His eyes were on her, but he said nothing, so she continued. Her words came faster as she watched him take a bite of the food in front of him.

"There's a group of guys here that depend on me. They rely on me to make good choices, to keep this ranch running so they can feed their families. So, that's not just those guys, but their families relying on me too and shit, that's a lot of pressure.

"Then on top of that, I have some asshole breaking in here, trying to find me, to do God knows what to me. Somebody, maybe the same asshole, putting threats on my truck. Frank Miller gets in my face. You. And all the sudden I feel like a scared little girl again, not that kick ass chick that I used to be."

Eric choked on the food he had swallowed and wiped his face before reaching for his iced tea. Then he looked at her with wide eyes. "What do you mean, me?"

"What?" Andy asked. She looked up from the spot on the counter that she had been looking at during her rant and locked eyes with him.

He took a drink and swallowed. "You said 'you'... as in me." He pointed to himself.

"No, I didn't," she said. She felt heat rising in her cheeks, and she was sure they were turning red. Her heart was in her throat. Had she said that?

"Yes. You did," he replied, taking another sip of his tea before leaning his forearms on top of the counter. He stared at her, his blue eyes searching her green ones. She exhaled but stayed silent, chewing on her bottom lip. Her mind was racing to figure out a way out of this, but she wasn't sure she could.

"Andy," he began, "Those guys that you feel responsible for would kill someone for you. Carl affirmed that to me when he was trying to intimidate me. That guy for sure would murder for you and probably have some really creative ways to dispose of the body, and we both know that.

"If you were in trouble on the ranch, if you needed help, they'd have your back. You're more than a boss to them. You're their daughter, their sister. Yeah, they depend on you, but I'm pretty sure you can depend on them too, if you let yourself." He paused, and she felt tears beginning to well in her eyes.

"The asshole breaking in...yeah. I can't do shit about that other than tell you to get a gun, which I know you won't do. But you're doing all the right things. Keeping things locked up, turning on the alarm, keeping your phone nearby. The only other thing you could do is go stay with Romeo or Carl or somebody."

He took a deep breath before continuing. "I don't know why he was here, I don't know what his motivations were, but you're smart, you're strong and hopefully he was some stupid dick scoping out the place and realized it wasn't worth it because a tall, dark and handsome deputy arrived so quickly."

She smiled and he couldn't help mirror the reaction. "The threats on your truck," he continued, "I don't know much more about that, but if you want me to file a report, I can. You say the word. Otherwise, if it happens again, you call me and we'll take it from there.

"Frank Miller, I don't know him well enough to know if he could be violent, but he's an asshole and the whole town knows it. And from what I've heard, you're respected ten fold over that guy," he paused again and took a deep breath.

"And that brings us to me," he said, leaning forward a little more and looking her in the eyes, "And I'm not sure what the problem is there. So please, enlighten me."

Her heart thudded in her chest and her brain felt cloudy. After a moment, she felt something wash over her. She realized this was the perfect shot. The old Andrea would embrace a moment like this. This might be the first step to finding that version of herself again. A sense of calm washed over her. Pushing herself away from the counter, she told herself it was now or never.

She moved around the island and he swiveled the seat of the stool to stay facing her as he watched her every move. As though being pulled by a magnet, she closed the distance between them. Trying to channel the confident woman she had once been, she took a deep breath. "I've been hurt, Eric, by a guy you remind me of. A handsome, charming guy who told me he'd love me and promised he'd give me the world and instead, broke my heart," she searched his face, but he wasn't reacting yet.

"And I dealt with it, and I got over it, and I promised myself I'd never let another guy like that hurt me again." She took a deep inhale, and let the breath out slowly, "And then you came around. And at first it was easy to ignore you existed, to blow you off and think you were another jackass who thought he was God's gift." He slid off the barstool and stood in front of her, his jaw clenched, watching her.

She took another step forward so there was no light passing between them. She could see his chest rising and falling more quickly as he breathed faster. "And then..." a small smile spread across her face as she saw the look of desire in his eyes and knew she was in control of this moment. She smiled more when she realized how much she liked this feeling. "You weren't. You weren't that guy at all. And I wanted you to be around more, and then I thought about what I would do if a moment like this would arise."

"And what would you do?" he asked, his hands in fists at his sides. She could smell his cologne, feel his breath. His Adam's apple bobbed up and down as he swallowed hard. Pressing her palm against his chest, she looked up into his eyes. All she could hear was her heart pounding as she grabbed the collar of his shirt, pulling him towards her. She raised up on the balls of her feet and pressed her lips against his.

His hand was on the small of her back. The other hand found her waist, and he pushed her body against his, deepening the kiss. She brought her hand to rest against his jaw. Feeling the heat spreading through her body, her breath was coming fast, her heart was racing. She traced his bottom lip with the tip of her tongue. With a firm hand, he pressed her even tighter against him, and she could feel the effect she was having on him.

His response encouraged her, and she brought her hand to the back of his neck and pressed the tips of her fingers into it. His lips were soft and warm. She wanted to feel them on other places of her body. She nipped at his lip with her teeth and heard him groan into her mouth.

His hand traveled down from her waist and cupped her ass. His tongue teased her and then slipped between her lips.

When his radio squelched to life, their lips parted, both of them panting. "All units, all units, possible B&E in progress at Weston's. All available units, please respond," a voice said. He groaned but kept his hand on the small of her back, keeping her tight against him.

"Shit," he whispered, as he caught his breath. She gave him a half smile, and he pushed the button and replied, "Unit 338, I'm about five minutes out." He groaned. "Shit," he whispered again. She pressed her hands against his chest and pushed gently. He released his hold on her and she took a step back, still smiling.

"Duty calls, deputy," she sighed, as he chewed the inside of his lip.

"This," he said, pointing to her, and then back to his chest, "isn't over." He grabbed his jacket, but before he dashed out the door, he took another long glance at her, and let out a mix between a sigh and a groan.

She watched the cruiser's red and blue lights flash as he sped down the driveway and then down the dirt road. After she locked the door, she leaned against it and exhaled. A huge smile was on her face and she pressed her fingers to her swollen lips. That damn radio.

22

After his shift ended, he dragged himself to his truck. He pointed toward his apartment and the events of the night before played over in his head, as they had done on a loop since he'd left Andy.

The call that had interrupted the moment he'd been dreaming about for months had been a bust. An employee who showed up to clean but had forgotten the code had tripped the alarm at the small hardware store. He suspected the kid was high, but let him go after a quick conversation with the store owner who had showed up, none too happy that he had to come talk to the police in his pajamas.

After that, there were a couple more calls for minor issues, but nothing of real importance. He was glad for the distractions that kept his mind off how Andy had felt beneath his hands and how much he'd wanted to rip off her clothes and explore her body. These were all things he was thinking about now, though.

With little thought, he drove past his apartment and out of town towards her ranch. If his brain been able to chime in over his heart, the warmth that spread through his body when he thought about her, or his sheer exhaustion, he wouldn't have pulled into her driveway in the middle of the morning when he was sure there were ranch hands milling around.

Fortunately, he didn't see anyone when he pulled in. He stepped out of his truck and looked around the ranch. The crisp November wind whipped across the field. He pulled his jacket collar up to stop the cold from nipping at his neck. Making his way to the nearest barn, he peeked into the open side door but didn't see anyone. He was preparing a quick lie in his head about checking in on things and what he might say to make it believable should someone stop him.

He was pulling his head out from the empty barn when he heard that raspy voice from behind him. "Something I can help you with, Deputy?"

He spun around and found himself face to face with Andy. She was wearing a tan Carhart jacket, jeans and work boots. She had an emerald green knit hat pulled down over her hair. He felt his breath catch in his chest when he saw her. He was dying to pull her into him and kiss her.

She stared at him, eyebrows raised, a slight smile on her face, and he felt heat rising in his cheeks. "I wasn't snooping, I swear," he said.

"Sure," she replied, her eyes still fixed on him as she took a step closer. "So, what were you doing?"

"I was looking for you. I told you last night that this wasn't over."

She smiled wider. "So you thought now would be a good time to pick up where we left off? Now, when it's about forty-two degrees out here, I've been walking through horse shit all morning and I have people working all over this place?"

"Yeah, well...ya know..." he stammered, "Not my best thought out plan."

"Look, some of the guys and I are going to hit The Lodge tonight to watch the game. But I'm free tomorrow night if you wanted to come over and...pick things up." She looked up at him from beneath her eyelashes, a wicked smile on her face. He felt blood rising in his cheeks as desire stirred within him. He didn't know how he was going to survive another whole day without touching her again.

"Tomorrow then, I'll bring dinner. Would six be safe?"

"Yeah," she smiled, "six is fine." She crossed the space between them and glanced all around before brushing her lips against his cold cheek. Then she turned on her heel and walked away, not looking back.

He didn't stop smiling the entire way home. Once he hit the door to his apartment, his exhaustion took over, and he barely got out of his boots before he collapsed in a heap on his bed.

23

The next day was filled with hard labor for Andy on the ranch yet again. When she was finally done, she contemplated a nap, but she knew the anxious feeling in the pit of her stomach would never allow her to drift to sleep. So instead, she settled for a long bath. Afterwards, she spent an embarrassingly long time preparing for the first "date" she'd had in years.

After many outfit changes, she was pleased with the reflection in at her in the mirror. She took one last look at her reflection and smiled. The person looking back at her reminded her of New York, Andrea. She was someone she had missed for a very long time, but hadn't realized how much. That Andrea had plenty of reasons to dress up, wear makeup and even heels. Spring Hills Andy had no more use for heels than she did for another hole in her head.

After starting a fire in the fireplace in the living room, she tried to relax. When she heard tires in the driveway, she glanced at the clock. He was right on time. She took a deep inhale, and blew out the breath slowly, making herself wait until she heard him knock at the door. It seemed like an eternity later when she heard his heavy boots on the porch and then a knock. She wiped her sweaty palms on her thighs before she answered, and she was sure she was smiling like an idiot when she opened the door.

It made her feel much better to see him standing there with a huge smile plastered on his face, too. She noticed his eyes moving down, then back up her frame, like he wanted her to know he was looking at her this way. "Come on in," she said. He entered and set a cooler and a bag down on the dining room table.

He took off his boots and hung his coat on a hook by the door. Then he took a few steps towards her and smiled again. "You look incredible."

She smiled, feeling the heat rising to her cheeks. "Thanks, Rancher Andy rarely has an excuse to wear much other than work jeans and flannel. It's nice to change it up a bit. You look nice too."

He was always handsome, but she seemed to notice more tonight how tight his shirt was across the muscles of his chest. "Well Rancher Andy looks damn good, but Date Andy, that's a whole different category." He smiled, and looked her up and down again, this time his eyes lingering a little longer. Tension hung heavy in the air between them. "I brought dinner," he said, gesturing toward the cooler.

"I'm intrigued."

"I hope you like it." He walked over to where he had set his things and pulled out a bottle of wine. "Can I interest you in a drink?"

"Absolutely," Andy said. She set two places across from each other at the table. Eric pulled out a chair and gestured for her to take a seat. She did, and he pushed her chair in. He leaned over her shoulder to pour her a glass of wine. She felt his chest near her back and could smell his cologne. She could feel warmth spreading from her core because of her proximity to him, and hoped her cheeks hadn't turned pink.

He took his place across from her and pulled the cooler closer. "Are you ready?" he asked, waggling his eyebrows.

She laughed. "I'm as ready as I'll ever be." She was curious about what the cooler could contain. A gasp flew from her mouth when he pulled the first container from it and sat it in front of her. He pulled five plastic containers with clear lids from the cooler.

"Sushi?" she exclaimed, putting her hand to her mouth. "The nearest sushi place is in the city. That's a two-hour drive!"

His smile spread from ear to ear, and the corners of his eyes crinkled. "So you like it?"

"Eric, oh my gosh, this is...this is amazing." Her eyes swept over the table, taking in the assortment of sushi he had brought. He dug his hand into the cooler one more time and pulled a handful of small, black plastic cups with lids out of it. She glanced up at him, questioning him with her eyes.

"Eel sauce," he said, "I asked for extra." Andy's mouth fell open, and her eyes stung with tears. He remembered from their conversation that seemed like it was so many weeks ago. When she looked up, she saw her smile was as big as his. This was one of the nicest things anyone had ever done for her on a date, maybe ever. She couldn't think of a time when Jake had been anywhere near this selfless to make her happy. Eric had spent his whole day driving to the city and back, just for sushi, because he knew she missed it.

She stared at him, drinking in the moment. "I don't know what to say. Just...thank you." A flood of emotions flowed through her at his gesture.

"That's plenty. Dig in!" Together they popped the plastic lids off of the containers and snapped apart their wooden chopsticks. When Andy put a piece into her mouth, she groaned out loud.

"Oh, that's so good," she said through her full mouth. He smiled at her and popped a piece into his mouth.

After about an hour of conversation that flowed comfortably, they were both stuffed. "I don't think I could eat another piece of fish right now if my life depended on it," she said, wiping her mouth and throwing her napkin on the table.

"So you're giving up, huh?" Eric asked. She nodded, and he said, "Me too. It was good, though." Together they put lids back on containers and cleared the table. After they had cleaned up, they stood facing each other in the kitchen, close enough that she could have taken a step forward and kissed him. Her gaze dropped to the floor. She tried to channel that fearless version of herself from the other night, but was struggling under his gaze.

"Well, I guess we could go to the living room," she suggested, attempting to temper the tension that was continuing to grow. He nodded, and they went to the next room.

The fire was crackling, but otherwise the room was silent. Andy stopped in front of one of the large picture windows in the room that looked out into the fields behind her home. "I will admit, this is the best place to see stars," she started, folding her arms across her chest.

"When I went to New York, I was so disappointed that there weren't any stars. I mean, I knew there wouldn't be, but once you go from this to that, it's still surprising. You asked me once what my favorite thing about Spring Hills was and I think it's this sky...those stars."

They were standing very close to one another, their arms brushing. She took a deep breath, willing herself to tap into the confidence and courage she'd had before. She turned to face him.

He stood looking at her, trying to decipher her intent, looking for an invitation or validation. That he wasn't making any moves and was letting her set the pace only helped solidify the fact that he differed from guys she'd dated before.

A slow smile crept over her face, and she put a hand on his waist. With a hand just above the pocket of her jeans he drew her a little closer towards him. "I really want to kiss you," he whispered.

"Then you should."

His hand slid behind her neck, and he pulled her, bringing his mouth to hers. He pressed his lips against hers and she felt her skin heating. He stopped and looked down into her eyes.

She placed a hand on his jaw and his gaze flicked to her lips. "So," she said in a near whisper, "Picking up where we left off..." then she stood on tiptoe and brought her lips back to his. Soon she felt his hands go to her hips.

The kiss deepened, and he wrapped his arms around her waist. She draped hers around his neck, their bodies pressed up against one another. One of her hands traveled into his hair as she tried to pull him closer. It felt like fireworks had erupted inside of her. She hadn't been kissed like this in so long. She hadn't felt the want building up inside her like this in years, and it scared her.

She took her lips off of his and they stood, looking into each other's eyes. Her breath came quickly now, her heart was pounding, and she could feel her stomach twisting itself in knots. She lowered herself down off the balls of her feet and pressed her forehead into his chest.

He kept his arms wrapped around her waist. "I'm scared, Eric," she whispered. Putting a finger under her chin, he tilted her face upward. He didn't look angry or frustrated that she had stopped things. He looked concerned, worried.

"Scared of what?" he asked.

"You. This," she said. "I was engaged before Eric. I had a life planned out with a man who probably never truly cared about me. He cheated on me when I was at my lowest point, and it was devastating. I had come home to be with my dying father and he had found at least one someone else to keep the bed warm. I don't want to be hurt again, Eric."

He smiled a sad smile. "I don't know if I could live with myself if I hurt you, Andy," he said and tucked an errant piece of hair behind her ear. He took a small step back, keeping his hands on her hips but creating some space between them. "I was married," he whispered.

Surprise washed over her, and she knew her eyes grew wide in response. "We were young. We rushed into things because we both thought it was love. Now I'm not so sure. So, I know what you mean. It's kind of scary for me too.

"I won't ever push you to move faster than you want to go. I never want to cause your pain. Jesus, you're pretty much all I've thought about since the first time I saw you at Dolly's, when you looked at me like I was a swamp creature."

"Really?" she asked, her mouth curving into a smile.

"Really. You can ask Mark if you want."

She took a step forward and kissed him, their lips touching for a few seconds. "I might have to."

He pressed his lips to hers again and then looked into her eyes. She was torn between wanting to kiss him all night and not wanting to move too fast. With Jake, there had been a few thousand miles between them to help her cope with her heartbreak. She wouldn't have that luxury if something went south with Eric. There would be no running away this time.

He seemed to sense that she was trying to slow things down. He glanced at the clock on the wall. "I think it's likely you have to be up early to go milk some cows or shoe a horse or something," he said and she laughed.

"Is that what you think I do all day, Deputy Grayson?" she asked, playfully pushing her hands against his chest.

"Honestly, I don't know." He smiled and pulled her in for a hug, pressing his cheek to the top of her head.

"Well, maybe one day you'll have to come put in an honest day's work," she replied, breathing in his scent.

"Hmm...I'll think about it. But for now, as much as it pains me to leave, I think I should let you get some sleep."

"One more thing, Eric. Can this stay between us for now? Until we figure this out, whatever this is? It's not that I'm embarrassed or anything, but dating in a small town has its unique challenges, like never ending gossip. Jesus, Joyce Newcome would die if she got word of this."

He put a hand on each of her arms. "Andy, I told you, I never want to be someone who hurts you. If you want to take it slow, if you want to keep it quiet, then that's what we'll do. You can call the shots. I'm guessing you like that anyway," he said with a wink. She smiled, and he pressed kissed her forehead. They both walked into the kitchen, where

Eric collected his things and got ready to go. He cast her one last glance and walked out into the night.

After she locked the door, she smiled to herself, realizing she was wishing he had stayed. She vowed to herself that the next time they were together, she would listen to her heart instead of her fear.

24

The next few days seemed to creep by. He and Andy spoke every night talking about odds and ends, at least briefly. However, between his work, her being needed on the ranch and plans they'd already made with other people; they weren't able to see each other in private. He caught a glance of her at The Lodge one night, when he was there with Mark and she was there with Carl, Romeo and another man he guessed worked for her.

Mark had laughed and called him out for stealing a few glances at her throughout the evening. She had caught him looking once and shot him a quick, sly smile and a wink. It had sent a jolt through him and he wished more than anything he could have grabbed her right then, but he was taking her request for both secrecy and pace seriously.

They had arranged to meet at her ranch that evening and he felt like he was drowning in anticipation. She had told him she would cook for him this time. He willed the day to go by quickly and thankfully, it did. Before he knew it, he was pulling into the driveway at Summers Ranch and knocking on her door.

When she answered, she was smiling. She wore a pair of tight, light blue jeans with a black shirt under a light cardigan, and a hand towel thrown over her left shoulder. "Come on in," she said, a huge smile plastered on her face.

"Something smells good," he said, perching himself atop a stool at the island. She shot him a smile and when he was settled, she offered him a glass of red wine and scurried back toward the stove.

"Well, I hope it tastes good. I haven't made this in years. My mom was an amazing cook, and this was one of my favorite meals she made. She'd always let me help her with this one," her voice seemed to trail off as she recalled the memory. "And so, it's the one thing besides chicken that I'm pretty comfortable making."

"I'm sure it'll be delicious," he said, smiling. "Anything I can help with?"

"Nope, you sit there and look pretty. I think I'm just about done," she replied as she opened the oven. He couldn't help but take in the view when she bent to check the contents before closing the door. She looked at him and smirked. He smiled back, knowing he'd been caught staring. She said nothing, but chuckled as she picked up a large serving bowl and carried it to the nearby table. On her way back through the kitchen, she grazed his thigh with her fingertips and then shot him a devilish smile.

"Two can play at that," he thought to himself, taking a drink of his wine. Andy stood at the counter, cutting a loaf of bread. She was in front of the cabinet he had seen her get the plates from the last time he had been here. "Let me help set the table," he said.

Stopping behind her, he rested a hand on her left hip and leaned his body against hers to reach into the cabinet. He dipped his head, brushing his lips against her neck, and heard her breath catch in her throat. With plates in hand and feeling a little victorious about his turn in this game, he set the table.

Shortly after, they were about to dig into the lasagna that Andy had made. "So you like Italian food, huh?" he asked, scooping some onto his plate.

"What's not to like? It's like 80% carbs and cheese!" she replied, making him laugh. "My mom and I would make this at least once a month. Although, she made her own sauce, and I used a jar from the store. I'm not sure I'll ever be quite on her level."

He had taken a bite while she had spoken and wiped the corners of his mouth with his napkin. "This is delicious Andy. Thank you for sharing it with me." She looked at him, but he couldn't quite figure out what she was thinking.

"You're welcome."

Like always, their conversation flowed. Thanksgiving was approaching, and Andy asked if he was going to go home for the holidays. He had told her he wasn't, that holidays in their home had always been more of a production than anything else. His mother would have the meal catered, they would all be instructed on what color palette to wear for the photo that mom would stage. Then they would eat in near silence while his father got shit faced. As soon as the meal was done, they'd all hole up in different parts of the house, avoiding each other until it was acceptable to leave.

Andy's holidays had been much different when her mom was around. She talked about the huge dinners her mom would make, with leftovers for days. After her mom died, they tried their best. Venison that her dad and brothers had scored took over for the turkey. The meals became less extravagant, but they still tried. After everyone grew up and went their separate ways, Andy missed a few Thanksgivings with her dad. She regretted that now, but the ones she was home for she remembered fondly. It became their tradition to make pizza and eat a whole pumpkin pie between the two of them.

Eric felt a swell of jealousy. She had such significant memories with her family, even after they had faced unimaginable challenges. He could count memories with his family he wanted to remember on one hand. Most of that could be blamed on his father's alcoholism, but if he was honest with himself, his mother was distant, and his brother was a prick. He could also admit that he had some responsibility for the way things were, too.

Chair legs scraping the floor interrupted his thoughts nearly an hour after they had started eating as Andy pushed back from the table. "I'll start cleaning up," she said.

"Let me help."

As they cleaned, it was obvious they were both trying to touch and tease each other as much as possible. Every touch that they pretended was accidental but was anything but electrified his skin and made his heart thump. Every time their fingers grazed, or her hand brushed against his chest or back, he felt his desire growing. She brushed against him again and walked away. Feeling at the end of his rope, he grabbed her by the wrist and she spun around.

He pulled her against his chest and kissed her. She kissed him back, grazing his bottom lip with her teeth. Then she looked up at him. "I win," she said. He laughed and kissed her again, but this felt different. She slid a hand up the back of his shirt, her fingertips digging into his muscles.

Each kiss grew more intense, hungrier. She bit his lip again, and he pushed her away, just slightly, his chest rising and falling quickly as his heart raced. He could feel where this was leading.

"Are you sure this is what you want, Andy?" he said, bringing a hand to her cheek. "You said you want to take things slow, and I'm OK with that. I am. But this doesn't feel slow, not that I'm complaining, because I'm not. I can't even tell you how much I want this Andy...but if you tell me to stop I will, any time. I don't want you to get caught up in this and do something you're going to regret."

25

Her breathing was quick and shallow. He was searching her with his eyes. His hand was warm against her cheek. She couldn't remember wanting anyone like this, not even Jake. She felt like if she didn't have him right now, her heart might burst out of her body. Pressing her palm to his chest, she could feel his heart pounding, too.

She didn't want to regret anything either, and if she crossed this line, she couldn't undo it. But God, she wanted to cross the line. Her body felt like it was on fire, and she wasn't sure how much more she could take. He stopped things to make sure she was okay. He was standing in front of her, ignoring what he wanted because he was worried about how she felt.

"I want this, Eric," she said, aware her raspy voice was even lower than it normally was. "I want you."

"You're allowed to change your mind, Andy." He stroked her cheek with his thumb, then dragged it across her bottom lip and the warmth between her legs grew. "Anytime you say the word and we will stop," he half whispered.

Never had a man said this to her. She had men call her a tease, she had men beg to keep going when she was ready to stop, but she had never had a man tell her she was in control. She nodded, even more turned on, and crashed her lips back to his.

He pulled her hips, so she was as close as possible to him. He slipped the cardigan she wore from one of her shoulders, exposing the strap of her camisole, and kissed the skin there. It was such a simple act, but desire was consuming her.

She pressed her lips against his, searching his mouth with her tongue as she unbuttoned his shirt. When it fell open, she ran her hands over his chest. She could feel his firm muscles under her fingertips. After she slipped the shirt from his shoulders and he slid out of the sleeves, she stepped back, drinking him in. She wasn't sure she had ever seen a more attractive man up close and in the flesh.

His jeans hung low enough that she could see the waistband of his underwear and the V of muscles there. He wasn't a man who spent every waking minute in the gym, but his muscles were defined, his shoulders broad, his stomach flat. She wasn't sure how much longer she could stand not feeling every inch of him against her. Her heart was racing. She bit her bottom lip before smiling at him and whispering, "Damn." She watched a smile cross his face.

"Do you approve?" he asked, holding his arms out to the side. Words were impossible. All she could do was nod. Moving back to him, she placed a kiss on his neck, which elicited a groan from him that spurred her on. She continued, trailing her lips and tongue down his chest before returning to his mouth. She could feel him growing harder under his jeans, and she pressed herself against him.

He slid his hands up her back, under her shirt, and she shivered. He dragged his fingers down her skin and the sensation made her want to melt. She felt him tug at her shirt hem and then stop. She could tell this was his way of letting her control the situation.

Stepping back again, she pulled her shirt up over her head, feeling grateful she still had some nice lingerie from New York. She saw his eyes take in her figure in the red, lacy number. "Jesus Christ," he breathed before pulling her into his arms again.

As they kissed more and more fervently, she ran her fingers along the waistband of his underwear and heard him take in a ragged gasp. She smiled against his lips, encouraged that she was having this effect on him. She dragged her fingers up his back, digging her nails into his skin. He groaned into her mouth and undid the top button of her jeans. She took another step back and his jaw clenched again.

She smiled as she slowly, and she hoped seductively, wriggled out of her jeans. When she stepped out of them, she looked at his face. She saw hunger and desire there. "Andy," he hissed. He didn't seem to get enough blood flow to his brain to find words. She pressed herself against him again, the intensity of the moment becoming almost unbearable.

His hands slid down to the back of her thighs, his fingertips digging into the flesh there, and then he was lifting her up. She wrapped her legs around his waist and pulled him closer, feeling his erection against her. She ground her hips against him and heard him moan. He stopped, and looked into her eyes, "Andy..." he started.

She shook her head, panting. Every inch of her felt filled with a need only he could fulfill. "I'm okay, Eric, I promise," she muttered. She kissed him again, her tongue tracing his lips.

"Where?"

"Upstairs." He carried her up the stairs as she kissed his neck and nibbled his ear.

"We might not make it to the top if you keep that up," he growled. She laughed and figured she'd try her luck, anyway.

"You passed it." She laughed again as he walked past her doorway. He spun back around, went in, and tossed her on the bed. She propped herself up on her elbows and looked at him. He had a mischievous grin on his face.

"I think you've earned some payback for that stuff on the stairs...slow...slow payback..."

She watched as he climbed onto the bed and ran his fingertips along her thighs as he moved over her body. He kissed her again, his tongue plunging into her mouth. She wrapped her legs around his waist and tried to pull him towards her. "Uh-uh," she heard Eric whisper.

"I said you were going to get payback..." he hissed into her ear as she felt his hand find the warmth between her legs. He slipped his hand into her underwear and when his fingertips found her most sensitive spot, she jolted against him. "I want to taste you."

"Please..." she begged, and he moved his mouth to her jaw, then her neck, creeping down her body, kissing and licking the skin in his path. In minutes, she was panting, pressing herself against him even more. He was expertly bringing her to the edge when finally her body shook and he looked up at her, smiling.

She pulled his face up to hers and kissed him, then rolled him onto his back. She pulled off his pants and kissed the skin around the edge of his underwear. He squirmed, and she dragged her fingers against him. "Jesus, Andy," she heard him say under his breath as she pulled off his underwear. Using her tongue and mouth, she brought him to the brink.

"Andy," he said, breathless, pulling her face back to his. "I want to feel all of you."

"Yes..." she gasped with one hand in her hair he pulled her lips back to his.

After what seemed like both an eternity and a moment of what she could only describe as bliss, she was watching him walk back into the room after going to clean up. He'd slid back on his boxer briefs and she swore he looked like he belonged in one of those sexy firefighter calendars.

He laid back down next to her and she stayed on her stomach, her hands tucked under the pillow that she rested her head upon. He kissed her shoulder, then laid his head down and dragged his fingers over her back. She closed her eyes. She wanted to seer every moment of what had happened in her mind. Lock away the memory of the pleasure that had coursed through her as she rocked her hips against his, the ecstasy that flooded through her nervous system when he had his mouth and hands on her.

She'd never been with someone as unselfish as Eric had been. He'd made sure she'd experienced pleasure before moving on to anything else. He'd told her to tell him if anything he did made her uncomfortable, which it didn't, or if at any moment she wanted to stop, which she hadn't. They laughed through the awkward parts, and nothing ever felt weird. Being with him that way felt easy.

"Are you asleep?" she heard him whisper.

"No," she said, opening her eyes and looking at him. "Just thinking."

"Penny for your thoughts?"

"Oh, they cost much more than that." She rolled to face him, pulling the sheet up over her chest.

"Maybe we can work out a barter." He smiled back as he pulled her towards him, kissing her swollen lips again.

"Mmmm, perhaps," she said against his mouth before kissing him again. Their kisses once again grew from tender to more passionate and soon they were entwined, his arms around her, her leg thrown across his body.

"Now will you tell me?" He started kissing her neck, and she moaned.

"I was thinking that I was so, so wrong about you."

He stopped kissing her and looked her in the eyes. "I hope that's a good thing," he said, stroking her cheek with his knuckles.

"A wonderful thing."

He put his head back on the pillow and rolled onto his back, positioning his arm around her and her head on his chest. For a few minutes, they laid together, soaking each other in. "Why don't you paint anymore?" he asked.

She thought for a moment, then took a deep breath. "It hurts too much," she answered, so honestly she almost shocked herself, which was beginning to be a trend with this man. "The Andrea who loved living in the city, who dressed up and drank fancy wine, who painted for hours on end...I think she died the day my dad did.

"I've tried to paint a couple times since then, but every time I go to get things set up, it hurts. It reminds me of everything I could have been, everything I could have done, and instead, I'm here. Instead of working with beautiful pieces of art and having showings in galleries,

I'm fixing fences and tending to cattle. Instead of discussing the masters and their work, dissecting pieces with other people who love art, I talk about the incoming cold fronts and the finer points of bovine breeding."

"You miss her, that version of you, that Andrea," he replied.

"I try not to. There's no sense in it. I'll never be that person again. I can't be. I made a promise and so I'm here." She pushed herself up onto her elbows so she could look at him and ran her fingers through his hair, then traced his jaw with her fingertips. He turned and pressed his lips to her palm. She didn't want a night that had been near perfect to turn so somber. "And right now, I'm pretty damn glad I am."

He smiled and pulled her back down to him, kissing her again. "I am too," he said, rolling her onto her back. She could feel him growing hard against her again.

"Deputy Grayson, are you sure you have it in you?"

"Oh, I'm damn sure I do," he whispered, as he trailed kisses down her body.

26

It had been very late, or very early, depending on how you looked at it, by the time Eric had dragged himself away from Andy. He knew he couldn't stay, the ranch hands would start rolling in about 4:30 and a strange truck in the driveway would be a dead giveaway that she had a guest. With the limited population in Spring Hills, it wouldn't take a rocket scientist to realize it was him.

He'd made it back to his apartment around two in the morning, but it'd taken him much longer to fall asleep. The event night kept running in his head. He could sit and talk to her like they'd done at dinner for hours.

He hadn't imagined that things would end the way they had, and he hoped she wasn't regretting it now that the heat of the moment had passed. His mind went to her standing in front of him after taking off her jeans, how she looked lying in the bed, the memory of how she reacted to his touch, to his mouth, how she felt, how she tasted. Now he was alone, trying to sleep, tossing and turning for what felt like a very long time.

He woke up a few hours later to a text from Mark asking him to meet for breakfast at Dolly's. He hadn't seen his friend in what felt like a while, so he agreed and figured he had to hope Grace wouldn't be there.

When he walked into the diner at their agreed upon time, his stomach was rumbling with hunger. Grace was standing behind the counter and all thoughts of a delicious omelet disappeared. He spotted Mark, who was smiling ear to ear, presumably reading his mind again.

Eric slid into the booth across from Mark, looking somber. "How much spit do you think I'll get in my food this morning? Should I risk it?"

"You don't have to," Mark replied, sipping his coffee. "Grace has moved on, sir. To that strapping young cowboy over there." Eric followed Mark's gaze to a young man in, of course, flannel smiling up at Grace as she placed a hand on his shoulder and giggled.

"Are you sure it's not a ploy to get a bigger tip?" Eric eyed Mark.

"I'm sure. Margie heard it from a lady at the salon that Grace is wrapped up in that guy now. Couldn't care less about you or your food is the way I hear it."

"Thank God." He wondered if one day he'd be the subject of salon gossip, then he realized he probably already had been, maybe more than once. One of the other servers came over and poured Eric a cup of coffee, and took their order. Mark talked about Margie and how things were going at home, and a few stories from his classroom. Eric half listened, his mind still drawn to the memories of the night before.

"Eric," Mark said at one point, "Earth to Eric!" He looked at Mark, confused. "I asked you how work was going for you?"

"Oh," Eric replied, "It's fine. Policing in a small town, ya know, busted tail lights and kids drinking in cornfields." He took a sip of his coffee as Mark stared at him.

"What happened? Was it Andy?"

"What are you talking about?" Eric hoped his cheeks weren't gaining any color. Mark glared at him. Then the server brought their breakfast, interrupting the inquisition.

"Something is going on with you, Grayson, and I'm gonna find out eventually, so you might as well tell me now," Mark said before piercing a piece of sausage with his fork and putting it in his mouth. While Eric would have loved to have been able to tell Mark that he had been wrong about his chances with Andy, he wouldn't dare betray her trust.

"Nothing is going on Deveraux. I didn't get much sleep last night, so I'm kind of out of it." It wasn't a lie. He had slept only a few hours. He just wouldn't tell Mark the reason.

"Well, I have to admit, I was sent here on a mission." The door to the diner dinged, halting Mark's train of thought. "Don't look now, Grayson, but the one girl in the county you seem to have it bad for just walked in." Eric didn't turn around. Then Mark's lips curled into a smile and he waved, "Hey Andy!"

When Eric looked up, she was standing beside their table. "Hey guys," she said, smiling. Her eyes flicked to Eric for only a brief moment, causing his heart to sink. He hoped she wasn't second guessing their night together.

"You're just in time. I have something to ask you both," Mark said, gesturing to the seat beside Eric. Eric moved over and Andy slid in beside him, perched on the edge of the bench seat. He was guessing she was trying not to touch him, but he wasn't sure why. She seemed so happy when he left. She had kissed him goodbye once, then grabbed him and kissed him again. Now she couldn't even look at him.

"I can't stay long. I popped in to get some breakfast for me and the guys. So far, it's been a rough one." Andy said, leaning her elbows on the table. Eric saw the dark circles under her eyes and felt a little guilty that he was partly responsible for them. The surly server came by and plopped a mug of coffee in front of her.

"Thanks Sue, you're an angel on this Earth," Andy said and Eric noted that the server smiled back before she walked away, something he hadn't seen her do to anyone else.

"So what's up?" Andy asked, taking a long drink of her coffee.

"Well, it's serendipitous that the two of you happen to both be here," Mark began. Eric saw the tiniest bit of pink creep up Andy's neck.

"Why's that?" she asked.

"Margie wanted me to invite you both to our place for Thanksgiving," Mark said, smiling. Andy and Eric exchanged a quick glance that Mark didn't seem to notice. "Margie's mom and dad are going to see one of her brothers over in Aspen for the week, so for the first time in years it'll be just the two of us. We don't want you two eating microwave meals or whatever, so we want you to come too."

"I volunteered to pick up Thanksgiving," Eric said, playing with the mug in front of him. "I figured the other guys have family in the area so I could work instead. Doesn't hurt that I get double time too."

Mark's face fell a bit. "Hmm, what about you Andy?"

"I try my best to work the ranch myself on holidays, strictly keeping cows and horses alive, obviously. The guys deserve a break, but it takes almost all day on my own," she said.

"Well, damn," Mark said, digging his phone out of his pocket. "Give me a second. I'm gonna call Margie and let her know." He slid out of his booth and walked across the diner and out the door.

Neither Eric nor Andy said anything to each other. Instead, both of them stared into their coffee. "Are you OK?" Eric asked. Andy looked at him, a tiny smile playing on her face.

"I'm doing great, thank you," she replied. He frowned. Something was off. He dropped his voice to a low whisper.

"Look about last night if you're having second thoughts—"

"Eric," she whispered back, interrupting him, "It's not that, I just -," Before she could finish her thought, Mark was back.

"Margie is not OK with the thought of the two of you not celebrating the holiday at all. Eric, do you work Saturday?" Mark asked and Eric shook his head no.

"And Andy, you'll be wrapped up on the ranch by Saturday afternoon?" He asked to her. She nodded, and Mark smiled. "Good! So Margie would like you both to come to a 'Friendsgiving,' on Saturday, instead then. She said you both need a home-cooked meal, and she wants to celebrate with our friends before the baby comes and changes everything."

Eric and Andy exchanged another quick glance, but this time, Mark noticed. "It's not a conspiracy to hook you guys up," Mark said. "Scout's honor!" He held two fingers up, recalling his old boy scout days. "Come on guys, my wife is pregnant. I'm trying to keep her happy. Gestating a child and teaching a bunch of other ones at the same time is difficult, and she lets me know that every chance she gets. I need a win here. And don't expect for one minute she won't call you herself if you say no."

The server came by and put a carrier filled with foam cups with lids and a brown bag with a grease spot already on it down in front of Andy. "Thanks Sue," Andy said, draining her mug and standing up. She looked from Eric to Mark and then said, "Sure Mark, I'll be there...for Margie." Eric noticed how pointedly she had added that last bit. Then Andy scooped up her order, said goodbye to them and was back out the door.

Eric felt a rotten feeling settling into the pit of his stomach. He wasn't sure what he had done wrong. "And you, my man?" Mark said to him.

"Yeah, sure. Tell Margie I'll be there," Eric replied, confusion and frustration bubbling up inside him.

"Outstanding!" Mark said. "Margie will be so happy. And that bit about it not being to set you guys up was partially true. I mean, it's not the only reason, but getting you two to spend some quality time together in a private setting can't hurt your chances, right?" Mark chuckled and continued eating.

Eric wasn't feeling quite so hungry and he pushed away his half finished omelet. "Or can it?" he thought to himself.

After a little more idle conversation, and paying the bill, Mark and Eric left the diner and went their separate ways. Eric climbed the stairs to his apartment and slumped onto his couch. He was bewildered. "What the hell went wrong?" he said aloud to no one. He couldn't bear another second of sitting around feeling sorry for himself, so he got up, threw on some sweats and his running shoes, and ran out into the chilly November air.

He had put his ear pods in, but partway through his run, he thought he heard someone yelling his name. Slowing to a jog, he pulled an ear bud out from under his knit hat, and looked around. Andy was perched on the seat of a quad that was running alongside the fence. When she saw him stop, she hopped off and walked to the fence. Wiping sweat from his face, he approached her, his heart in his stomach. He was dreading what she might say after how she acted earlier.

"Hey," she said. He thought she looked like a tan marshmallow. She wore insulated overalls under a matching coat. A hat was pulled down over her ears and her cheeks and the tip of her nose were rosy.

"Did I do something wrong?" he blurted out before saying anything else.

Confusion washed over her face. "What?"

"In the diner, it seemed like you wanted to be anywhere else but next to me. I thought you were having second thoughts about what happened last night," he replied.

Her eyes crinkled in the corners as she smiled. "Oh, Eric," she said softly, pulling off one of her gloves. She leaned against the fence with her still gloved hand and put the other one on his cheek, her warm palm against his air chilled skin.

"I don't regret what happened, not even a little. I don't know how to act with you in front of other people yet. I'm afraid if I look at you too long I'll either start thinking about how good being with you felt, how good you felt and I'm going to blush, or not being able to control myself and climb on top of you," she said with a chuckle. He smiled as relief flooded through him.

"I can't tell you how much better that makes me feel." Then he looked around. "This isn't your property, is it? What are you doing all the way out here?"

"Another rancher called me. He was shorthanded this week. Frank Miller hired a couple of his hands out from under him. He had some stuff that he needed help with and asked if I could send anybody. I try to make Sunday's light for the guys, so I came over to give him a hand instead."

"Can I see you tonight?" he asked, for once not caring if he sounded desperate with a woman. He had always tried to seem strong, waiting a day or two after a date to call because he was "supposed" to, but he didn't give a damn right now, not with the memory of what her curves felt like under his hands.

A broad smile stretched across her face and she bit her bottom lip, "I have rancher poker tonight."

"Rancher poker?" he asked.

"For years, a bunch of ranchers get together on Sunday night and play poker. I always thought it was funny they gambled on 'the Lord's day.' When dad died I got his seat, so every Sunday night we head over to Roger Hills' house, drink beer and whiskey and bet $50 on poker. Winner takes all."

He stared, trying to imagine this slight, blond woman in a room full of old, weatherworn, cranky ranchers playing poker. He shook the image out of his head and said, "So you can't see me because you're hanging out with other guys, huh?"

She laughed hard at that. "Oh yeah, you've got some stiff competition all right."

"Hmmm," he said. "I'll have to work harder."

She raised her eyebrows at him. "I'm both intrigued and terrified trying to imagine that." She looked over her shoulder at the quad. "I need to get back to helping Tom if I'm going to be done before the game starts."

She smiled at him and went to turn away before changing her mind and coming back to the fence. She grabbed a handful of the front of his sweatshirt, pulled him toward her, and kissed him. Her tongue met his, but before he could touch her, she broke away. "Just to tide me over," she said with a wink. Before he could respond, she was back on the quad and driving away into the distance.

Still smiling, he turned and ran back to his apartment, feeling much lighter than he had at the beginning of his run.

27

Andy had worked far later than she thought she would and showed up for poker just in time. As strange as it was, she enjoyed her poker nights with the other ranchers. First, she was a skilful player, and walked away with a good chunk of change now and then. Second, these men had played with her father every Sunday. This group of old, weather worn ranchers, most with either a cigar or a wad of chew stuffed under their lip, sometimes felt like the closest connection she had to him.

These poker nights were also what she considered the last line of defense against Frank Miller. Often during the game someone would mention a trouble, a concern or an idea. With the other small ranchers all in one room, they could figure out a solution or give a much needed opinion. Andy excelled at creatively solving one rancher's issue without leaving another feeling imposed upon.

During this particular game, there was some talk about bulls and cows, but much of the conversation was about family and Thanksgiving plans. Most of the ranchers would work in the mornings while their wives prepared a meal. Then they'd release their hands and sit down with their families, some of them at tables with eighteen people or more.

When they'd asked her what her plans were, she told them she was giving her hands the whole day off, working the ranch herself, and then she'd eat some leftovers. By their reactions, a person watching would have thought she told them Waylon Jennings was a traitor. They'd guffawed and told her that hands expect to work. She rebuffed that, told them she'd run her ranch the way she saw fit, and that ended that conversation.

When she'd looked around the table, she tried to count the number of men the other ranchers had lost to Frank Miller, whereas not a single one of her guys had left her since she'd taken over. Four of them had been at the ranch since before her dad died and she'd added a few more to that count as her ranch grew.

She gave them as many holidays off as she could muster and she shared a portion of profits with them. They got first dibs on any work truck she was going to get rid of. She'd sell them each a cow to butcher at cost every year too. The other ranchers thought her hands were taking advantage of her. She thought she was treating them like the valuable human beings they were. It was hard to find a good, experienced ranch hand, which was why they all mourned when Frank took one of theirs because he could throw more money at them.

But that game, and those conversations, were turning into a hazy memory as she got ready for Eric to come over. She wasn't sure what to wear and couldn't believe that she was caring again. Like so many things that he was causing to bubble up to the surface, she liked it. There were so many clothes in her closet that she never wore anymore. So many fine fabrics in rich colors and interesting cuts. She stood in front of them, running her fingers along the collection of heels languishing on shelves.

As she stared at the clothes, she grew frustrated. She grabbed her phone and fell flat back onto her bed, shooting a text to Eric before she thought it through. "I can't find anything to wear. Sweats OK?"

She saw the dots in the left-hand corner and a quick response came through, "I know for a fact you would look great in anything." She smiled to herself. More dots popped up in the corner. "I have a crazy idea though," he texted back, then her phone rang.

"If it's swimsuits I'm out," she said when she answered, causing him to laugh.

"No, no. I mean, I'd be all for seeing you in a swimsuit, but it is November, after all," he replied. "I was thinking about how you've mentioned that you didn't have a reason to dress up, but I imagine you did once."

"Right," she answered, already seeing where he was going.

"Around here we will only have rare opportunities to see each other dressed in anything other than jeans. So, even though it's not like we are going anywhere fancy, maybe we can still spiffy up a bit. Dress like we're going somewhere you would go in New York, and I will too."

"Are you going to wear a suit?"

"Agree to this and then you'll find out."

She heard the smile in his voice. "OK," she replied, unable to stop grinning.

"Perfect. I'll bring grub and look dashing. You won't be able to resist me, Miss Summers."

"Awfully confident, aren't we Deputy Grayson?"

"Oh course I am. Once you see how well I clean up, you'll understand why. See you soon," he said and ended the call. She lifted herself off the bed, feeling a little giddy about putting something on that she hadn't in ages. She went to the closet and one of her favorite dresses caught her eye.

She did her hair, pinning it so gentle curls cascaded over one shoulder. After rifling through her old makeup, she pulled out some things that, thankfully, hadn't expired. She raided the heels in her closet and settled on a simple black pair. When she looked in the mirror, she noted how great her ass looked in this emerald green, mid thigh, tight dress that showed just the right amount of cleavage. For the first time in a long time, she thought she could walk into a restaurant in NYC after strolling through a gallery.

Loud knocks shook her from her thoughts. She had lost track of the time and went down the stairs as quickly as she could manage in the heels. Taking a deep breath, she straightened out her skirt before opening the door.

She already thought Eric was handsome, but when she saw him standing on the step wearing a dark navy blue suit, she was blown away. He could have fit in on wall street, or at a Hollywood premiere as far as she was concerned. When he flashed her a million-dollar smile, she felt that now familiar longing rising within her.

He came in and pulled a to-go bag from Dolly's from behind his back. "My options were limited," he said, smiling. "Pretend it's something super classy and not diner food." He kissed her on the cheek and she looked at him with surprise.

She asked with raised eyebrows, shocked at his tepid greeting. "That's all I get?"

"Sorry," he said smiling, "My ex was very against kissing on the lips if she was wearing makeup. I guess I'm more conditioned than I thought."

The jealousy rising within her took her by surprise. She knew he'd been married before. Obviously, that came with physical intimacy, but hearing him say it made it more real.

She went to him and pressed her mouth to his. He pulled her closer, and she slipped her tongue between his lips. When they parted, she smiled up at him. "Well, with me, I guess it's whether you can deal with having lipstick on your face," she said as she wiped the smudge away from his mouth with her thumb, and he did the same to her.

"It could be a good look for me." He winked, and she rolled her eyes.

The evening went by in a blur of laughter and pleasant conversation. They'd eaten their less than classy dinners and spent the rest of the evening sitting beside one another on the couch. Touching, interlocking fingers and tracing lines and circles on each other with fingertips while they talked about everything and nothing.

Jake had been an excellent conversationalist too, but she'd never felt like she connected to him like she felt like she was connecting with Eric. Underneath the surface, though, there was one thing bothering her. One answer that she'd like to have before things between them went further, before she'd let herself fall even harder for him.

She got them both a fresh drink and then sat beside him on the couch. "Eric, I want to ask you something, but I'm kind of afraid to. I feel like it's something that might be important for me to know, but I don't want to upset you either," she began. Eric set down his beer on a coaster on the coffee table and put his arm on the back of the couch behind her, turning to face her.

"Lay it on me," he said.

She noticed he had exhaled, preparing for the question that was coming at him. "Why did you leave LA?"

"Oh," he said, and his body language shifted. He tensed and leaned forward, resting his elbows on his knees. She stayed quiet, waiting for him to speak. A thousand terrible scenarios ran through her mind: he had committed a crime, the LAPD fired him for something terrible, he had a wife and kids he had run away from.

He took a deep breath and she could feel the tension rolling off of him in waves.

28

His knuckles turned white as he clenched his hands into fists. "I was doing well, even after the divorce. I realized through it all that we weren't compatible. Work was going great. I was even studying to take the detective's exam and my superiors were supportive. I'd raked in some commendations and I felt like everything was on the right track.

"And then...shit." He rubbed his hands over his face.

Staying silent, she moved even closer to him, so their thighs pressed against each other. She put her drink on the table and her hand on his arm.

He took another deep breath and continued. "There was a breaking and entering call in this bad part of town that we patrolled that night. I mean, there are lots of unpleasant places in the city, but this was one of those where you always made sure your windows and doors were locked, even if you were driving through.

"We rolled up on it, my partner and I. The alarm in this place was going nuts. The window was smashed in. We entered and announced ourselves. Then we heard some crashing from the back and I saw someone running. They went out the back door and I followed.

"I kept announcing myself as police and shouted for them to stop. My partner was slower than me, an older guy, so he had jumped in the car to head us off, radioing for backup while I took off after this guy. Next thing I know, the guy shoots at me.

"We were running through alleys and back streets. From what I remember, he got about five shots off on me during the pursuit. Finally, I had this guy cornered. He had hit a brick wall. So I announced again, at this guy who had just shot at me five times, 'LAPD, freeze'," Eric took another drink and then put the beer on the table in front of them. He closed his eyes tight and continued.

"And for a second, he did. He had his back to me, but he put his hands up. I could see the gun in his hand. I yelled at him to drop it. But he didn't. Jesus, I remember my heart was pounding so hard I could barely hear myself. I was praying that he would put the damn thing down.

"He turned around and I swear by that time I've told him to drop his gun about four times. But now he's turning to face me. I yelled at him again to drop the gun, but he got another shot off...so I pulled the trigger. Twice, like we're trained to do. Pop. Pop. And he dropped.

Eric's head was in his hands as he pulled out these memories that he'd wanted to keep buried. She kept one arm wrapped around him and a hand on his arm.

"So I moved forward, kicked the weapon out of reach and kept mine on him, like I was supposed to. That's when I saw him." He continued, his voice breaking throughout. "He was a kid. Turns out he was only 18. The robbery was a gang initiation. I'll never forget his face." He looked at her and she could see tears on his cheeks. She rested her head on his shoulder.

"I killed a kid. He was some lost boy trying to find his way, and I killed him. I took away a boy from his family. In the end, he had been a scared kid who didn't know what to do and made the wrong choice. Who knows what he could have become if he'd been able to get on the right track?"

Sliding off the couch, she perched herself on the edge of the coffee table in front of him. She rested her forehead against his, her hands on either side of his face.

"I couldn't live with myself. When I closed my eyes, I saw that boy on the pavement, his eyes wide open but not seeing. I couldn't sleep. Ever. So I drank, like my goddamn father. I was spiraling out of control and I knew it.

"One night I was sitting there, surrounded by empties, and I started crying. This wasn't what I wanted, this wasn't how I wanted to live. I needed someone. My mom wouldn't give a shit. She'd lived with an alcoholic for my whole life. As long as her son looked like the shiny hero, she wouldn't care what was going on underneath."

He took a long, rasping breath. "My dad had never, ever been there for me and will never be. So I called my brother, Will. He answered, and I remember breaking down and sobbing. All he said was, 'And what do you expect me to do about it?' and then he hung up. I was so shocked, so hurt, I didn't know what to do for a second.

"So I did the only thing I could think to do. I called Mark, and he showed up at my apartment the next day. He had hopped on a plane at god knows what expense and rushed to be with me when the guy I share blood with couldn't even stay on the phone with me. But that's who Mark is."

Tears slid down Eric's face, but he didn't bother to wipe them away. "He sat with me through the weekend, got me to take a shower, forced food down my throat. Then, he told me he wanted me to come back to Spring Hills with him. He wanted me to get away from LA. Every night until I could, Mark would call me and check in to make sure I was doing OK.

"Then a few weeks later, he found out about the opening here. So I applied. And I'm pretty sure Mark greased some wheels, or Margie, or Margie's dad. I'm not sure, but I had an interview over a video call not too long after. A day after the interview, I got the job. I turned in my gun and my badge in LA right away. And here I am," he finished, his head hanging low.

She pulled his face towards hers and kissed his cheeks, tasting the salt of his tears. He leaned into her and she wrapped her arms around him, resting her cheek on the top of his head. They sat that way for a few minutes. Then he pulled back and looked at her.

"Eric, I'm so sorry I made you relive that. I was imagining all the reasons you'd leave LA, and I figured the truth was better than what I was coming up with," she said, searching his eyes.

"You don't have to apologize. You deserve to know. I mean, I can't imagine what you thought could have made me run a thousand of miles away from LA. You would have found out, eventually..."

"Eric," she whispered, "This doesn't change what I think or feel about you. I can't imagine having to go through that. I know nothing I say is going to make you feel better about what happened, but when I look at you, I still see the same guy I saw when you walked in here tonight."

He looked at her again, his eyes searching her face for something. She saw pain there and wanted to take that from him. Putting a hand behind his neck, and pulled him to her.

He buried his face in the space between her neck and her shoulder. Her hands ran the length of his back to provide some comfort. They stayed like that; him breathing her in for quite some time. She pulled away and took his tear-stained face in her hands.

She kissed him, and then slipped her hand into his. When she stood, she pulled, urging him to his feet. "Andy?" he whispered.

Without speaking, she led him up the stairs and into her bedroom. They stood facing each other, and she unbuttoned his shirt. His hand wandering the curves of her body before it found the zipper on her side. She felt the dress become loose and then fall from her body as he gently pushed the straps down her arms.

When they were in nothing but their underwear, Andy took his hand in hers and led him to the bed. He sat on it, his back against the headboard. She climbed in and settled into the space between his legs, curling up against his chest. He put his arms around her, holding her tight against his body.

She wasn't sure how long they sat together, his warmth seeping into her bones. A feeling of safety, of contentment, of warmth filled her. She knew she was falling hard for this man, but realized it didn't scare her anymore.

She turned and looked into his eyes. A sense of calm had settled around him. She smiled and asked, "Penny for your thoughts?"

"I'd be robbing you if I charged you that much," he said, a big grin spreading across his face. She punched him on the arm and he laughed. "I'm thinking that you're amazing. I'm thinking that while that's a painful time in my life to talk about, I'm kind of glad you know. I'm thinking that I've got to be the luckiest guy in the world to have you next to me."

She pressed her lips to his and felt his warm hands on the exposed parts of her skin. His hand cupped her jaw, and hers moved to his neck. Warmth grew between her legs and stopped herself.

"Eric," she whispered against his lips, "we don't have to do this tonight. I know it was hard for you to have to talk about all of that—"

"Andy, if you think for one second I don't want to keep doing this while you are half naked and gorgeous, sitting between my legs, you're crazy."

29

Thanksgiving came the next day and Andy cursed when the alarm went off at 3:30 AM. Eric had left around 11:30 the night before since they both knew she had a long day ahead of her, but it still wasn't enough sleep.

She hit the snooze button, which she never did. When that buzzed, she groaned and smashed her palm against the clock to make it stop beeping. Bleary-eyed, she threw on her clothes and shuffled to the kitchen, where she made an entire pot of coffee and put what she would fit into the largest travel cup she owned.

She pulled up her thick, insulated overalls, slid her feet into her work boots, shrugged into her coat, and put on her gloves and hat. Then, clutching her coffee, she headed out into the cold to do the work of at least four men.

It was seven o'clock at night by the time she dragged herself back towards the house. Every part of her body ached and her stomach growled. She was tired, hungry, and grumpy. She kept telling herself two things. The first was that it was worth it. It was worth busting her ass all day to give her guys one day off with their families. Although, the niggling response in the back of her head was that no one was there to give her a day off. The second thing was that these late nights with Eric, albeit enjoyable, may be the death of her.

As she approached the door at the side of the house, she saw something laying on the porch. When she got closer, she saw it was a frozen pizza with a white box from the bakery in town on top of it. A slip of paper was taped to the box. She pulled off her gloves and shoved them in her coat pocket, then pulled off the note and read it.

"Can't break tradition. Happy Thanksgiving. E."

She scooped up the boxes and went inside. When she opened the white box, she saw a beautiful, perfect, dark orange pumpkin pie.

It was a combination of exhaustion, loneliness, memories of what this holiday used to be and the fact that Eric not only remembered the conversation they'd had but also that he was taking care of her. But when she saw that pie, she cried. Big, ugly sobbing tears.

She left the boxes on the counter and went to rid her body of the day's grime. After her shower, she slid into a pair of sweats and her mom's sweater and went downstairs to have her Thanksgiving dinner of pizza and pumpkin pie.

After she slid the pizza into the oven, she shot a text to Eric, who she knew was working. "Thank you. You're amazing."

He shot back a blushing emoji beside a heart eye emoji. "Hopefully in more ways than one," he replied.

"Way more than one," she texted back, smiling at the screen.

30

Margie's Friendsgiving was upon them. Eric hadn't seen Andy in person since the night he'd ended up telling her about LA. He'd felt like one big raw nerve when he told her, completely vulnerable. It wasn't a secret. A big swath of the city had known about the shooting. There were no big protests or major outcry after the body cam footage was released, but that hadn't mattered to him. He hadn't cared that it was ruled a "good shoot."

He had gone to the boy's internment, standing off to the side so no one would see him. He didn't know why he went, but he felt he had to. Watching the boy's mother sob as they lowered the cheap casket into the ground had made his stomach churn and his heart race. His throat had felt like it was being squeezed.

He had wished it was him being lowered into the darkness and not a young boy. It all felt like too much. Too much to bear, too much to witness. He had twisted on his heel and made it to the driver's seat of his car before he started sobbing in the cemetery. On his way home, he picked up another bottle of vodka.

Now he stood in his bathroom looking at himself in the mirror, battling back the memories that were resurfacing after talking to Andy.

"There's nothing I can do to change the past," he said to his reflection. Then he turned and walked out, heading for Mark and Margie's place.

When he pulled into the driveway, he noticed Andy's truck right behind him. He parked and climbed out of his vehicle, waiting for her to do the same. "You ready for this?" he said to her, smiling as they walked up to the door.

"Eating one of Margie's home-cooked meals while staring at your handsome face and thinking about all the things that tongue of yours can do?" she said with a wink. "I was born ready." His hands itched to pull her close and the smell of her stirred him, but he kept his hands to himself and instead they both turned and walked up the steps of the big porch.

Eric rapped his knuckles on the door and Mark answered, a smile that turned confused when he saw them standing there together. "Hey man," Eric said, then felt the urge to explain. "We pulled up at the same time."

"Oh! Come on in guys!" Mark said with a smile.

Eric let Andy go ahead of him, and Mark shot him a wink. Eric smiled but shook his head, stifling a laugh as he hung up his coat and took off his shoes. "Margie," he yelled from the hall, making his way to the kitchen, with Andy behind him. "That smells incredible!"

He walked into the room and saw her form with its now burgeoning belly at the stove. She had an apron covering her front, but hadn't been able to tie the strings around her waist.

"Margie," Andy said, pushing past him and going to her. "If you're standing there stirring gravy, that is something I can handle. Have you sat down at all today?" Without letting Margie respond, she took the wooden spoon from her and began stirring the liquid.

Margie dabbed at the beads of sweat on her forehead with the towel she had on her shoulder. "I'll sit down soon, I promise," she muttered, short of breath.

"What else could you have to do?" Andy said, scowling at her.

"Mostly putting stuff out." Margie huffed as her hands went to her lower back and her fingers made circles against the muscles there. The counter was littered with bowls and serving trays with lids. "I have to finish the gravy and pull the rolls out when they're done."

"Margie, we will get the table set. I'll finish up this gravy and throw the rolls in this basket." Andy held up the wicker basket that Margie had lined with a light blue towel. "You will go sit down and put your feet up."

"I've been trying to tell her that all day," Mark piped in from behind them. Margie looked conflicted.

"Mark," Andy barked in her raspy voice, still stirring the gravy. "Get this woman a big glass of water and take her somewhere to sit. Do not let her get until it's time for her to enjoy all this hard work. Eric, start taking some of these bowls out to the dinner table...please."

Eric smirked and threw a salute before grabbing a couple of bowls and taking them to the table. Mark filled a glass and took Margie by the arm, and although she was protesting, she did as Andy said.

Eric smiled to himself, thinking they just got a taste of how Andy must take charge at the ranch. He had to admit it excited him to think about what happened when she took control of other, more private venues.

He returned to the kitchen to get something else to take to the table, but the sight of her standing at the stove distracted him. "Still stirring?" he said, going to her.

"Gotta stir it until it boils or it'll be lumpy, then Margie would banish me from her kitchen for life, and blame me for ruining her dinner. Who knows with those hormones?"

He peeked over his shoulder and then moved to stand behind her, putting his hands on her hips and pulling her to his body.

"Eric," she hissed.

"They're in the other room, under your direct orders," he whispered into her ear before kissing her neck. He could feel her shoulders relax.

"Mark could walk in here at any moment."

Eric put his arms around her waist and kissed her neck again. "I'll tell him I was performing the Heimlich."

"Will you stop and go put some of that stuff on the table?" she hissed. He laughed and released her waist, swatting her butt before he took another round of stuff to the table.

When he returned to the kitchen, she held the basket of rolls out to him. "Can you take these?" she asked, looking around the kitchen.

He went to her and took the basket in one hand and put his other arm around her and drew her in for a kiss. She relaxed against his body, kissing him back. Then he felt her push her hand against on his chest, "They're going to catch us."

"If you say so, Miss Summers, but you have to admit, it adds a little something, that possibility of being caught." He winked at her and turned to leave before he felt her grab his arm. He turned, and she pulled him back up against her. She kissed him again, the kind of kiss that makes you feel hot and sweaty all over in the matter of seconds. He kissed her back, the basket of rolls still in his hand. His other hand traveled down her back before cupping her backside.

The sound of someone clearing their throat brought them back down to earth. "Sorry for interrupting," Mark's voice said. They broke apart, like a couple of high schoolers caught behind the bleachers. Andy brought a hand to her mouth. Both of them were looking at Mark like deer in the headlights while he stood there, his mouth slack and his eyes wide. Andy buried her face in Eric's chest.

Eric was sure he was wearing a shit-eating grin. "Hey Mark," he said, "Wanna take these rolls out to the table so we can finish up here?"

"Hell no," Mark said, "Nobody better be finishing up anything in my kitchen. But I can take the rolls for you." He took the basket from Eric and went out to the dining table, whistling a happy little tune.

Andy punched Eric on the arm. Her eyes were enormous, green saucers. "Shit, Eric!"

"Hey," he said, grabbing another bowl of food. "That last one was all you, Miss Summers."

She paused, seeming to replay the moment in her mind. She groaned and put her hands up to her cheeks. "Mark's gonna tell Margie," she hissed.

"One hundred percent he will." He heard her groan again as he took the bowl into the dining room.

Mark was standing next to the table, his arms over his chest. "What the hell, man?" he hissed, hitting Eric in the shoulder, not nearly as playfully as Andy had.

"What was that for?" Eric asked after he put the bowl down, smiling from ear to ear, knowing what it was for.

"You and Andy? How long has that been going on for, man? Why the hell haven't you told me?"

"It's not been long, a few weeks-"

"A few weeks?" Mark interrupted in a hushed yell. He raised his hand as to hit Eric again.

"Andy wanted to keep things private until we figured things out for ourselves. She said dating in a town like Spring Hills can be challenging."

"Yeah," Mark said as he nodded and lowered his hand. "Like everybody in the whole county knowing your business about two minutes after it happens."

"So what are the odds you won't tell Margie what you saw?"

"Slim. And by slim, I mean zero," Mark replied, his eyes sparkling.

"And what are the odds we could convince her not to tell anybody?"

"High. She and Andy were close in high school. They're still friends now. She wouldn't do anything to hurt her."

"OK," Eric said, feeling a twinge of relief. "Will you let me tell Margie myself?"

"As long as it's today, because she's gonna talk to me about how things went and if we think ya'll have a connection tonight, as a tiny human punches her insides and prevents her from sleeping."

Eric nodded and went back to the kitchen. Andy had grabbed the bottles of wine that had been set on the counter. "So," he said with a sigh, "I say we tell Margie and beg her to keep it a secret. Mark is of the opinion that she'll be OK with that." Andy nodded, but looked mournful.

"What's the worst thing that could happen?" Eric asked, rubbing his hands over her arms.

She raised her eyebrows to the ceiling. "The worst that could happen? The whole town finds out we're screwing. Then we call things off. Then I have to see you all the time, knowing that the whole town knows we used to be involved. I lose credibility on the ranch because my guys think my head's not in the game. I lose all my hands, I lose the ranch and I have to sell to Frank Miller!" And although she was whispering, Eric knew she would have been yelling if she weren't trying to be discrete.

"Wow, okay. There's a lot to unpack there. First, is that all we are doing? Screwing?"

She looked at him, and her face softened. "No...but they won't know that."

"And do you trust Margie?" he said, taking another step closer to her. She closed her eyes and thought for a moment.

"Yeah."

"Are you thinking what I'm thinking?" he whispered, putting an arm around her back and brushing a strand of hair from her face. She looked at him and blinked.

"What are you thinking?"

"That we need to find a way to have sex in this kitchen to mess with Mark."

"Oh God," Andy said, rolling her eyes and walking away. He caught her arm and pulled her back to him.

"It's going to be alright Andy, they're our friends." He gave her a quick, gentle kiss. "And I won't let anything bad happen to you. Promise."

He followed her back to the dining table and popped his head into the living room, where Mark and Margie were watching something on TV. Margie had her feet up, which he was glad to see.

"I think we're ready for you," he said. Mark helped Margie off the couch and followed behind her as she waddled into the next room. They sat together on one side of the table. Eric and Andy on the other.

"Oh," said Margie, tears welling up in her eyes, "You guys did such a great job. Everything looks beautiful."

"Margie," Andy said, chuckling, "You did all the work. We just put bowls on the table."

Margie smiled back at her and wiped a tear. "Well, you did a great job of it. Shall we say grace?" she asked, and Mark and Margie dipped their heads.

After they were done praying Margie's eyes lit up and she said, "Well let's dig in ya'll!"

Eric had never had a Thanksgiving spread that had been this good before. Margie had made a phenomenal meal with everything they could have hoped for. They talked comfortably and soon over an hour had passed. Eric hadn't been blind to Mark's pointed looks at him, and as the conversation seemed to come to a lull, Eric figured it was now or never.

"So, uh, Margie," he said, then shot a look at Andy, who dropped her gaze and stared at her wine. "I know that inviting us here today was because you didn't want us to miss out on Thanksgiving. But I know it was also a little to get Andy and me to spend more time together."

Margie's eyes got big, and they flicked from Eric to Andy and back again. "Well, I thought...I didn't mean any-"

"No, it's OK Margie," Eric said, smiling, trying not to laugh at Margie, who would never have been able to lie even if she'd wanted to. "I thought you should know that the latter part is unnecessary because Andy and I have been spending time together, anyway."

Margie looked confused until she saw the look that Eric and Andy exchanged. "What? You're...oh!" Margie clapped her hands together. "You guys are...together?" she asked, her voice hopeful.

"We're figuring things out, Margie," Andy piped in. "But it's still pretty new, and we'd appreciate it if you didn't tell anyone."

"Oh, I promise! You tell me when it's not under wraps anymore, but until then, my lips are sealed." She pushed her chair back the best she could and got to her feet. "Oh, I'm so happy for you both!" Eric stood up to meet her embrace, as did Andy.

"Once the baby is a little older, we can have my parents watch the little one and we can go on a double date! Won't that be wonderful?" Margie's cheerfulness was almost contagious. She sat back down and looked at them thoughtfully. "Why are you telling me now if you're keeping this a secret, which I will honor, by the way?"

"Well," said Eric, "The two of us were in close proximity in the kitchen together earlier and Mark may have walked in on us stealing a private moment." Margie laughed and Mark joined in. Eric and Andy followed, the laughter around the table infectious. "And we will clear the table and do the dishes since you provided such a wonderful meal for us."

"Likely excuse Grayson, you just want some more of those 'private moments.'" Mark said, smiling.

Eric put his arm around Andy and looked at her, a smile creeping across his face as he said, "Well, I'd be lying if I didn't say the thought hadn't crossed my mind." A slight pink rose in Andy's cheeks as she swatted him in the chest with the back of her hand. Eric caught her by the fingers and brought her palm to his lips, causing Margie to sigh happily.

Eric and Andy cleared the table and did the dishes, stealing quite a few "private moments." Then they sat in the living room side by side, his arm around her. He was surprised at how relieved he was that he didn't have to pretend they were just friends. They both noticed Margie growing tired and said their goodbyes and hugged the Deverauxs before going back into the cold November night air.

"So," Andy said when they reached the door of her truck.

"So," Eric repeated, standing beside her.

"Are you interested in a nightcap?"

"Is that how you got the guys back to your place in New York?"

She winked at him. "I'll never divulge my secrets, Mr. Grayson." Peeking over his shoulder to make sure no one was looking through the closed blinds, she took his jacket in each of her hands. She pulled him towards her and kissed him, her tongue searching his mouth.

"Well, I mean, I was going to say yes anyway," he said, when they'd broken apart. "But I don't mind the convincing."

31

A few days later, a call came in a few hours before Eric's shift was over. "Attention all units, reports of an incident involving trespassing at Summers Ranch. Any units in the area?" His heart jumped into his throat, and the only thing he could think of was making sure that Andy was safe.

"338, I'm in the vicinity, I'll respond," he flipped the lights on, not sure what he was driving towards but trying to get there as quickly as possible. When he turned into the driveway, he flicked the lights off and strode towards the house.

He was ready to bang on the door when he heard Carl's voice. "Deputy!" he shouted, "Over here!" He followed Carl back to the barn, where he knew the cows were kept. "Brace yourself, Deputy," the older man said before pressing a palm against the small side door.

Eric entered, blinking as his eyes adjusted to the light. When they did, the reason he had been called in was obvious. A cow lay dead in the middle of the cement floor, its throat slit. Dark red blood dried around the edges, surrounded the body. More disturbing though was what was on the wall, written in the cow's blood, "You're next whore," the big, dark red letters read.

Eric flexed his fists, anger consuming him as he looked over the scene. He took a few deep breaths before turning and walking out into the still dark morning. Carl was standing beside Romeo, their heads together as they talked in hushed tones. Andy stood off to the side, one arm shielding her chest, the other covering her mouth. The other hands lingered around until Carl bellowed, "Don't you pecker heads have shit to do?" They scattered like roaches when you turn on the light.

"Carl," Eric called, and the man turned and walked towards him. They walked a little farther away before Eric asked questions. Carl's face was bright red, beads of sweat formed on his brow even though it was well below freezing outside.

"I need you to tell me what happened this morning, Carl," Eric said.

"Me and Romeo pulled in right around the same time. We're the first ones here. Andy walked out at the same time we pulled in, like always. We were bullshitting, goin' over what we had to do today when we walked up to the side door. Andy and I were behind Romeo.

"Romeo stopped all the sudden and was like, 'Hey look at this,' and he pointed to the doorknob that looked smashed in. He pushed the door open and shoved Andy back. I've never seen him like that.

"Maybe some of that high school basketball shit came back to her, but she slipped past Romeo and ended up looking in there before we could stop her. Andy stood there a minute, like she was tryin' to take it all in.

"Then she looked up at me and I swear Eric she was that like six-year-old girl lookin' up at me after her brother fell off a horse and broke his arm. So I pulled her outta there, and we called 911. She ended up getting sick over there behind the house. What kind of psycho would do something like this?"

Eric shook his head, unsure of how to answer that question. "It's gonna take me some time to work the scene. I'll let you know when you can get back in there," he said quietly.

Carl didn't look happy about it, but he understood. Then Eric talked to Romeo, whose version of events matched Carl's. He got a small digital camera from his cruiser and started taking images of the scene. No CSI to be called out here.

Eric dusted the door for fingerprints, although he had assumed correctly it would be fruitless. In December, everyone around here wore gloves to protect their skin from the cold. When he was sure there wasn't anything he missed, he went back out into the cold air.

Carl, Romeo and Andy had disappeared from where they once stood. He walked to the horse barn and found Romeo tending to an animal. "Hey Romeo," Eric called, "I need to talk to Andy."

"We sent her inside. She didn't fight us, which tells me she's not OK. We were trying to give her some space before we checked on her," Romeo replied.

Eric went back to the house and knocked on the door. Andy answered, her eyes bloodshot and her cheeks puffy. She turned and walked back into the kitchen, leaving the door open for him.

Andy kept her back to him after he closed the door. He slipped his hands in the pockets of his parka until her shoulders started shaking. Closing the space between them quickly, he enveloped her in his arms. She turned and buried her face in his chest. Her arms wrapped around his waist as she cried. He didn't talk; he didn't shush her, he let her cry and held her close.

Within a few minutes, her eyes met his and his heart broke at how distraught she looked. He kissed her forehead, and she was still for a moment. He took a step back from her so they were an arm's length apart. "Tell me what happened," he asked. She sighed and sat on a chair at the table.

"I headed out and met Carl and Romeo when they got here and we headed toward the barn. Romeo noticed the doorknob was damaged, and he went in. He tried to stop me. Dammit, I should have listened. But me being me, I didn't. You saw it Eric…"

He plucked a tissue from the box nearby and handed it to her. She blew her nose and then crumpled the tissue in her hand. Fresh tears welled in her eyes. "What am I going to do?" He sat on a chair next to hers, turning so he was facing her, and she continued.

"How can I stay here, with someone who might be the same person who broke into my home, prowling around out there? How am I supposed to sleep, or shower, or watch TV without feeling like someone is right out there waiting to hurt me? How do I feel safe?" Her tears rolled down her cheeks faster now.

"I will do everything I can to keep you safe," he said, wiping one of her tears. "Any night I'm not working, I'll be here. When I can't be, you can go to Romeo's, or Carl's, or Mark and Margie's?"

She shook her head and leaned further into his palm. "Run and hide?" she asked.

"No," he replied, fighting to keep his cool. "Stay safe. You're right, this guy came in here once. If it's the same guy who left the note on your truck, he's getting bolder now. Like you said, this shows he's violent. He could hurt you, Andy." She was quiet and closed her eyes for a moment. "Did you hear anything last night, Andy?"

"No, nothing. Look, I need to get out there," she said, standing. "Sitting in here all day by myself will help nothing and no one." She stood up before he could say anything and had her tan marshmallow suit on in no time. She pulled her gloves onto her hands and he stood up and went to her, putting his hands on her waist. He pulled her towards him and lowered his lips to hers, just for a moment. She looked at him, her eyes still sad and afraid, and went to the door.

Once he got back in his cruiser, the desire to drive straight to Frank Miller's house and confront him bubbled within him. He started in that direction and then sense took over him. He pulled to the side of the road and slammed his hand against the steering wheel.

As good as it would feel to handle this himself, he knew he couldn't. If he moved on to this case and his involvement with Andy ever came to light, it could screw things up. He sighed and instead turned his cruiser toward the station. He called his sergeant on the way and asked to meet with him in an hour.

When he arrived, he sat at a desk and typed up the report regarding what he'd seen in Andy's barn. He typed up a separate, unofficial document, with the threats he'd heard Frank Miller make against Andy, and also the note she'd found on her truck. He was grabbing everything off the printer when the sergeant walked in and motioned to the office.

Then he sat across from one of the more experienced sergeants in the Sheriff's department. He was an older guy with a slight gut, but one who was respected by everyone in the department. "Thank you for meeting with me, Sergeant James," Eric began.

"You bet, Grayson, what can I do for you?" he said, giving Eric his full attention.

"I took a report on a call over at Summers Ranch this morning," he began.

"I heard that come over on the radio," James responded.

"It was a lot worse than I thought it'd be. One of her cows was left dead in her barn, and a threat was written on the wall in its blood. I've typed up the report on it."

"Jesus," James said, rubbing his jaw. "Okay, good start. You got any leads or anything you want to follow on this? You know we've talked about this before. We aren't segmented like LAPD, you pop a case, you work the case. We don't have fancy detectives. You're on nights, so that will be harder, but you'd coordinate with someone on days and you'd still be lead on the case."

"Yes, sir. That's why I need to speak with you." Eric took a deep breath. "I'm telling you this, hoping it can remain confidential." The sergeant's eyes narrowed. "I know I've only been here for four or five months, but I assume that, like with the LAPD, the personal involvement of an investigating officer with the victim of a crime would be a reason that the case should be reassigned." The sergeant took a moment for the information to register and then nodded his head in understanding.

"I see. So you're saying this case needs to be reassigned?"

"Yes sir. I've typed up the report with witness statements and included the photographs I took this morning. I've also included an unofficial document with additional information that wasn't reported by the victim but may be relevant now, all of which I have witnessed."

"And why wasn't it reported?" James asked, taking the pages from him.

"The first instance was of an altercation between Andy, I mean, Andrea Summers and Frank Miller. Later, she found a note on her truck and I was in the area. She asked me to look at the note, and I did, but she wanted nothing reported. The next instance with Frank Miller was in a crowded diner. He was angry about a deal Summers had made with another rancher that didn't benefit him." Sergeant James slipped a pair of glasses onto his face, turned towards his computer, and typed. He scanned the screen for a moment.

"You were the responding officer on a break in that occurred at the same address a few months ago. You're coming to me now excluding yourself because of personal involvement but haven't done so previously."

"Yes sir, that's correct. There was no, uh, involvement at the time of that crime and my report. This is a more recent development..."

"You can stop there, son," James said, putting a hand up and taking his glasses off. "I know how things work, boy meets girl, yada yada yada," he smiled at Eric. "I respect you did the right thing coming here and telling me this. I respect you didn't haul ass over to Miller's place, who it seems like you've pegged as a suspect, and rough him up like I'm sure you want to.

"I expect you will not respond to further calls at this residence, unless, of course, it's an emergent scenario. In that circumstance, I expect you to respond and turn over the call to the next responding officer if possible.

"You're a good kid, you're a good deputy, and you've done good work with us so far. I'll assign someone else to this case and give them some bullshit reason. I can be pretty convincing, Deputy, and your request for confidentiality will be honored."

"Thank you sir," Eric said.

"I appreciate your professionalism and as I understand it, you have some investigation skills from the LAPD."

"Yes, sir."

"I have a day shift position opening up soon. A guy there is retiring. They're usually the ones knocking on doors, piecing any puzzles that we get together. While you don't have the seniority here with this department, you have a lot of experience and have policed longer than a lot of my night shifters. I've had conversations with LAPD and they were all disappointed you'd left the department. They sang your praises and your skills would be a great asset to us. I'd like you to consider switching over to days when that position opens up."

"I will, sir," Eric said, getting to his feet.

32

Andy had been pretty shaken up after seeing that poor animal laying in the middle of the concrete floor in a puddle of dried, dark red blood. She hoped the cow hadn't suffered and the person who had killed her had known what they were doing. After Eric told them they could go back in the barn, Romeo and Carl took care of the cleanup. Some hands had scrubbed with bleach water, but the dark patch on the concrete remained. Luckily, the metal barn wall was able to be cleaned, and it looked like nothing had ever happened.

She'd ended the day trying to say goodbye to the guys. Before she knew it, they had formed a half circle around her. "Andy," Romeo began. "So, we've been kind of thinking and talking, and we don't think you should stay here tonight."

Anger clouded her vision. She could feel herself flushing, sure that telltale red splotches were forming on her chest, and she was glad for the multiple layers of clothing that were hiding them. "Let me explain," Romeo said. She could see he was struggling under her angry stare.

Carl took a step forward. He was much more gruff and aggressive than soft spoken Romeo. He cleared his throat. "Listen Andy, cut the bullshit. Every single one of us cares about you and respects the hell out of you.

"This," he said, gesturing to the matte splotch on the barn, "is getting out of hand. This is scary shit, Andy. You're here, in this house, by yourself. We wanted to have this conversation with you after the break in, but knew you'd react the way you are now.

"But now, with this, with Frank coming at you in the diner," some hands whispered to each other, not knowing about that incident. Andy could feel herself bristling, but Carl continued, "It's not OK. We wouldn't be doing right by you, by your father, if we didn't say so. Any of us would take you in until they figure out who's doing this, until we are sure you're safe."

She heard the fear in his voice and it put her on edge, chipping away at the wall she had built up to keep her emotions in check. She took a step towards him. "If I run away," she continued, her voice cracking, "Isn't that showing this prick, this psycho, that he's winning? Isn't it showing that I'm some little chicken shit, turning tail and running because of their threats?

"Would you be telling any man here to do that? Or would you smack them on the shoulder and tell them to stay strong and show that asshole that they're not scared? Would you tell them to show this guy what kind of man they are?" The group was quiet. Carl and Romeo looked at each other and then back at her, unsure of how to respond.

She gulped down some of her anger. "Look," she said, taking a step back and addressing the entire group. "I get it. This is a fucked up situation. I have an alarm that got the cops here last time. I've got the place locked down every time I walk through the door. I'll even look into a camera system, but I can't run away. I can't turn around and show this guy that he's gotten to me. I can't let him win."

"God dammit Andy, this ain't about winning!" Carl shouted. She and the rest of the guys were taken aback. Carl had yelled before, but not like this. This was the first time that she could remember him sounding afraid. "You aren't the only one who made a promise to your daddy, Andy! If anything happened to you–" his voice broke. A wave of understanding washed over her.

"Guys, I need to talk to Carl alone. I appreciate every one of you being concerned about me I do. I'll figure this out, and I'll see you guys bright and early tomorrow morning. But for now, go, be with your families, hit the bar, do whatever you guys do. You've put in a hard day's work. You deserve to be doing that, not standing here in the cold arguing with me."

At first, they stood looking at her. Then one of them took a step forward, clapped her on the shoulder and headed towards his truck. One by one, the rest of them followed suit. Romeo had taken both of her arms and stared at her a moment before saying, "Mija, we are just a call away. If you need anything, pick up the phone." He nodded at her before turning and leaving. Then it was only her and Carl.

She gestured toward the house, and he followed her. They both took off their Carhart's and overalls. She poured them each a whiskey and sat down across from him at the table. Her phone buzzed, but she ignored it, letting it dance on the counter.

Carl swallowed his whole glass in one gulp. She took a sip of hers and set it back on the table. "You're being stubborn, Andy," he said.

"What'd you promise my dad, Carl?" she asked.

"I promised him that'd I'd keep you safe," he replied, his voice barely above a whisper. "I promised him that no harm would come to you. I promised him that if you were ever in over your head, or I could see that you were losing yourself, that I'd convince you to sell this place and leave Spring Hills."

Stunned, she sat staring back at him. "Your dad knew you were made for other things than this ranch, Andy. He wrestled for a long time with that and wanting to keep this place in your family. Your brothers proved themselves to be unworthy of this place, so the decision was almost made for him. But he made me promise that if I ever thought you were slipping, if I was ever worried you'd become so unhappy you wouldn't be able to claw yourself out, that I'd convince you to sell it.

"And Andy, I gotta be honest with you. Until recently, I thought that's where we were heading. I was preparing myself to go to the other guys in the area and see if they could buy you out, or talking to the bank about a loan." She stayed quiet, tipping the rest of the whiskey into her mouth and letting it burn down her throat to stop the tears that were threatening to spill down her face.

"Then, in the last few weeks, it's like you've got this light back. You're laughing more, joking around with us more. And then this shit happens. So now I've got to keep my promise, Andy. I've gotta convince you to leave."

"Well," Andy said, taking a deep breath. "He put us in a shitty situation. One of us is going to break our promise to him. Either you can't get me to leave, or I do, and this ranch leaves our family forever." They were both quiet, looking at each other.

"Andy, you know you're like another daughter to me. You're as much a kid of mine as my own kids are. Probably more since I see your ass damn near every day and they are all off doing whatever they do."

"I know Carl."

"You can not stay here tonight." Before she could respond, there was a knock at the door. She got up and looked through the peephole. On the other side stood Eric, his face scrunched with worry.

"Shit," she thought and glanced back at Carl. She heard the pounding on the door again and resigned herself to the fact that Eric was likely to break it down if she didn't answer. She opened it wide so Eric could see Carl behind her at the table.

"Andy," he started, sounding relieved, then he glimpsed the old ranch hand at the table and sighed. "I'm sorry. I called, and you didn't answer. I didn't know if you were in trouble. After what happened this morning, I thought the worst..."

"Come on in, join the party," she grumbled and walked into the kitchen, grabbed a beer out of the fridge and popped off the cap. She set it on the table and Eric slid into the chair behind it.

Andy could feel Eric looking at her, and she watched as understanding spread over Carl's face.

"It's you," he said, looking at Eric, his jaw going slack for a moment. Then he looked at Andy, "Been goin' on just a little while, a few weeks maybe?" He asked, and she nodded before looking away. "Well, I'll be damned..." Carl said, drifting off.

"Look Carl," she began, "this isn't something we want the world to know–"

"Oh come on Andy," Carl laughed, "I respect you enough not to go talking about your private life. Secret's safe with me. I won't even whisper about it to Linda." He turned to Eric, "You staying here tonight?"

"That's up to her, sir," he stammered, taken aback by the forward question. Andy felt the familiar flush of red spread up her chest at the thought of Carl knowing she might have someone sharing her bed that night.

Carl turned to Andy, "Andy?"

"Would it get you off my ass, Carl?"

"Sure would, at least for tonight," Carl said. "I'm going to tell myself he's sleeping on the couch, though," he added with a smile. She nodded, and he stood up. He slid back on his heavy coat, threw his overalls over his arm, and stuffed his feet into his muddy boots.

"Don't worry about his truck in the drive tomorrow morning," Carl began. "I'll make sure I'm here first. I'll tell the guys the only way I'd agree to let you stay here is if I hired the Deputy to keep an eye on the place. I'll make them think I told him to check in with you early to report on how things were overnight. Deputies take side security jobs, right?" Eric nodded his reply.

Carl continued, "I'll get them thinking it was the deal we struck. You'd be able to stay in your house, pride intact, and I'll be able to live with myself. After your little speech earlier, it'll be easy to believe."

Andy nodded, and Carl smiled half-heartedly. Then he turned and left. She locked the door, set the alarm and then turned to Eric, feeling too tired to be angry, but still trying her damnedest.

"What the hell, Eric?" she said, exhaustion clear in her voice.

"I know Andy. I'm sorry," he replied. "I called, and you didn't answer. You hadn't answered a couple of my texts I sent you earlier, and I was worried about the shit this morning. I didn't think that somebody would still be here. I figured all the guys would have gone by now." She sighed and grabbed her and Carl's empty glasses from the table and set them in the sink.

He followed her, and when she turned around, he was looking into her eyes. He took her in his arms and held her. She felt his warmth against her body and wrapped her arms around him, her anger ebbing. "There's something I need to tell you, Andy," he breathed. She pulled away and saw him searching her face. "My sergeant knows I'm involved with you, too." She sighed and pushed him away, throwing her hands in the air.

"Why don't you hire a damn skywriter, Eric? Or get a t-shirt that says 'I'm screwing Summers' across your chest!" She pushed past him and stomped into the living room. He followed her.

"Andy I had to!" She turned and stared at him, daring him to explain. "I was the first to respond this morning. The responding officer is lead on the case. If I was lead on this, and they found out about us later, it'd be bad. Like throw the case out bad.

"If we can find the asshole that's doing this to you, I want to make sure he gets what he deserves. I don't want to be the reason he gets a slap on the wrist and a pass. I told my sergeant that it needed to be confidential. He got it, Andy."

Stared at the ceiling, she ran her hands through her hair. She was aware of how disgusting she smelled after working all day. She stood like that for a minute, trying to absorb everything that had happened since she woke up this morning. When she looked at Eric again, she felt herself relax a little. He almost looked scared. His eyes searched her face, like he was trying to figure out what she was thinking, and he was chewing his bottom lip.

She thought about all the sweet things he did for her; how kind he was, how good and right things felt with him. She reminded herself that he was trying to protect her. That was the only reason he'd come, to make sure she was safe. Everything he had done was for her. She exhaled and her heart rate slowed. The anger flowed out of her again.

"I need to take a shower," she said. She turned and went to the stairs. She reached the first step and looked back at him. He hadn't moved. "Well, are you going to join me or not?" she said and started up the stairs without waiting for an answer. His footsteps followed behind her a moment later.

After she turned the shower on to warm up, she heard him close the door. She pulled off the long-sleeved t-shirt she wore and then the long johns she was wearing under that. It wasn't until she was down to her sports bra and jeans that she felt him touch the small of her back.

"Andy," he whispered. "I need you to know I would never hurt you on purpose. I'm not trying to let the world know about us before you're ready."

She sighed and turned, then put a hand on his chest before lowering her forehead to rest against him. "I know. I lost my temper back there, and I'm sorry." She took a deep inhale. "It's just...this is my first whatever this is since I've taken over the ranch. I don't want any of my guys, any of the other ranchers thinking I'm soft, or weak, or I don't know. I can't afford to lose any of the respect I've fought so hard to earn."

"I didn't think of it like that. I'm sorry," he said, looping his thumbs through the belt loops above her back pockets and resting his hands there. She felt her pulse quicken at his touch. She brought her lips to his and felt every ounce of anger she had left drained out of her.

He pulled her closer, and she kissed his neck, then trailed her lips up to his ear, nibbling on his earlobe before whispering, "You can't shower with your clothes on."

"Hmm, we should fix that," he replied, his voice low. She pulled his shirt up over his head and raked her fingertips over his chest.

She hooked her fingers into the front pockets of his jeans. "And these?" she smiled at him.

"You first," he replied, undoing the top button of her jeans. She slid them off, along with her long thermal underwear. Then she pulled her sports bra up over her head. Looking him in the eyes, she slid her underwear down and stepped out of them. She could see his eyes traveling over her body.

"What are you waiting for?" she said softly.

"I could use some help," he said. She smiled and went to him, unbuttoning and unzipping his pants and sliding them down his legs so they fell to the floor. She slid her fingertips into the waistband of his boxer briefs before pulling them down and letting them fall. He pulled her body against his, his hands moving over her skin.

33

It wasn't until after the shower, then the bedroom, that she heard her stomach growling. He'd shown up after Andy had worked all day. Before that, she hadn't had an appetite because of the cow in the barn. As they lay in a tangle of limbs, she heard his stomach growl too. "I think we both need some food if we're going to keep up our strength after such strenuous activity," he said. She chuckled.

"Well, put on some pants and we'll see what we can rustle up," she said. She slipped away into the bathroom and when she came back, she threw his underwear and jeans at him. While he pulled on his jeans, she slipped into his t-shirt.

"Never looks that good on me," he said, pulling her in for a kiss.

"I would disagree," she smiled back. They went downstairs and raided her fridge. They made some sandwiches and stood at the counter, devouring them. "You know, this is going to be the first time you sleep over?" she said.

"Yeah," he said, "the thought had occurred to me."

"I have a serious question," she said, locking eyes with him. He looked concerned for a moment. Then she asked, "Do you snore?"

He laughed. "Only when I'm drunk or sick. What about you?"

"Not that I know of, but you can tell me in the morning," she winked and then yawned.

"Tired?" he asked, hugging her from behind. She put her hands on top of his and leaned into him.

"Yeah, I had that nightmare again last night, didn't sleep very well. Then the barn thing. I think it's all catching up to me." Without warning, he spun her around and then scooped her up and held her with one arm behind her back and another under her knees. She wrapped her arms around his neck and rested her head against him. He carried her up the stairs and set her down when they reached the top.

"I think I might have an extra toothbrush around here, one of those dentist freebies," she said, digging in the cabinet under the sink before pulling one out and handing it to him. They brushed their teeth side by side and she realized how this felt like a very intimate thing. Yes, they'd explored every inch of each other's bodies, but this was different. It was domestic, something a couple would do. Then they walked into the bedroom and stood at the foot of the bed.

"What side do you sleep on?" he asked.

"This side," she said as she climbed into the bed on the side farthest from the door and crawled to the pillow. He pulled off his jeans, turned off the light, and got in on the opposite side. He put an arm around her and she laid her head on his shoulder.

They woke up to her alarm's shrill beeping the following morning. She blinked her eyes open and felt like they were puffy and dry. Eric groaned and only then did she remember he was in her bed. Rolling onto her stomach, she inched close to him, throwing a leg over his and resting her head on his chest. She laid like that, listening to his heartbeat as he stroked his fingers in her hair, massaging her scalp. "Mmmmm," she groaned, "If I don't move now, I never will."

"That wouldn't be so bad," he whispered.

After rolling away and dragging herself out of the bed she got ready for the day, and slipped downstairs. She was making breakfast when Eric came up behind her and kissed her neck. "Good mornin," he said, his voice was still gruff with sleep

"Hmmm," she said. "Says the man who can go back to his place and sleep more." He chuckled and settled himself onto a stool as she stood at the island across from him. She pushed a plate of eggs towards him and they ate in a comfortable silence.

"You know, I could get used to this," he said after he took another bite.

"What's that?"

"Waking up next to a beautiful woman, eating breakfast with her..." Then they heard tires on gravel.

He hopped from the stool he'd been perched on and went to her. He put his hands on her lower back and pulled her to him, kissing her and leaving her wanting so much more.

"Show time," he said with a wink. He threw on his boots and coat and headed outside.

She slid into her gear and headed out the door in time to see Carl sauntering up to the house. Another truck had just pulled in, too. Eric made his way over to Carl and they had a quick conversation. By the time Andy had gotten to where they had congregated, Eric was waving goodbye and heading back to his truck.

She walked with Carl to the barn, and Romeo met them. Soon all the hands were there and Andy was running through the things that needed to be taken care of and doling out daily assignments. When she'd finished, almost all the hands dispersed, except for one who lingered behind and approached her.

"Hey Andy," he said, "I didn't know Braxton was back around." Andy stared at him, bewildered.

"What are you talking about?" she asked.

"My mom was over in Bellridge. She said she was at the store there and thought Braxton Summers was walking down the street."

"Was she sure it was Braxton?"

"Well, I mean, she said it looked like him. We were friends before he...changed, so she knows what he looks like pretty well. But it was through a store window, so I dunno, could have been someone who looked like him, I guess."

He turned and walked away, leaving Andy to mull this information over. It was possible that Braxton was in Bellridge. She hadn't talked to him since the reading of her father's will, and they'd barely been able to track him down for that. As far as Andy knew, Braxton could be anywhere, but why would he be here?

She worked hard for the rest of the day, thoughts of Braxton kept popping into her head. If it was him, what on earth was he doing in the even smaller town of Bellridge? Maybe it was a drug mecca she wasn't aware of? She knew small towns were having a lot of issues with meth and opiates these days, and anything was possible.

When they'd wrapped up their work, she'd bid farewell to her hands. Carl lingered back again and when the other hands were out of earshot, he approached her. "Hey Andy," he said quietly.

"What's up Carl?"

"Eric coming by again tonight?" he asked, like he wanted to get the words out of his mouth.

"Yeah, I think that's the plan," she replied, staring at the ground and nudging a stone with her boot.

"Well, look Andy. Your dad gave me this, told me to give it to you if I ever thought you'd need it. I'm feelin' like now might be that time." He handed her a white envelope. She turned the envelope over and saw her name written on the front in her father's handwriting.

"What is this, Carl?"

"Like I said, Andy, you and me, we both made promises." Without another word, he left the barn. She dashed to the house and once inside, stripped off her gear and sat at the kitchen table.

Her hands shook as she opened the envelope and pulled out the piece of paper covered in her father's scrawl.

Andy,

My sweet girl, my days are numbered now. I can feel it, and in the end I'm going to ask you to take this ranch. It's not fair, and I know it, but I don't know what else to do Andy. In my heart, I know that asking you to do it is wrong. You are so much more, so much bigger than this place. But I made a promise to my father, years ago, that this place would belong to a Summers as long as there was a Summers alive.

You are so special, Andy. We knew that from the moment you came screaming into this world. These last few weeks have shown me that while you may look like me, you have your mama's heart. You came when I needed you and now here I am about to betray you by burdening you with this place.

Andy, I'm going to make you promise me the same thing my daddy made me promise him, even though it breaks my heart to do it. Even though I know you deserve so much more. You deserve to be somewhere as bright as you are, somewhere full of lights and sound, painting and doing the things you've talked about doing forever. You deserve everything you've ever dreamed of.

But you're going to agree when I ask, because that's who you are. Your heart will break into a million pieces, but you'll promise me. I'll swallow all this regret down, because if you make that promise, then I've kept mine. But here's the thing Andy, the part of the promise I'm going to write here, the thing I won't be able to say out loud: promise you won't lose your joy.

If you ever start to feel you've lost a sense of who you are, or your happiness...you need to leave. Sell this place, get rid of it. I'd like to see it go to someone who deserves it, like Carl or Romeo, someone who loves it like I do. But Andy, don't lose yourself to this place, don't lose yourself to a promise made to a stubborn, dying old man. Paint Andy. Do what makes your heart full and happy.

So this is the promise I want you to keep. This one I should be binding you to, but I'm not strong enough to do that out loud. Give the ranch thing a try. Hopefully, you'll find a way to love it. But if you don't, don't walk away, run.

You are one of the best things I ever did, Andy. I wouldn't be doing right by you if I bound you to this place with no way out. So promise me now, do whatever it takes to be happy. You get only one life...you have every right to live it the way you want.

I love you Andy. You are an amazing woman, and I credit your mother for that. I wish I could see you grow old. I wish I could see everything you're going to accomplish because I know whatever it is, you're

going to be great. I hope you are happy honey, and if you aren't, do what
you have to do to get there.

Promise me.

Love you always,

Daddy

Fat tears rolled down Andy's cheeks as she folded the letter back up and pressed it to her chest. Her body shook with sobs. She'd always known her father had loved her, but he had never said the things he'd written to her before. Part of her felt a sense of relief wash over her. She was free. She could go back to New York if she wanted to.

She looked out the window at the rolling pastures she owned. The old bright red barn her great grandfather had built, and the more modern silver metal barn her father had erected, both stood tall and proud in the distance. No matter how she felt, this was a piece of her heritage, her family and of herself.

34

Eric gripped the steering wheel hard as he drove away from the Sheriff's office. He hadn't been on duty, but the sergeant had called him to let him know they were bringing Frank Miller in for questioning regarding the incident at Andy's ranch. The evidence they had against him was circumstantial at best, and he was considered a cooperating witness since they had nothing they could hold him on.

Eric wasn't allowed in the room. Instead, he watched through the two-way mirror as Frank was questioned. The shit-eating grin he'd had plastered on his face the whole time enraged Eric, who kept his arms crossed across his chest to stop himself from barging into the interrogation room and beating Frank's ass.

Unfortunately, but not unsurprisingly, Frank denied everything. With nothing except hearsay and overheard threats to link him to the crime, he'd been able to walk out of the station. As Frank left, he'd seen Eric and loud enough for him to hear, said, "I didn't do shit to Andy, but I'd like to buy a beer for whoever did." Luckily, he'd stayed calm and instead of throwing his fist into Frank's face, he flexed it at his side, watching him walk away.

Almost without realizing he'd driven that far, he pulled into the driveway of the ranch. He parked and walked up to the door, trying not to let the weight of the day's events show on his face. He didn't know how to tell Andy that they still had no idea who was terrorizing her like this.

She'd taken a little longer than normal to answer the door. When she did, her eyes were red, her cheeks tear stained. His heart sank. "Did something happen? What's wrong?"

She stepped aside so he could walk in and went to the table. Saying nothing, she handed him a piece of paper and crossed her arms tight across her chest. When he read the words on the page, his stomach churned.

"Wow Andy..." his heart felt like it was being twisted. He wouldn't try to influence her, but he knew she now had her dad's permission to leave all this behind. She could leave him. Would she? He went to her and embraced her. He felt her melt into him and her arms went around him. "Are you OK?" he whispered into her hair.

"I don't know," she replied. "I'm confused."

"Want to talk about it?" he asked, his lips still against her scalp. He felt her shake her head no. Then she pressed her lips against his, tenderly at first, but it quickly turned into more. He felt her tongue teasing against his bottom lip.

"What do you need, Andy?" he asked, pulling her tighter against his body.

"Make me forget. Make me forget everything else that's going on right now, Eric."

He heard the desperation in her voice and didn't need to be asked twice as he crashed his lips against hers. He placed her on top of the counter and was looking up at her. She ran her fingers through his hair as he kissed the soft skin of her neck. Her pulse increased under his lips and a slight moan escaped her.

He pulled her shirt over her head and took her in with his eyes. He had never seen a more beautiful woman than Andy. The thought that he could lose her rocked him to his core. He stared into her green eyes. He knew he loved this woman. With everything he had, he wanted to keep her safe and hold her against him for as long as he drew breath.

Her eyes searched his face, a question unasked. To admit this out loud was too much. Instead, he brought his lips back to hers and kissed her reverently, hoping she could feel what she meant to him through his touch.

Her fingers found the bottom of his t-shirt and she pulled it up over his head. He pulled her as close to his body as he could. He didn't know if he could ever get enough of her. Enough of her scent, her touch, her taste.

He carried her to the bedroom and did his damnedest to do what she had asked and make her forget about everything that was going on outside of those four walls.

After he'd given his best effort to comply with her request, they lay in her bed, limbs tangled, her head on his chest. His fingers grazed her skin as he stared at the ceiling, lost in thought.

"Hey Andy," he whispered.

"Hmm?" she mumbled back.

"If you think back to a time where you felt confused, where you were stuck, or couldn't figure out what to do next, what'd you do?"

"I painted."

He raised his eyebrows, and she stared up at him. They looked at each other before she stood up and scooped his shirt off the floor and slid into it. "Come on," she said, holding out a hand. He stood up and pulled on his jeans, then took her hand and followed her.

She led him down the hallway to a door near the end. Her hand was suspended above the doorknob. She shot him a wary glance before opening it. The air in the room was stale and when she flicked on the light, he could see a layer of dust was covering everything in it.

"This was my 'studio'," she said, making air quotes with her fingers as she turned to look at him. "It was Eddie's room. Then, when he went away to college, Theo moved in. After Theo passed, my mom convinced my dad to make it a space for me to paint.

"Whenever she would fall asleep, I'd creep in here and paint. I'd paint when I was sad, or happy, or whatever." Andy crossed the room and went to a stack of canvasses that were resting against the wall. She flipped a couple against her leg until she pulled out the one she was looking for and pushed the rest back into place.

"This was her. The original Andrea Summers," she said, holding the canvas out to him. He gasped when he saw the paint laid on top of it, shocked it wasn't a photograph.

"You did this?" he asked, still trying to battle the disbelief that this woman, with ranch worn hands, skin tanned from hard labor and a propensity for whiskey and swearing, could have painted this. Andy gave him a half smile and nodded.

"That was the last time I painted her. She was so weak from the treatments by then, but she still agreed to sit for me."

She brushed her fingertips over the paint. He noted the woman's sunken in and hollow cheeks, the pink floral scarf wrapped around her head instead of a crown of hair. The thing that struck him the most was her eyes. Even from the canvas, they seemed to sparkle.

"Her eyes, Andy, they almost look...alive," he said in a near whisper. Andy smiled bigger now.

"Her eyes were always beautiful and bright. Even towards the end, one look from her and you'd feel like somehow things were going to be alright. That was the piece I submitted to get into art school. My favorite note I'd received was that even though I'd painted the subject in one of her weakest moments, I could still capture her light."

Eric motioned to the multiple stacks of canvasses against the far wall. "Are those all your pieces?" Andy nodded and Eric stood for a moment, taking in the scale of work. "Are there any others you can share with me?"

Andy looked up at him, contemplating. "You can look at any of them you'd like."

He handed her the piece of her mother, which she continued to look down at, and went to a stack. He wondered if there was any method to the arranging and almost asked when she said, "They're piled up in any which way. That box is stuff I brought home from college.

He went to the box first and opened it. The painting on top was abstract, a swirl of bright colors that brought a smile to his face. He felt her move behind him. "I painted that right after Jake proposed to me," she said quietly. "I was so happy. How stupid I was." She knelt down beside him and she explained each piece in the box to him as he pulled them out.

The breadth of her talent amazed him. She had painted portraits and still life, landscapes and abstract pieces. Anything she had wanted to capture with paint, she could. When they'd finished looking at the last piece in the box, he lifted himself off his knees and sat on the floor, stretching his legs out in front of him and crossing them at the ankles.

"Andy, you're amazing," he said, and he watched a shy smile spread across her face. "No, seriously. You are so talented. I don't think I've ever known anyone in real life who can paint like you do."

"Thank you," she replied and moved over to where he sat. She crawled up his legs and knelt in front of him, straddling his thighs. "Any favorites?" she asked, running a finger along his jaw.

"Too many to choose one. You should paint again, Andy."

He tucked a piece of hair back behind her ear. A look crossed her face, and he wasn't sure what it was, a mix between fear and excitement, maybe.

"Being in here makes me want to pick up a brush right now and start putting paint down," she smiled a little before she bit her bottom lip. "But I feel like I filed that part of me away."

"You don't have to keep it that way. You're so good, so talented. If this is what you did to help you figure things out before, why not try it now? Maybe you'll surprise yourself and the answer will appear."

He felt deep in his gut that the second she picked up a brush, she'd be gone from him. She would decide to go back to New York, or Paris, or somewhere else far away because her talent couldn't be wasted here on this ranch. His stomach lurched at the thought, but he couldn't hold her back. He couldn't discourage her in this, or he could never live with himself.

She was looking at him now, a slight smile turning up the corner of her lips. Her eyes danced across his face. She put a hand on either side of his jaw and brought her lips to his. She kissed him again and then dropped her mouth to his neck, kissing and dragging the tip of her tongue against the sensitive skin there.

He put his arms around her and kissed her. She ground her hips against him as her tongue passed his lips, fire growing inside him again.

He wrapped one arm around her waist and another under one of her legs and rolled while lowering her to the floor. She smiled at him. "Smooth move, Grayson."

35

She'd kissed Eric before he had gone out to report to Carl the next morning. After she watched his headlights back down the driveway, she snagged the letter from the table and walked out into the chilly morning air.

"Hey Carl," she called. He turned and waited for her to catch up. When she did, she held the letter out to him. "Do you know what this says?"

Carl shook his head, his expression solemn. "Your dad told me it was your 'escape clause.' That's all I know. Why, what's it say?"

"Basically, that he wants me to be happy, and if that means selling the ranch, that's what he wanted me to do," she said, kicking a stone in the grass.

"Hmm," said Carl, looking past her. He was quiet, then his eyes found hers again.

"Well, ain't like you have to decide today. Eric said he's gotta work tonight. So where are you gonna stay? You're welcome to stay at our place. I'm sure Linda wouldn't mind."

Then the soft voice of Romeo came from behind him. "I am on strict orders to bring Andy back to our house tonight. Rosa said whatever Andy wants for dinner, she'll make. She also said if Andy tried to fight, then she would come over here herself..." Romeo's voice trailed off as he smiled. He knew Andy wouldn't be able to refuse Rosa.

"That's not fair," Andy replied, finding another rock and booting it with her toe. "For the record, I hate this, and I think it's unnecessary and stupid."

"Got it kid. And for the record, we don't give a flying fuck," Carl said, and walked toward the barn after winking at her.

"What should I tell Rosa you'd like to eat, Andy?"

She glared at Romeo for a second. "Whatever she wants to make is fine, Romeo," she said, then turned around and stalked off.

After all their work had been done, Romeo waited in the kitchen, drinking a tall glass of iced tea while she got a bag set up for the next two nights of staying with him and Rosa. She tossed everything into an old duffel bag she had and slung it over her shoulder. When she went back into the kitchen, Romeo stood up and smiled at her, then put his glass in the sink. "Rosa is going to be so happy to have you, Andy," he said, throwing an arm over her shoulder as they walked out.

When they pulled up to Romeo and Rosa's small home, he hopped out of the old truck and grabbed Andy's bag. Andy trudged up the driveway and as soon as her boots hit the porch, the door flung open and Rosa's arms wrapped around her in a hug. "Mija! I am so happy you are here!" she said, dragging Andy over the threshold. Andy glanced back at Romeo, who wasn't even trying to contain his laughter.

Andy hung her things on the hook by the door. "How have I not noticed how skinny you've gotten, mija?" Rosa grabbed her by the hips and spun her around. "Are you eating? Is it the stress? You should come stay with us for good until they find this lunatic. I'll make sure you get some meat on your bones for winter!"

"Mi reina!" Romeo laughed as he slid off his boots. "Let the girl breathe!"

After Rosa had taken Andy to the guest room and gotten her settled in, they went back to the kitchen. She got both Andy and Romeo a beer and they sat at the small table and chatted for a long time. Rosa served them some soup she had made. Andy didn't know what kind it was, but it was fantastic. Andy helped clean up, and as she was drying her hands, her cell phone buzzed in her back pocket.

She pulled it out and saw Eric's name on the screen. After excusing herself to the other room, she answered, "Hey."

"So, who has commandeered you this evening?" Eric's voice asked.

"Romeo and Rosa, how'd you know someone was commandeering me?" She flopped down on the bed she'd been given for the night.

"Carl told me and I quote, 'There is no way in Hell that girl is staying in that house tonight. If I gotta tie her up and throw her in the bed of my truck, I will.'"

She giggled at his spot on Carl impression. "The Deputy did nothing when someone threatened a kidnapping? I am appalled, sir."

"The Deputy wasn't opposed to said kidnapping if it kept the one being kidnapped safe. I'm sure Rosa is taking good care of you, though," Eric said, and Andy could hear his smile on the other end.

"She's already told me she needs to fatten me up. She offered me permanent residence, and then provided me with an excellent dinner. So yes, she's great."

"A permanent residence, huh? That might put a damper on my security side hustle."

"Nah, I have a lot more fun when you're on your security detail."

"I thought about what we did in your studio about a thousand times today."

Her mind flashed back to the night before, and she smiled. "Hmmm...I can tell you it's nothing that room has ever seen before. Perhaps we'll have to think about what other rooms we can test drive."

"I hope you're not teasing me," he said in a growl that made her laugh.

"Well, I should go back out there. Rosa will be in to check on me if I take much longer."

"Alright babe, sweet dreams. I wish I was there."

When she felt the butterflies in her stomach flutter, she realized it was the first time he'd ever called her anything other than her name. A smile spread across her face. "Good night. Be safe," she said, then pushed the red button on the screen.

When she'd gone back out, Rosa and Romeo were still at the table talking. The three of them started a card game together and played until both Romeo and Andy said they needed to turn in if they were going to wake up on time in the morning. Andy showered and then climbed under the warm covers.

The next morning, she had dressed and crept out into the kitchen, expecting Rosa to still be asleep. She should have realized that wouldn't be the case, but was still a little surprised to see her up and in front of the stove. "Mija!" Rosa exclaimed when she noticed Andy. "Sit, sit," she said, gesturing to a chair at the table.

Before Andy could process what was happening, she had a steaming mug of coffee and a full plate of breakfast in front of her, including eggs, sausage, and a small stack of pancakes. Rosa set another plate down in front of the empty chair and then brought her own and sat down beside Andy.

Romeo came out of their room not long after and sat at the table with them. "Romeo," Andy began after swallowing a bite of the most delicious, fluffy pancakes she had ever had, "Does Rosa cook for you like this...every...morning?"

Romeo smiled. "I don't get pancakes often, but something like this, yeah."

"Rosa," Andy said after she took a sip of her coffee, "Will you marry me? I promise I'll give you a good life." Rosa laughed and slapped the table.

"Romeo is my one and only, but I'd adopt you," Rosa replied with a wink. Andy looked around the table and felt sad for a moment. Last night and this morning she'd felt more a part of a family than she had in a very long time. Part of her wondered if that was a serious offer, because if it were, she may consider it.

Within the next thirty minutes, Andy and Romeo had eaten their breakfasts, downed their coffee, donned their overalls and coats, been handed travel mugs of more hot coffee and bags of lunch and headed towards the ranch. Romeo was quiet. "Rosa is amazing, Romeo. You're so lucky," Andy said with a grin.

Romeo took a deep sigh. "She is incredible. My only regret is that we never had a child. I see her with you and I think how wonderful a mother she would have been. I know she wishes we could have had one, but with you around, she feels like she does. That's why she's always making me bring food to you."

"She stepped up for me when my mom died. I see her as something like a surrogate mom."

Romeo made a face. "Does that make me your dad?"

"Eh, I figure you're more of a brother," Andy laughed.

"Thank God. I know the kind of kid you were, Andy. I wouldn't want to deal with that."

Andy swatted him on the arm and his laugh filled the cab of the truck as they pulled into the ranch's long driveway and parked behind the big barn.

36

After a few nights of sleeping in a small twin bed, Andy was looking forward to staying in her own house. She was excited to see Eric, but she also wanted a couple of hours of time to herself. She'd called Eric and explained that to him and while he didn't like the thought of her being alone in the house by herself any more than she had to be, he agreed. He told her he'd come over around seven and bring some food Margie had dropped off to him.

When she and the ranch hands finished, it was four o'clock, meaning she'd have three hours to do whatever she wanted, by herself. For someone who lived alone for the past three years, having people around 24/7 was a little exhausting.

After a quick shower, she threw on a pair of leggings and an oversized t-shirt, and pulled her hair back into a ponytail. Without hesitation, she padded down the hallway and into the studio. She stood in the room with the sunlight streaming in through the dusty window.

The last few nights at Romeo's, she'd lay in her bed wondering what she was going to do. Carl's voice kept replaying in her head, telling her she didn't need to decide right away, but she still felt it weighing on her.

She felt like she'd been deceitful sitting in Romeo and Rosa's kitchen talking about the future when she didn't know where her's was going to lead her. So, after tossing and turning last night, she decided Eric might be right. Maybe she could find some clarity doing the one thing she had always turned to before.

She prepared the space and placed a canvas on the easel. The blank surface in front of her taunted her, and her teeth made marks on the pencil she had gripped between them. Sometimes she knew what she wanted to paint ahead of time, other times, like now, she waited for something to come to her. Just when she was thinking it was stupid, that she'd lost her knack, an image flashed in her head.

A small smile crept over her face as she drew a rough sketch on the canvas. She loaded up her palette with paint and dipped a brush into the first color. Her heart was pounding and she could feel a layer of sweat on her skin, like she was about to open the door to a big dark room and she wasn't sure what was inside.

The first pass of the brush on the canvas was slow and methodical, but God, it felt good. She swiped the brush over the canvas again and felt the tension in her shoulders dissolving, the crease in her forehead disappearing. With each bit of paint she applied to the canvas, she felt lighter, and before she knew it, she was lost in what she was doing.

She nearly had a heart attack when she noticed Eric standing in the doorway. "You scared me half to death!" she exclaimed as she put down her brush and a smile spread across his face. "What are you doing here? You said you were coming at seven!"

"It is seven," he replied with a low chuckle. "Good thing you gave me your code. I was knocking out there forever. I called you too."

"Oh shit," she said, wiping the back of her hand across her forehead. "I left my phone downstairs and I must have lost track of time..." Her eyes swept back to the canvas in front of her.

"You're painting," he said, his smile growing wider.

"Yeah, I am," she said, feeling self-conscious. She wasn't sure why. He'd seen her work before, but this felt different. "It's not my best work. I'm a little rusty," she said, looking at the canvas again.

"May I?" he asked, still looking like some sort of Greek god as he leaned against the door frame, smiling at her, his blue eyes watching her every move. She glanced from the painting, then back to him and nodded. He came around the easel and stood beside her.

She watched his face as he took the painted silhouette of a woman in the foreground. One half of the background was dark colors, blues and black, the other half was warm colors, reds and yellows. Tendrils from each half wrapped around the figure.

"You did this all today?" he asked, turning to her. She nodded, chewing her bottom lip. He took a deep inhale and put his hands in his pockets. "You're incredible Andy. This is what you should be doing. I know you're a good rancher, too. I hear it all over town, and it's clear how loyal your guys are. But Andy, this is amazing," he said, running a hand through his hair, a sad look in his eyes.

Andy stayed quiet, but took a long inhale. She took a step forward and leaned against Eric's chest, feeling him wrap his arms around her. "I don't know, Eric," she sighed. "I don't think I'm ready to decide yet."

He nodded and rested his cheek on the top of her head. "You know what you need? You need to get away from the ranch. How about tomorrow night? You take a couple hours after you're done working to paint, then you can meet me at the bar. I'll see if Mark and Margie can come, too. We show up, you stroll in a little later, nobody will think you came to meet us there. It can all look like a lucky coincidence. We can talk and drink shitty beer and you can take a break from all of this."

She chuckled a little. "That sounds nice."

"It's a date then. I'll text Mark and Margie and see if they're in."

"And what about tonight, then? Any plans for us?" she asked, looking up at him, a glint in her eye.

"Well...I'm sure we can come up with something," he whispered and then brought his lips to hers. His hands settled on her waist and she felt heat rush through her body. He lowered his mouth to her neck and pressed his lips to it, then brushed his tongue against her skin. "I missed you," he whispered, and her body ached for him. His hands crept up under the back of her shirt and her heart pounded.

"I missed you too," she said and brought her hands down the sides of his torso, slipping them under his shirt and settling them on the waistband of his jeans. She tucked a finger on each hand under the fabric and pulled him as close as possible to her.

His blue eyes danced across her face before she brought her lips to his, tracing his lip with her tongue and hearing him groan. She took a small step back and unbuttoned his shirt. With each button undone, she would kiss the skin that had been exposed all the way down until his shirt was open and she hovered above his waistband. She smiled up at him, but he gripped her shoulders and pulled her to her feet.

Bringing his mouth to her ear, he whispered, "You first." A shudder of anticipation ran through her. He pulled off her shirt, then traced his tongue from her ear down to her breasts, teasing her. Then he lifted her off her feet, and she wrapped her legs around him. He lowered himself to his knees and laid her down on her back. Kneeling between her legs, he unbuttoned her jeans, pulled down the zipper, and dragged them off.

Still between her knees, he ran the tips of his fingers down her inner thighs. He grazed them over her underwear and then slipped a finger under the waistband, pulling the fabric down. He gave her a grin as her heart rate climbed further and her breathing became shallow, and kissed the skin that had been uncovered.

37

Eric had arranged for Mark and Margie to meet him at The Lodge the next night. They were both happy to get out of the house as much as possible before the baby came.

Eric sat in a booth alone and while he waited, he replayed the activities of the previous night in his head as he swirled the beer in his bottle. Images of Andy throwing her head back, clamping her thighs around him as she moaned his name, played on a loop. Louisa came by the table, breaking him from the highlight reel in his head.

He had already avoided her first advance when he came in. He was watching the door like a hawk as Louisa bent low over the table, asking him if he had plans later. Thankfully, Mark and Margie walked in and he waved at them enthusiastically. Louisa stood back up, put her hands on her hips, gave him a wink and sauntered back to the bar.

Mark shot Eric a glance. "Don't," Eric warned.

Within minutes, the three of them had filled the air with comfortable chatter. They had asked Eric what his Christmas plans were, and he revealed he was going to stay in Spring Hills. He was hoping he'd be able to spend the holiday with Andy. In his estimation that would be a lot better than listening to his drunk father berate everyone in the family for their individual failures and shortcomings, one of his least favorite family Christmas traditions.

They talked and when he glanced at his phone, he was surprised to see that was 7:15. Andy was supposed to meet them there at seven, and she was pretty punctual. He called her phone, but she didn't answer. He felt his pulse quickening. She didn't respond to a text either. He called again, but there was still no answer.

When he felt his phone vibrate in his hand and her name popped on the screen, relief flooded through him. "Hey," he answered.

"Eric," a gruff voice on the other end of the line replied. His heart dropped, and he gripped the top of the table. "It's Carl."

"Carl? Where's Andy? What's going on?" Mark and Margie had stopped talking and were staring at him, wide eyed, sensing the alarm in his voice.

"Andy's OK," Carl responded. "Well, she's shaken up, but she'll be alright. We're at the corner of Main and Westbrook. They called me first, and I'm sure she's going to hate me for asking you, but I think you should be here."

Before Carl had finished speaking, Eric stood up, threw a ten-dollar bill on the table and whispered to his friends that he would call them. He felt terrible leaving when both sets of their eyes went wide, but his body was almost moving without his input.

He told Carl he'd be right there and jumped in his truck. As he pointed the vehicle toward the intersection, he felt nauseous, his heart was racing and he could feel the sweat prickling up on his skin. He drove in silence, his knuckles turning white as he gripped the steering wheel, half moons forming on his palms where his nails dug into his flesh.

The red and blue lights flashing from a police cruiser and an ambulance that had pulled up to the intersection were almost blinding. His headlights hit Andy's vehicle, and he felt a fresh wave of panic.

Her silver truck was halfway in the ditch. The front of it had smashed into a large fence post, the metal twisting around the wood. He scanned the scene but couldn't find Andy. His heart was pounding in his ears as he parked the truck and got out.

He could hear voices and went towards the vehicles. When he rounded the back of the ambulance, he saw the doors were open and Andy was perched on the edge of its interior. An EMT was murmuring to her as she stared at her hands. Carl stood beside them.

"I don't need to go to the hospital, Johnny," she insisted. The EMT was replying, but Eric couldn't register what was being said. He took another step forward and Andy's eyes flashed up at him as his boots crunched on the road.

Her mouth dropped into a small O, and he took in the large bandage across her forehead. "Eric," she said softly.

Before he could stop himself, he was at the back of the ambulance. He felt her body go stiff against his as he wrapped his arms around her. He buried his face into the space between her shoulder and her neck and then felt her body relax and her arms go around his waist.

They stayed like that for a moment as he took deep breaths, calming himself down before he tried to speak. Then he separated from her and put a hand on each side of her face. "What happened?" he said, searching her face with his eyes.

He heard a throat clear and saw Carl beside them, looking down at his feet. The EMT had a smirk and a deputy he knew as Brad Farwell stood beside them, too. Both Brad and the EMT's eyes were wide, but Brad was smiling at Eric with a knowing grin.

Andy seemed to take in the expressions of the other men and brought a hand to her face and stroked the uninjured side of her forehead. Realization that he had outed them to these two, and thus to the entire community, struck Eric too late. He looked back at Andy, expecting her to look angry, but she had tears forming in her eyes.

Brad took another step forward. "Looks like someone fucked with her truck." Eric spun to face him. "What?" he asked as he felt anger rising in his chest.

"As she tells it, Andy was going into town. Things had been normal when the brakes and steering both went out. She was lucky she hit that fence and not something bigger," the deputy responded matter-of-factly.

Eric whipped his attention to the EMT. "Is she OK?"

"She's got a pretty good cut over her eye there. Since she hit her head, I'm trying to convince her to go to the hospital, but in true Summers' fashion, she's being stubborn as hell," the EMT replied as he stripped a blue glove from his hand.

Eric turned back to Andy, who was looking down. He laid a hand on her thighs and she looked up at him. "Why don't you go get checked out, Andy? Just to be safe?"

She glared up at him. "I don't do hospitals," she retorted. He thought about her mom and her treatments and understood why Andy was reluctant to go. "Unless I am dying, I would rather go home, if you all don't mind." Her eyes whipped to the EMT. "Am I dying?" she asked with an edge of sarcasm.

"Not as far as I can tell," he replied, resigned to the fact that he would not talk her into anything.

"Do you need anything else from me?" she asked, turning her attention to the deputy.

"Not tonight. I've taken your statement, and you did the breathalyzer." Eric's eyes flashed to him and Brad put both hands up. "You know damn well that's standard procedure, Grayson. We'll get the truck towed and see if somebody can figure out what happened." Then Brad turned on his heel and pushed the button on his radio to tell dispatch to send a tow truck.

"Great," Andy said, and gently pushed Eric's hands off her legs before hopping down from the ambulance. She turned her glare to Carl. "You and I can talk more about all this tomorrow." Without another word, she made her way to Eric's truck, yanked the door open and slid into the passenger seat while Carl, Eric and the EMT stood still, unsure of what to do with the tension that hung in the air.

"I uh..." Eric began as he started toward the truck. "I'm going to make sure she gets home OK." He turned and saw the EMT smirking and Carl scowling.

When he got to the truck, he pulled himself in and looked at Andy. Her arms were crossed over her chest and she was staring straight ahead. The atmosphere was thick, and he wasn't sure what to do or say to change it, so instead he started the truck and headed towards the ranch.

When they got there, Andy got out and stalked toward the house. Eric scrambled to catch up to her and had slipped in the door behind her before she spun on her heel to look at him.

"Didn't you think Eric? The whole damn town is going to know about us now!" She said in a voice that was just below a yell.

"No Andy," he replied, taking a step towards her. "I didn't think. Not for a single second. Carl called me and said I had to come. So the entire drive there, I was imagining everything that could be wrong. And then I see you, in an ambulance, with this..." he stroked his thumb over her bandage and rested his palm along her jaw.

"I was so relieved to see you in one piece and so upset to see you hurt, I needed to hold you to make sure it was real, I just-" He was cut off mid sentence as Andy stepped into the space that had been between them and put her lips against his.

Her hands slid up his back as she brought his body closer to hers. She pulled her lips away from his and looked up at him before pressing her cheek against his chest. They stood in silence for a moment, arms wrapped around each other, his cheek resting on top of her head.

"What happened, Andy?" he whispered.

"I was heading out to see you," she said, and he could hear the tremor in her voice. "Everything was fine, and I tried to stop and the brakes felt like I was pushing the pedal down on a toy car. Nothing happened. Then when I tried to steer it was so hard, like cranking the wheel of an old tractor. Everything happened so fast."

"I'm glad it was a fence post and not something else." He pressed a kiss into her hair.

"Eric," she whispered, her voice shaking. "Someone is trying to kill me."

38

Rage flew through him as he screamed out into the night. He had watched her for months. He knew her routine. She wasn't supposed to leave that night. She was supposed to go the other direction in the morning. Towards Jim Bishop's place, to check on things like she did every fucking week.

She should have driven down the big hill with the giant oak tree at the intersection. Then she would have smashed into the tree like he had imagined time and time again, her body flopping against the steering wheel like a rag doll.

"FUCK!" he screamed at no one. He'd been watching from his usual spot when she left. His heart dropped to his stomach when she turned in the other direction and he tried to visualize if there was anything she was headed toward that could cause the effect he wanted. He cursed under his breath when he realized there wasn't.

When he'd driven past the scene to confirm his suspicions, he'd seen her in the back of the ambulance and had to talk himself out of aiming the beat up old Chevy at her.

Now he paced back and forth in the field. Anger was the only thing he could feel. He had been patient, so patient. The time for patience was over. She had to die, and it had to be quick, and now it had to be at his hands. He wouldn't be satisfied unless he watched her take her last breath.

~ele~

Andy winced as she stood in front of the bathroom mirror, trying to pull her hair up into a ponytail. She was much more sore than she expected.

She closed her eyes and took a deep breath as she thought about the whirlwind that had been last night. The panic that had coursed through her when the brakes didn't respond, the terror when the steering wheel wouldn't budge, the sound of the metal crunching with the fence post, the searing pain and the sticky feeling of the blood that dripped into her eyes from the gash on her forehead.

The adrenaline that had been pumping through her veins had worn off, and she fell asleep in Eric's arms. She hadn't dreamt. In fact, she hadn't even stirred when her alarm woke her up in the morning. She had looked over at Eric's sleeping form, realizing the whole town would be buzzing about them today. There was no way the deputy and EMT were keeping their mouths shut about something as juicy as Andy Summers, notoriously closed off bachelorette and the hot-bod deputy shacking up.

She took another deep breath as she raised her arms to her hair and felt shooting pain in her back. She hissed through her teeth and squeezed her eyes shut. "Let me," she heard Eric's sleepy voice say from behind her and her eyes flicked back open. She noticed his reflection in the mirror as he approached her, his hair messed from sleep and his chest bare. She could honestly say she'd never seen someone who had just woken up look more attractive.

He plucked the hair tie from her fingertips and put it between his teeth without waiting for an answer. She watched him while he pulled her hair back and then held it in one hand. With his other, he took the hair tie from between his perfect lips and wrapped it around her hair, tight enough to hold, but not tight enough to hurt.

In the mirror, she could see his eyes on hers and he put his arms around her, his hands resting on her stomach, his chest against her back. "If you are too sore to put your hair up, you shouldn't go out and do all the shit you do out there," he whispered, his lips grazing her ear and sending shivers up her spine.

She sighed and rested her body against him. She felt his lips go to the sensitive skin of her neck. Warmth bloomed between her legs. She felt his breath, followed by his tongue, brush against her. "How do you know how to do that so well?"

"What? Turn you on?" he asked, pressing his lips to her earlobe.

"My hair," she replied, feeling his teeth on her skin, making her breath faster.

"I had long hair back in high school." He kissed her neck again, trying to distract her.

"I can't even picture that." She struggled to keep back a giggle as the familiar feeling of desire spread through her body. He drifted his hand lower, down her stomach, toward the button on her jeans, but she caught his hand in hers and laced her fingers through his.

"I have to get out there," she whispered.

He sighed and pressed his lips to her cheek. Then brought his hands to her shoulders and pushed his fingers into her muscles. She bit back a moan as he worked the knots there. "I'm worried about you," he breathed.

She opened her eyes and saw him watching her in the mirror again. "You're pushing yourself too hard, Andy."

She spun and put her arms around him and stared up at him.

"You know I want to be mad that the whole damn place is going to know about us," she said. He looked concerned, and a smile tugged at the corners of her mouth. "But it will be nice to go places with you and not pretend I don't want to do this."

"Is that all you want to do?" he whispered. She smiled, and then they heard a loud banging on the door downstairs. She glanced at Eric and went downstairs to answer.

She looked through the peephole and standing at her door were none other than Carl and Romeo. She took a deep breath, anticipating what was coming, and opened the door. Both came in without a word. Then Carl looked past her and asked, "How is she?"

She spun around and saw Eric coming down the stairs. She felt relieved he had thrown on his t-shirt. He nodded at Carl. "Sore," he replied and took a seat at the table.

Carl spun to meet Andy's eyes and surveyed her. "You're not settin' foot on that ranch today, Andy."

"Like hell I'm not," she spat back and went to the kitchen to make coffee.

"Andy," Carl began, but she cut him off.

"You realize I'm a grown adult and I can decide by myself." She reached for the coffee grounds and instantly regretted it. Pain shot through her upper back and she couldn't stop herself from sucking air in through her teeth.

She looked over her shoulder and saw all three men looking at her. Carl looked so angry his eyes were almost slits. Romeo's eyes were wide and his mouth was open slightly. Eric looked up at her from under his eyelashes, trying to hide a smile, knowing she had been caught.

"You may be an adult," Carl growled, "But you have a tendency to make shitty decisions."

She threw her head back and sighed, before muttering under her breath. "Like keeping you around to ride my ass."

"That wasn't your decision. It was your daddy's, and it was a damn good one," he snapped as he plucked the coffee grounds off the shelf they sat on and handed them to Andy.

"I don't want to sit here all day, Carl. I'll go crazy."

"You able to be with her today?" Carl asked, looking at Eric.

"Yeah. Tomorrow I start on day shift, so I'm off today," Eric replied.

"So your solution is to have me pent up in this house with him? Goodness knows what we'll do to pass the time..." Andy's voice trailed off as a smirk played with the corners of her mouth.

Carl's face went white before pink flashed across his cheeks. "You," he said, turning to Eric, "She needs to go to the feed supply and put in an order. Take her there, get her some breakfast while you're out. And she should go over to Jim Bishop's place and see how things are going."

Andy was surprised that Eric nodded and rose to his feet. "Yes sir. I'll go get cleaned up and we can head out."

"Good, it's settled." Carl shoved his hat back on his head and looked at Eric, pointing a finger at him. "Behave," he said in a low voice.

"Yes sir," Eric replied, but a smile spread across his face as Carl and Romeo went out into the cold air.

Eric and Andy were soon sitting in his truck as he drove down the gravel road. She had thought about how to hide the bandage across her forehead and then decided it was a waste of time, anyway. She was sure the whole town knew about what had happened. Besides the deputy and EMT, there were a bunch of people with police scanners who must have heard too. She imagined the ladies at the salon talking about Andy's accident and how Eric showed up out of the blue. The two of them were probably all the old hens in town could talk about.

She sighed to herself. Then she felt Eric take her hand and slide his fingers through hers. He kept a hold of her hand while he drove, but said nothing for a while. "You hungry?" he asked.

"Yeah, I could eat," she replied. Then she thought of all the glances the two of them would suffer at Dolly's.

He squeezed her hand tight as if he could read her thoughts. "Don't worry about it. If anybody says anything, it's because they are jealous that I get to do this and they don't." He brought the back of her hand to his lips and she smiled in spite of herself.

Eric held the door of the diner open for her and when she passed through it, she felt eyes on her. She drew in a sharp breath of air and felt Eric's arm go around her waist. She shot a warning glance at him, but he smiled back at her and led her to a booth.

She slid into it, and to her chagrin, he slid in beside her instead of sitting across the table. He put a hand on her knee and she saw a mischievous look in his eyes and a playful smile on his face.

She rolled her eyes at him but couldn't help smiling back. She heard other diners whispering, but in that moment she decided she was done caring. Let them talk. If they didn't talk about her because of her relationship with Eric, they'd find something else to say about her. She didn't know what came over her, but she pressed her lips to Eric's cheek and was rewarded with a shocked expression on his face.

They had eaten in relative peace aside from feeling eyes boring holes in them and the whispers that were continuous. They'd visited Jim, and his wife had smiled at both of them, but had said nothing.

The most jarring incident happened when Andy had popped into the bakery to pick up something for the guys at the ranch. Even though it was they who told her she couldn't work that day, that didn't stop her from feeling guilty. She had stepped back out onto the sidewalk with a box of cookies and almost collided with none other than Joyce Newcome.

Andy swore to herself and tried to figure out how she could get back to the truck where Eric was sitting as quickly as possible. But of course, Joyce would have none of that. "Oh, Andy Summers! How are you? I heard about the accident. How's your head, darling?" she began. She sounded like she cared, but Andy caught the glint in her eyes.

"I'm alright Joyce, thanks for asking," Andy said, her eyes shooting to the truck. "See you around then."

But before she could escape, Joyce had placed a hand on Andy's arm. "I have one more quick question for you, dear." Joyce kept her red talons on Andy's sleeve. "Someone mentioned they heard Eric Grayson came over to the accident last night, but somebody else said they saw him at The Lodge. I can't imagine a fine man like him drinking if he was on duty..."

"He wasn't." Andy tried to push the annoyance she was feeling down.

"Oh my. So then why did he come on out at all, honey? I didn't realize you two were that close..." the corners of Joyce's started mouth turning up as the words passed her lips. Andy knew Joyce was playing dumb, and it was pissing her off. She looked Joyce in the eyes and opened her mouth to speak when she heard Eric's voice.

"What kind of boyfriend would I be if I didn't go to her when I heard she'd been hurt, Mrs. Newcome?" he said, taking the bakery box from her and putting an arm around Andy's shoulders. She felt her cheeks flame and saw Joyce's victorious smirk.

"Boyfriend huh?" Joyce repeated. Andy's mind raced. They hadn't put a label on this thing that they were doing, but thinking of Eric as her boyfriend didn't feel wrong at all. Eric said nothing but kept eye contact with Joyce. "Who'd have thunk it, huh? Andy has a reputation for being a little cold and withdrawn. I can't imagine how she paired up with such a warm man like you, Deputy," Joyce purred.

"Oh, come on now, Mrs. Newcome. Andy isn't cold or withdrawn at all. I think she tries to keep it short and polite with people that rub her the wrong way or try to get too involved in her personal business. Right, Andy?" Eric replied, a smile still on his face. Andy caught the not-so-subtle dig at Joyce and smiled as well.

"You know, Eric, I think you're right," Andy replied, and snaked her arm around his waist. "Now if you'll excuse us, Joyce," she added, and they turned and walked back to the truck. Andy was trying not to laugh as she imagined the look on Joyce's face.

39

It was two days after his last failed attempt to kill Andy Summers. He had been waiting for hours. She wouldn't slip away this time. Since early this morning, he had been hidden. That had been the only time he could get this close without being detected. He had watched the ranch hands arrive. He had seen her walk out into the cold air, zipping her coat up to her nose as she headed towards the barn. He had watched that asshole deputy pull out of the driveway.

There would be a very narrow window of time from when the last ranch hand left until the deputy returned. His legs ached to be stretched out and his shoulders and back throbbed with pain from staying still in his hiding place for so long. He'd had nothing to eat or drink, but he ignored the pain in his stomach. This would be worth all the sacrifices he'd made.

Rolling his neck, the only thing he had much space to do in the cramped space under the porch, he tried to combat the stiffness in his muscles. Finally, he heard the noises of ranch hands bidding their goodbyes, and his heart soared. The sounds of truck engines turning over and the crunch of tires on gravel made him smile as the blood pumped faster through his veins. He waited to hear her boots on the porch, but he heard a man's voice. He couldn't make out what the man was saying.

"Yeah Carl, come on in," Andy said above him. Then he heard the loud stomps of two people as they made their way to the door. Anger boiled up inside him. He considered enacting his plan now, but he didn't think he could handle both of them alone. He'd give Carl an hour. If he didn't leave before then, he would have to die with Andy.

Thankfully, forty-five minutes later, he heard heavy steps on the porch that got farther away, and finally the engine of a truck in the distance. It was now or never. Based on his observations of her, he figured she would set the alarm and go to the shower. He hadn't known about the alarm the first time he'd entered the house, but now he was prepared.

He waited five minutes and then picked the lock of the door. The shrill beeping of the alarm drew his attention. He went to it and held the small device he'd spent so much money on up to it. It began working and soon the beeping stopped and the alarm showed it was disarmed. He smiled and felt the excitement growing within him. It would all be over tonight.

—*ele*—

Eric was chatting with Mark on his cell phone while he drove home from work. Mark had asked if he and Andy would join them for dinner that night. He threw the truck into park and was about to say he would call Mark back after he talked to Andy when he saw it.

The door to the house was open. His heart rate increased. He knew this was not something Andy would ever do. "Mark," Eric said, "If I don't call you back within ten minutes, call the police and send them here."

"Eric," Mark said, an edge of panic in his voice. "What's going on?"

"Mark, ten minutes," he repeated and hung up. When he climbed out of the truck, every one of his senses buzzed. Something wasn't right. He could feel it. Andy would never have left the door open, not even a little.

His training kicked in, and he reached for his sidearm. When his hand felt nothing but the denim of his jeans, he cursed, and remembered it was locked away at the station. He pressed his palm against the door, pushing it open, and his breath felt like it had been stolen away from him. Two of the dining room chairs were knocked over. There had been a struggle. "Andy!" he yelled as he rushed inside.

His eyes darted around the room. Nausea struck him when he glimpsed dark red drops of what he knew had to be blood near the island. He raced up the stairs, taking them two at a time, yelling for her. When he flung open the bedroom door, the room was empty. He checked the rest of the bedrooms upstairs and each was the same: dark and empty.

He went to the bathroom and noticed water drops in the tub. The towel on the hook was damp, too. He spun around, looking for some other trace of her, but found nothing. After running back down the stairs as fast as he could, he burst out into the icy air.

His breath was coming fast now, creating small puffs that floated in front of him before they disappeared. He scanned the horizon, searching for some sign of her, anything.

Then he noticed it, a beam of light from the old barn. He started towards it, putting his hand in his pocket to pull out his phone, but it wasn't there. He glanced at the truck and remembered tossing it on the passenger seat in his panic. Hoping that Mark would follow through, he crossed the grass, wasting no time and trying to be as quiet as he could.

40

Andy blinked her eyes a few times. The bright lights started coming into a hazy focus. Her head was pounding and her mouth tasted like metal. She tried to figure out where she was, her memories coming back to her in brief flashes.

A voice, a twisted smile, shoving the chair towards him, feeling his hand in her hair as he pulled her back. Something hard connecting with the back of her head, then pain and darkness. Trying to lift her hand to where she'd been struck, she found she couldn't. Blinking her eyes open again, she could see her hands bound to the arms of a wooden chair.

There was the sound of footsteps in front of her, but everything beyond her hands was still fuzzy. Blinking a few more times brought things into focus a bit more. She could make out a pair of feet moving in front of her as someone paced. The person they belonged to seemed to realize she'd come to, and they turned and hurried toward her. She felt long fingers wrap around her throat.

"You bitch," the person snarled. It was a man's voice, a familiar voice. She tried to place it, but her brain felt muddy. She opened her eyes and shook her head, as if she was going to move the blurriness from her vision. Finally, the face in front of her was clear. Shock washed over her and she tried to say something, but her tongue felt like it was wrapped in cotton.

"Surprised to see me?" he asked, before yelling, "After you and that asshole we called a father ruined my whole goddamn life!"

She'd never seen her brother look like this before. Spit flew from his mouth when he spoke, and there was something off about his eyes.

His skin was sallow, his face gaunt, purple rings surrounded his sunken eyes. The number of tattoos peeking out from under his rolled-up sleeves had multiplied since she had seen him last. On his lower arms she could see bruises and cuts, along with a few dark, perhaps infected puncture marks.

"Braxton," she whispered.

It was almost like her saying his name wounded him. He yanked his hand from her throat like he'd been burned and resumed pacing. He put his hands on the back of his head as he walked back and forth. It was then she noticed the gun tucked in the waistband of his pants.

"Braxton," she croaked again. "What are you doing?"

This time the sound of her voice didn't seem to wound him, but enrage him. He crossed the room in what seemed like only two steps and punched her in the face. Pain streaked through her and she cried out. Blood dripped onto the leg of her jeans.

"What am I doing? You have the audacity to ask me what I'm doing?" he hissed, inches from her face. "The prodigal daughter and the ruined son...it's almost biblical, huh?" He laughed, a hollow laugh, a sound she'd never heard come from him, almost sadistic, taunting.

"Ya know," he continued, pointing a shaking finger at her, "I thought once that asshole died, he'd make amends for the things that happened to me, the things he shoved under the rug. But he didn't.

Instead, he gave you everything. That fucker couldn't even throw me a goddamn bone.

"What'd you do Andy? Whisper in his ear every night that you were the only one who mattered? Get a lawyer to come in and doctor some things up while dad was too out of it to notice? Why the hell couldn't he care about ME for once in his fucking life?"

"It's not like that Brax—" Andy started, her voice clearer now than it had been.

"Bullshit! Either you played this, or he was a bigger piece of shit than I ever could have imagined. What'd you do Andy? Why you?"

Andy closed her eyes tight and could see her father's face as tears streamed down his cheeks in his dying days. It had been the only time since her mother had passed that she had seen him cry. He had wept over the fact that he believed his sons had forgotten him.

"And where were you, Brax?" she whispered, trying not to let the anger inside of her overflow. She didn't know what he was capable of anymore, but she knew she needed to buy time.

"What?" he snarled as he whipped around. Her eyes snapped back open, and she stared into his.

"When dad was dying, where were you?"

"How dare you—" he said, coming towards her again.

"No Brax!" The anger and resentment that she'd felt for years burst through the dam she'd built to contain it. He stopped in his tracks, glaring at her with wide eyes. "No one else came. He called all of us, even you, and said he was sick and I came. You didn't. Eddie didn't. He was dying, and I was there. Where were you? Where were you when he was dying? Where were you when he took his last breath? Because god dammit, Braxton, I left everything! I was here with him! I watched him die just like I watched mom!"

"Where was I?" he growled and put his face so close she could feel his breath on her skin. His face contorted into something ugly, something she would have never imagined he could be.

"I was staying as far away from this fucking hellhole as I could." She looked at him, but before she could say another word, he continued. "You have no idea what I went through, do you? He wouldn't even talk about it on his deathbed, huh?" Andy kept staring at him and a malicious smile spread across Braxton's thin face.

"I'll take that as a no," he sneered and paced the room again. "You remember that old ranch hand that used to work here, Buddy? He had a beer gut and smelled like he didn't know what deodorant was, but dad swore he was a good guy, even after I told him he gave me the creeps," Andy nodded, a memory of the man coming back to her.

"Well, our wonderful father was wrong. Buddy wasn't a good guy, Buddy was a fucking pedophile. I was what, nine or ten when it started? Right here, in this god damn barn. He told me he'd kill all of you if I told anyone. He told me he'd hurt you.

"It went on for years, years Andy! I'll spare you the details of what that monster did to me, what he made me do to him... Then one time Buddy wasn't so lucky and dad walked in on it. He saw what he was doing to me. Andy, I swear to God I thought dad was going to kill him. I wish he had. He came close. There was blood everywhere. I felt like I'd been saved.

"And then dad sent him on his way. Fired him, told him to leave town. Never called the cops. Never reported it. He let him go, Andy.

And ever since then I've been left to wonder, how many other kids did that guy terrorize?

"Do you know how scared I was, thinking he'd come back to find me again? You can't imagine what the smell of this place does to me, the memories that terrorize me when I smell these goddamn cows?"

"Braxton, I didn't—," Andy sputtered. The horror of his words spread through her, making her nauseous.

"You didn't know? Yeah, I'm not even sure mom knew. She was sick by then. I couldn't bear to see her in any more pain, so I went to Dad. I told him how I had nightmares, how I thought I needed help, how I was having these terrible thoughts, how much I was hurting. But like the good ole' cowboy he was, he said I needed to man up and put it all behind me.

"Every time I went to him he wouldn't look me in the eye. He'd just say, 'What doesn't kill you makes you stronger, so put your chin up and move on.' But Jesus, Andy, how do you move on from that? From the things he did to me? How? I was a fucking kid!"

"Is that why you started using?" She asked, tears running down her face as she processed this revelation.

"It was the only thing that could take any of it away. The only thing that could numb it, the only way I could sleep without seeing him, without feeling him on my skin. And then whatever it was, after a while it would start not working as well, and I'd have to try more, or something new. Do you know how it feels to close your eyes and be...scared? To feel you have no control? Like you have no idea if or when you're going to be hurt again."

"Yes," Andy whispered and Braxton spun around to look at her again, eyes narrowed, suspicious. "Was it you? This whole time, was it you?" she asked. Braxton stayed silent, studying her face. "The break in, the note on my truck, the cow, my brakes. Was it all you?"

He said nothing, but a malicious smile that made it all the way to his eyes crept across his face. His betrayal rocked her and the anger she felt raged up inside her again. "You terrorized me, Braxton! Yes, I know what it's like to be afraid of someone every time you close your eyes because I was afraid of you! You became the monster Braxton! You were my monster!"

Her last words seemed to cut through him. His eyes widened and his mouth turned from a smile to a sneer. "You don't know a thing about monsters, Andy," he snarled.

"And what's your endgame, Braxton?"

"I'm going to kill you." His steely gaze was fixed on Andy as she felt her breath catch in her throat. He'd said it like he was taking out the trash. "You see, when dad died I thought he'd try to make it up to me. I figured he'd give me a slice of the pie. We'd sell the ranch and each get a fair share. For once in my adult life I wouldn't have to worry about money. Maybe I'd be able to get my shit together.

"But he gave it to you. All of it. It proved that he never gave a shit about me. It wasn't cowboy pride that made him turn his back on me all those years ago. It was just that he couldn't be bothered to give a damn about me.

"Eddie though, I was surprised he'd cut him out. The old man respected Eddie for being a sports star, and when shit turned for the guy, he still went out and made it on his own. He's everything I will never be. A suit with a beautiful wife and a huge house.

"Ya know, if Theo was still here, I'm sure it would have been him getting everything. The old man loved Theo even more than you. You know that's true, you have to." Her heart was pounding in her chest.

Her mind was reeling. She was helpless, tied to a chair in front of a man with a gun who told her he wanted to kill her. She was trying to conjure up a plan when something out of the corner of her eye near the door to the barn caught her attention.

41

Braxton must have seen her eyes flit towards the door because he pulled the gun from his waistband and spun in that direction. Eric hadn't been fast enough to hide. He stopped moving when he realized the weapon was trained on him, raising his hands to show he was unarmed. His stomach lurched when he looked past the man with the gun at Andy.

"Hey man," he said, trying to tap into the hostage negotiation training he'd taken ages ago. "I'm Eric."

"I know who you are," the man retorted. "You're fucking my sister." Eric's mind raced, trying to remember the names of the brothers that Andy had talked to him about. Eddie popped into his head, but he'd been some big shot. The scrawny tweaker in front of him was not a big city lawyer. Theo had died.

"You must be Braxton. Andy's told me a lot about you," he said after it had hit him like a bolt of lightning. "So man, talk to me. What's going on?"

"Shut the fuck up!" Braxton yelled. "You're not gonna use any of your cop psycho babble bullshit on me right now. So shut your mouth and go sit over there." He gestured in Andy's direction. "Don't get too close there, Casanova. I might not be the best shot, but I've got plenty of bullets."

Eric made his way toward Andy with his hands still over his head. He locked eyes with her for a moment, his stomach turned at the sight of her beautiful face covered in blood, her eyes filled with terror. He looked away when Braxton's voice rang out again. "Sit down."

Eric complied, sitting a few feet to Andy's left. Braxton's hands were shaking as he held the gun out towards them and Eric figured that based on what he knew, Braxton needed a fix. How long had he been waiting for a chance to grab Andy? He'd heard bits and pieces of the conversation before he'd made the calculated risk of entering the barn.

Braxton clicked his tongue in his mouth. "Tut tut tut, damn shame deputy," he said. "You didn't need to die tonight, too, but it is what it is."

"Why does anybody need to die tonight, man? We could all walk out of here."

"Well, while my dear sister is smart and driven," Braxton sneered, "I doubt she's made a will yet. Young, healthy little thing like her. So that makes me and Eddie her next of kin. If she were to meet some terrible end, we'd get the ranch.

"I asked Eddie a while ago. He told me that's what would happen. Good to have a lawyer in the family. Then me and him, we'll sell this shit hole and I'll get what I deserve."

"What makes you so certain she hasn't made a will? Like you said, she's smart. That was probably the first thing she did when your dad died. Would have been the first thing I did if it were me." Eric wasn't sure Andy had a will or not, but if there was any way to plant doubt in this man's mind, or at least draw this out until he could think of a plan, he was going to try it. Braxton turned and stared at Andy.

Eric kept going, doing whatever he could to stall Braxton's next move. "She's got a lot of people in this town she loves. Maybe she left it all to the group of ranchers your dad played poker with? I don't know if this place could be in better hands. She wouldn't have risked it going to the wrong person, I'd guarantee that. Not with Frank Miller sniffing around like he has been."

Andy stayed silent beside him. Braxton's eyes never left her face. "You paint anymore, sis?" Braxton said, his voice tender.

Eric could hear the pain in her voice when she spoke, "I had to give up everything when I came here. This wasn't my plan. I didn't want this Braxton. Let me help you. Please, untie me. We'll walk out of here together. I'll help you. I'll help you get you clean. You can start over."

"Yeah, sure, gave up everything huh?" he asked. He turned his back to her and dropped his head. "You ever have to sell your body, Andy? Did you ever have to give yourself over to someone so you can get what you need to not feel sick? So that you don't have to lay, sweating and shaking, throwing up all over yourself because you can't move?"

When Andy didn't answer, Braxton turned back to her and smiled that now familiar, ugly smile. "Didn't think so." Then Braxton raised the gun and pointed it at her. "Do you have a will, Andy?"

Eric looked at Andy and could almost see the wheels churning in her head as she weighed out the options that lay before her. "You always took care of me, Brax. You always made sure I was OK. When I painted something, you were the first person I would show it to because I knew even if you hated it you'd find some nice way to critique it."

Andy's voice shook as she tried to keep her composure. "When Eddie left, it was me and you. Theo was too old, too cool for us. Then when Theo died...it was just me and you. Don't you remember? Don't you remember how much I love you? How much you loved me?" Tears kept dripping from her eyes, mixing with blood on their way down her cheeks.

"I remember," Braxton croaked. Tears rimmed his eyes, too. He choked back a sob. "What do I do Andy?"

It was at that exact moment they heard the tires on the gravel. Eric's mind flashed to the conversation with Mark. He could only hope that he called the police and hadn't tried to come here himself.

Unfortunately, Braxton heard it too. His face, that had been contemplative a moment before, had turned hard again. "What the hell? Who the fuck is that?" he asked. He rubbed his forehead as he realized his plan was deteriorating before his eyes. His hands shook more than they had a few minutes ago.

"Braxton, you don't have to do this. You took care of me, it's my turn to take care of you. Please..." Andy begged, her voice breaking. Braxton looked around the barn, weighing out his options when they heard another car pull on to the gravel. Then Eric heard the familiar squelch of a police radio.

Braxton looked at Andy and his face fell, then hardened again. "Yes...I do," he whispered.

Before Eric could blink, Braxton had raised the gun. Eric screamed, "No!" and Braxton squeezed the trigger. The bullet struck Andy, and she gasped. Her beautiful green eyes went wide with shock. The chair she was bound to fell backward from the force. Without hesitation, Eric crawled towards her. He heard Braxton say, "Your turn."

He heard the familiar sound of two pops of gunfire and waited to feel the hot, searing pain of a bullet tearing through him, but it never came. Instead, Braxton crumpled to the ground like a paper doll, blood spreading on the concrete floor beneath him. Eric glanced to the door and saw deputies swarming in, guns raised.

Eric scrambled across the floor to Andy. The bullet had hit her in the shoulder and a crimson pool had blossomed out under her. He tore off the coat he wore and pressed it against the wound. "Call an ambulance!" he yelled, hearing the panic in his own voice. "I need a knife over here!"

He heard one of the deputy's key up his radio and request an ambulance. Another scurried over with a multi-tool and cut the binding that secured Andy's feet to the legs of the chair and her wrists to the arms. Her eyes fluttered.

"I'm right here, Andy," he whispered, pulling her head into his lap and keeping the coat pressed against her shoulder. "Stay with me OK baby? Help is coming OK? Don't leave me. Please...stay with me...please Andy. I love you, you can't leave me..." He felt the tightness in his chest grow even more when she stayed still.

Tears burned his eyes as he looked down and saw the thick fabric he held to her shoulder had already become soaked in blood. He glanced over to where Braxton's body lay. One deputy had already kicked the weapon away.

All Eric could think was that this couldn't be happening. This wasn't real. He was going to wake up from this nightmare soon and he would be in her bed. When he woke up, he'd pull her warm body into his and bury his face in her hair.

After what seemed like an eternity, he heard the whooping of an ambulance siren. EMTs came in, but Eric couldn't move until he felt a hand on his shoulder. "Sir, we need room."

Eric slid over, then got to his feet. He looked down at his hands and saw they were covered in her blood. His stomach roiled. Within minutes, the EMTs had Andy on a stretcher and were heading toward an ambulance. "I'm coming with her," Eric said.

The sea of red and blue lights in the driveway blinded him for a moment. "Family only. You'll have to meet us at the hospital," one of the EMTs replied as he jogged, pushing the stretcher toward the waiting ambulance.

They had her in the back and had closed the doors before Eric could process what had happened enough to object. He watched them pull away and heard a familiar voice. He spun around and saw Sergeant James running toward him.

"Was that Andy in there?" he asked. Eric nodded.

"Come on," James said, and they ran toward his cruiser. Eric slid into the passenger seat and James threw on the lights and sirens, spraying up gravel as he stomped on the accelerator.

"How did they know to come?" Eric said, a few minutes into the drive.

"What, son?" James asked, not taking his eyes off the road.

"The deputies...how'd they know we were in trouble?"

"Your buddy Mark called it in, said something was off, and you told him to call if you hadn't contacted him."

During the ride, Eric borrowed the sergeant's phone and called Mark. He didn't give any details about what had happened and told him Andy was on her way to the hospital in an ambulance and he was behind it. He ended the call before hearing Mark say anything in response.

James pulled up near the hospital. "Go in, I'll park and be right there," he said.

Eric ran through the doors and rushed to the desk. The woman there listened to him as words flew out of his mouth faster than they may have ever done before.

"OK, are you her husband?" she responded.

"No, she's...she's my girlfriend," he said quietly.

"OK honey. Have a seat. I'll see what we can find out."

He looked down at his hands, still covered in blood. Then to his jeans, which were also stained with large, dark red spots.

"Ma'am," he said. "Is there anywhere I can get cleaned up?" She looked confused for a moment until her eyes landed on his hands. Then her mouth fell agape and her eyes went wide. As he felt his anger rising, a hand squeezed his shoulder.

He turned his head and saw Sergeant James standing beside him. "Excuse me, ma'am," he said, flashing his badge at the woman behind the desk. "Can you tell me where Andrea Summers is? She's a GSW that was brought in."

The woman clicked some keys on her keyboard. "Looks like they're taking her to surgery," she said, watching Eric. Sergeant James must have noticed her stony stare.

"Ma'am, do you think you have anywhere this young man can get cleaned up?" James asked, but the woman continued to look at Eric.

"Dorothy," James said after looking down at the woman's name tag. "If it will provide the answer to my question more quickly, I would like you to know this young man did not hurt that woman. On the contrary, he may have saved her life. I need to question what he witnessed, and I need a private area to do that in. So, where can he get cleaned up and where may I speak with him?"

Her body visibly relaxed at Sergeant James' words. The woman nodded and turned and spoke in a hushed tone to another woman behind the desk. She stood up and asked them to follow her.

The woman showed the Sergeant to a small room with a placard by the door that read, "Consult 3." Then she took Eric to a bathroom nearby.

He walked into the bathroom and locked the door behind him. The blood on his hands had dried, and he scrubbed it off in the sink, turning the water dark pink. Tears fell from his eyes as he washed her blood away and watched it swirl down the drain. He pictured her in his mind, lying on the cold concrete, unmoving, unresponsive.

After he had cleaned himself the best he could, he walked back to the consult room. He closed the door and sat down across from the sergeant, very aware of what was about to happen. James set a voice recorder on the table.

"I'm going to tape this OK?" his voice was gentle. Eric nodded and James turned on the device. "Alright son, tell me what happened."

Eric knelt forward with his elbows on his knees and rested his head in his hands. He took a deep breath, then launched into what had happened. He talked about how when he'd arrived, he'd heard voices from the barn. He explained he had stood outside listening for a while and told the sergeant what he'd heard Braxton say. James sucked in a breath when Eric spoke about the abuse Braxton had revealed.

He told him how he'd tried to get into the barn undetected and failed. How he'd ended up at the end of the barrel of the gun that had shot Andy. He told that he'd heard the two shots, saw Braxton fall and then how he scrambled to Andy to save her.

"Do we know if she's...if she's alive?" he could barely utter the words when he'd finished telling his version of events. Sergeant James turned off the recorder and stood up, sliding it into his pocket.

"Let me see what I can find out for you," he said, and he slipped out of the room. Eric leaned back in the less than comfortable chair and laid an arm across his face as more tears fell from his eyes.

A quiet knock on the door announced the sergeant's return. "She's alive. She's still in surgery, but there's somewhere you can wait," he said.

He gestured for Eric to follow. They ended up in a large lobby that was empty except for a couple waiting in the far corner. The sergeant clapped a hand on Eric's shoulder and gave him a sad smile. "The hospital is wondering if we know how to get in touch with Andy's next of kin."

"Shit," Eric sighed. "It'd be her brother, Eddie. I don't know how to get a hold of him though. I can call my friend and see if she knows how."

James shook his head. "Don't trouble yourself with that right now. I'll see what we can do." James put his hands on his hips and stood silent for a moment. "I'm sorry you're going through this, Eric. I am confident a woman like Andy Summers is going to pull through this alright. You're using some of those vacation days you've been neglecting for the rest of your shifts this week. I'll call you to let you know when you're on next."

"Yes sergeant. Thank you." Eric watched him walk away and collapsed into a hard chair covered in green vinyl.

He closed his eyes as tightly as he could, trying to block out the images from the last couple of hours that came rushing back to him. After only a few minutes, he heard someone hurrying toward him. He snapped his eyes open, expecting a surgeon, but saw Mark and Margie instead.

"What are you guys doing here?" Eric leapt to his feet and accepted embraces from them both.

"We were so worried," Margie said, squeezing his hand. "That call with Mark, and then we didn't hear anything...and now Andy's here..."

"You saved us," he choked and squeezed his eyes tight again, trying to stop the tears he felt coming.

Then he felt Margie's arms go around him, and he couldn't contain it any longer. His shoulders shook violently as he cried. Then he felt Mark's arms around him too, and they stood like that, both Mark and Margie holding Eric until he could compose himself. When he'd been able to breathe again, the three of them sat down together, Margie book ended by Eric and Mark, who were both leaning forward, elbows on knees.

"What happened man?" Mark asked, his forehead creased.

Eric was quiet. His mouth felt dry and scratchy and he felt sweat forming when he recalled what had happened. "It was Braxton...her brother. He shot her."

"What?" Mark said in disbelief.

"He wanted to inherit the ranch as Andy's next of kin and sell it. In order to do that, he had to kill her. He's the one that broke in. He left the message in the barn. He messed with her truck and then..." his voice trailed off and he dropped his head, not able to say the words again.

"He wouldn't have gotten it," Margie said. "Andy came over to our place one night not too long after she moved back. We shared a bottle of wine and while she was a little tipsy, Andy told me she'd already met with the same lawyer her dad had. She told me that if anything ever happened to her, the ranch would go to an estate. Romeo and Carl would have been the executors, they would have gotten the ranch.

"She figured that would be the best way to keep it as close to the family as possible, like she promised her dad. She was sure Braxton and Eddie would have sold it the second they could."

Eric's mind unwillingly pulled up the picture of her, lying in the puddle of blood, her blond hair fanned out behind her. He buried his head in his hands, pressing the heels of his palms into his eyes to block the image out. "Shit," he whispered. "She lost a lot of blood."

"Eric," Margie said, rubbing a warm, comforting hand on his back. "Andy Summers is by far one of the strongest women I know. She will get through this, out of sheer stubbornness, if nothing else."

42

It seemed like an eternity passed before anyone came to talk to him. Mark had got a hold of Romeo and Carl, and not long after the phone calls were made, they and Rosa were sitting in the same corner as Eric and the others. Mark had told them what he knew about what had happened since Eric couldn't muster up the strength to recall it a third time.

He had gotten Mark and Margie to go home after a few hours of sitting in the uncomfortable chairs. Poor Margie was trying to be a trooper, but Eric could see it was taking a toll on her pregnant body. Only after he promised that he would call as soon as anyone heard something, they hugged everyone and left.

Then it was just him and her ranch family. At about four in the morning, Carl went outside to call one of the other hands and give updates and orders for what was to be done that day. Other than that, the group was silent. Rosa and Romeo were holding each other's hands. Carl was pacing, back and forth, back and forth. Eric was surprised the carpet hadn't started to wear in his path.

He had stayed in his uncomfortable chair, feeling too drained of both emotional and physical energy to do much other than replay that same terrible scene in his head. Eric's eyes snapped up as he heard a gentle voice. "Are you here for Andrea Summers?"

He found himself looking at a man in light blue scrubs with a fabric cap covering his head. He nodded and before he could stand, the man settled into the green chair beside him. Eric's heart started beating faster. Rosa brought a hand to her mouth, like she was trying to keep whatever words or sounds she had from spilling out. Carl sat on Eric's other side, leaning so far forward to see the doctor that he was close to sliding out of the chair.

"My name is Dr. Wilson. We just wrapped up with Andrea. Her brother told us we could come and speak with you," he said quietly. He looked at Eric and must have seen the fear on his face because he added, "She's OK, she's in recovery now." Eric let out a breath and felt tears sting his eyes again. He dropped his head into his hands and felt his shoulders shake as he was overcome with a mixture of relief and exhaustion.

Carl put a hand on his shoulder and left it there. The doctor continued, "She's alright. She lost a lot of blood, but we could get her stabilized. Unfortunately, we weren't able to retrieve the actual bullet." Eric could compose himself enough to look up at the doctor and he continued. "I don't think she'll have much impact on her movement, or day-to-day life, but she'll have that reminder in her body for the rest of her life."

"Thank you, doctor," Eric croaked out. "If she had...if you couldn't..."

"But we did." The surgeon set a hand on Eric's other shoulder and stood to his feet. He turned to them and added, "She's going to need a lot of help over the next couple weeks." Eric nodded. "She's going to be in recovery for a while. Maybe you all want to get home and get some sleep, grab a shower?"

Eric shook his head. "I need to be here when she wakes up. She can't wake up alone."

The doctor nodded. "I'll let the nurses know to come get you once she gets in a room."

The doctor walked away and Eric heard Rosa cry softly. Romeo had taken her in his arms and was crying himself. Carl hadn't taken his hand from Eric's shoulder and when Eric's eyes landed on the old man's face, his weathered cheeks were covered in trails of tears.

Carl looked over at Eric. He brushed the tears off his face and cleared his throat. "You saved her," he whispered. Eric felt Rosa and Romeo look over at them and when he looked up Rosa had a little sad smile on her face. Carl continued, "If you hadn't been there, Jesus...I can't even think about that," then his voice cracked and he trailed off.

Rosa let out a sob and before Eric could realize what was happening, she had her arms around him. He hugged her back and felt his own tears fall again. She released him from her grasp and held his face in her hands. She smiled that sad smile again and kissed him on each cheek. Romeo patted him on the shoulder, his eyes bloodshot too.

Carl's phone rang from within his pocket and when he pulled it out, he cursed under his breath and stomped away as he answered. After a few minutes, he returned, still cursing. "Romeo, I swear to God those fucking idiots wouldn't know their heads from their asses if they didn't have a nose," he glanced up at Rosa and added, "Sorry."

"If you guys need to go, please, by all means," Eric said, and Romeo and Carl exchanged a glance. "Look, I know Andy would be pissed if her ranch went to hell because she was in this place. You could sit here and wait for hours, or you can go take care of things and come back, and when you do, she might be awake." Romeo cocked his head at Carl and Carl nodded.

"You're gonna be here when she wakes up, though, right?" Carl asked.

"I'm not going anywhere."

"Alright, then we will do the bare minimum to keep those dip shits from burning it to the ground. We'll come back later."

Eric had asked if they could bring him his truck when they came back and handed over his keys when they obliged. Rosa gave him another quick squeeze and then the three turned and walked away. He'd also gotten them to agree to call Mark and give an update on Andy's condition, since his phone was still in his truck.

When he slumped back into the chair, his stomach rumbled. He realized he hadn't eaten since lunch yesterday and wondered where he might find some food, but he didn't want to leave in case a nurse came to get him. A few minutes later, that exact thing happened.

He followed her through some hallways and up an elevator, down another hallway, and into the room where Andy was. When he saw her, he had to swallow down a lump that formed in his throat.

She looked so small in the hospital bed. Tubes and wires were connecting machines around the bed to her body. "She's alright sweety," the older nurse said, noting his hesitation.

Nodding, he crossed the threshold into the room. The antiseptic they had used on her, that definitive hospital smell, assaulted his senses.

Anger and sadness washed over him all at once when he saw her face. He dropped his head and squeezed his eyes shut once again against the image of her with blood running down her face. He shook his head and pulled a chair next to the bed.

After settling into it, he decided it was an upgrade from the waiting area, but still a far cry from comfortable. Taking care not to touch the IV that ran from the back of her hand to a bag of clear liquid hanging from a tall silver stand, he took her fingers in his own. Feeling the warmth of her skin brought him a sense of relief.

He didn't know what he would have done had he lost her. He had fallen in love with Andy Summers and he would do anything in his power to make sure she was safe and happy. He sat beside her mulling over what this meant for a while before exhaustion took over and he drifted to sleep.

43

She was becoming aware of sounds around her. There was a soft, rhythmic beeping, hushed voices in the distance, shoes squeaking on the tile. She smelled something that was out of place, something that made her nose wrinkle. It was a scent she recognized, and it made her uncomfortable. She was aware she was lying on something and felt fabric beneath the fingers on one hand, and her other hand was touching something warm.

Finally, she could open her eyes, but her eyelids fell again. She fought against the heaviness she felt and opened them again, squinting and blinking until her eyes could adjust to the light. She panicked when she realized she didn't know where she was. Then her eyes landed on the head resting beside her hip and the hand entwined with hers.

When she saw Eric, asleep with his head on his arm, slumped onto the bed from the chair he sat in, she could breathe. Then she realized that she was in a hospital. Flashes of the night before popped into her head: Braxton, the barn, Eric sitting beside her on the concrete. She tried to swallow and felt like her throat was on fire.

She must have winced at the pain, because Eric's eyes flew open and he lifted his head. When he saw her eyes open, he smiled a little and brought his hand to her cheek. "Welcome back," he whispered. She tried to speak and again felt the scratching burn in her throat.

"Don't talk yet," he said. "Let me get a nurse." He disappeared, but quickly he returned with a slight woman in scrubs following behind.

"Good morning Sleeping Beauty!" she said and went to some machines beside Andy. She flipped a few switches and pushed a couple buttons, then adjusted the bed so Andy was sitting up a little. "I'm guessing your throat is bothering you a bit, which is normal. During surgery, you had a tube down your throat to help you breathe and that can irritate things."

Andy squeezed her eyes shut again, trying to remember what the hell happened. "Here, drink some of this," the nurse said, offering a white Styrofoam cup.

Andy took the straw in her mouth. Once she felt the cool liquid slide down her throat, she realized how thirsty she was and took a few more long pulls from the straw. "Thank you," she could finally whisper.

The nurse smiled down at her again. "Everything looks good. I'm going to go let the doctor know you are awake and he'll be in to check on you," the nurse said and left the room.

She closed her eyes for a moment, again trying to figure out why she was here. "What happened?" she whispered. When she opened her eyes, they landed on Eric's face. His eyes were downcast. He sat back in the chair and took her hand in both of his, rubbing his thumbs along the back of it.

"Do you remember anything?" he asked.

"Not much, just Braxton being in the barn." She closed her eyes again and tried to will herself to remember. "You were next to me.

Braxton, he was angry…" She opened her eyes again and looked at him, waiting for him to fill in the blanks.

He cleared his throat, still rubbing his thumbs along her skin, his eyes not meeting hers. "I got to your house, and the door was open. The kitchen was a mess. A light was on in the barn and when I got there, Braxton had you in there. You were tied to a chair and your face was bleeding. I heard him talking. He…he was going to kill you Andy."

Andy's stomach felt like it had fallen to her toes. She looked at him, her brows knitting together, and then the images started rushing back like a macabre slide show. She could see Braxton with a gun, she could hear his voice, she heard him talking about the ranch hand, the abuse. She inhaled. "What happened? I can remember him now, I remember him talking, but I don't remember what happened next."

"He shot you, Andy," Eric said, but his voice was caring and his eyes met hers. She felt like his words slapped her in the face. "Thank God he's a bad shot, and he got you in the shoulder. When I got to the house, I was on the phone with Mark, something felt wrong and I told him to call the police if I didn't call him back, and he did. The deputy's arrived after Braxton had shot you. He's gone Andy. Braxton's dead." The words he'd said seemed to reverberate in her ears.

Her brother had shot her and then was killed. It didn't make any sense. Eric must have seen the confusion on her face. "He wanted the ranch. He wanted to sell it. He wanted the money, he-he thought he needed the money." He squeezed her hand.

They sat in silence for a few minutes as she absorbed everything he had told her. "Are you OK?" he asked. She shook her head.

"I don't know what I am…" her voice drifted off, and she pushed her head back against the pillow and fell asleep.

44

Over the course of the day, she had several visitors. First Carl, Romeo and Rosa arrived. Carl had driven Eric's truck back so he could go to his apartment and shower and change. It was only after much prodding that he reluctantly agreed. He kissed her on the forehead before he left the room, prompting Rosa to smile from ear to ear.

The first nurse that walked into the room balked at Andy having three visitors at once, but Rosa sweet-talked her into letting them stay. They visited for a while, never once mentioning Braxton or the events of that night, for which Andy was grateful.

When Mark and Margie arrived, the other three left, not wanting to bring on the wrath of an angry nurse. Carl had gently held her hand, and Andy could have sworn tears dripped from the corners of his eyes. Rosa had given her a half hug on her good side and kissed her cheek, and Romeo tipped his hat and winked at her, patting her leg before following the others.

Margie sat in the chair beside the bed and held Andy's hand, tears spilling down her cheeks. She apologized multiple times, blaming her pregnancy hormones for her outpouring of emotion. They chatted for a bit and although it seemed like a question had been on the tip of

Margie's tongue a couple times, they too avoided all mention of the cause of her hospitalization.

The two of them left when the doctor came to assess her with a young medical student in tow. They had spoken about her being shot, and the doctor asked the medical student a bunch of questions. Andy tuned them out until the doctor told her she'd be discharged the next day, assuming nothing changed with her healing.

After they left, she fell asleep for a little while and when she woke, Eric's familiar figure sat in the chair in the corner. He was flipping through a magazine Margie had brought, unaware that Andy was awake. She watched him, taking him in. She noticed the subtle twitch of his arm muscles when he flipped a page, the steady rise and fall of his chest as he breathed, the slight turn of his mouth as he read something amusing.

Then she remembered the feeling she had when Braxton had pointed the gun at him. The dread that had rushed through her at the thought of her brother hurting him. She remembered she had almost begged Braxton not to hurt him. She remembered thinking that she couldn't bear to lose the man she loved. As she watched him, she realized it was true. She loved this man with everything she had.

"Hey," she whispered, trying not to frighten him.

He spun toward her and tossed the magazine onto the table. Then he took her hand in his and held it, the warmth of his skin against hers, his calming presence bringing a smile to her face. He lifted her hand and kissed the back of her fingers, avoiding her IV. Then he brought her palm to his cheek and held it there for a moment.

Tears formed in her eyes at his tenderness, and he smiled at her. He leaned over her bed and brought his lips down on hers. Then she heard someone clearing their throat from the doorway.

Eric stood and turned, but didn't let go of her hand. A man in a long coat stood in the doorway. His hair was the same color blond as hers, but he had gray patches at his temples. He had the same light eyes as her, too. "Eddie..." Andy half stated, half asked from the bed.

"Andy," the man replied. He looked like he'd stepped out of a J. Crew catalog. He wore a light green sweater that played off of the color in his eyes and khaki pants with shiny, brown leather shoes. A far cry from the ensembles most of the people around here wore. His hair was coiffed and she could almost feel the arrogance rolling off of him.

"And you are?" Eddie asked, turning towards Eric.

"Eric Grayson," he said, walking towards Eddie with his hand extended. "I've heard a lot about you. Nice to meet you."

Eddie gave a perfunctory handshake in return before pushing his hand back into the pocket of his coat. He let his gaze drift across Eric. An unimpressed look formed on his face, like he'd taken a bite of something he didn't like.

"Knowing your probable source, if you've heard a lot about me, I don't know how you could say it would be nice to meet me," he replied.

Eric raised his eyebrows and put both hands up and took a step back, showing he didn't want to get dragged into a verbal sparring match. Andy sighed from behind Eric and he turned to her. "Do you want me to go?" She shook her head no, and she heard Eddie protest. Eric must have noticed it too, but he ignored it and returned to the chair in the corner without looking back at her brother. He grabbed a magazine and put his feet up on the small table, crossing his long legs at the ankle. He shook open the magazine, but she could tell he wasn't reading it.

"I was hoping we might have a private conversation," Eddie said, taking a few steps into the room.

"Whatever you have to say to me, he can hear," she responded, an edge to her voice. "I'm surprised to see you here."

Eddie moved closer and stood a foot or so beyond the end of the bed. She pressed the little button on the remote to move into a sitting position and they stared at each other until he took a deep breath.

"The police called and told me what had happened." Andy noticed how formal Eddie sounded, almost like he was in a courtroom. "They said someone would need to come to identify the body."

Andy felt her stomach sour at the thought of Braxton's dead body and she almost lost it when at the idea of how close she had been to being the one that needed to be identified. "When he called me, I had no idea this is what it would come to," he continued.

"He called you?" she asked, feeling prickles on her skin. She heard Eric stir beside her, but didn't tear her gaze away from Eddie.

"A while ago, out of the blue. He called and asked questions about next of kin if someone wasn't married. I'm so upset with myself that I didn't put two and two together..."

She heard Eric pull his feet from the table and put them on the floor but kept her eyes on the man in front of her. "When had you heard from him before that Eddie?" Anger began to swell inside her.

"Not since the will was read," Eddie said.

"So you're telling me, after years, out of the blue, he calls you. He asks about next of kin, and who that would be, and what would happen to someone's property if that person wasn't married and that didn't raise any red flags for you?" She glared at Eddie, but he didn't move.

"I would never fathom he would have been capable of this, Andy," Eddie said, his hands still in his pockets.

She squeezed her eyes shut and the memory of Braxton talking about his abuse swirled into her mind. "Did you know about what happened to Braxton? About the things that happened to him when he was a kid?" she asked, not able to say the word. Eddie cast his eyes downward and cleared his throat again. "You knew?" She heard the magazine Eric had been holding hit the table.

"He came to me in Chicago once, before we had the kids. He was using. I let him sleep in my basement. He told me then. He was so high I don't think he even knew what he was doing."

"And you kept that information to yourself? You didn't try to get him help Eddie?"

"That was not my responsibility, Andy. He was a grown man."

"He was a human being who was haunted by demons that you and I could never understand!" Her voice was rising. "So you knew he suffered? You knew he was running away from his pain? Then he calls you and asks you very specific questions, but somehow, you had no idea that he might mean me?"

Eddie's eyes rose to meet her stare, but he didn't say a word. She heard Eric rise, the chair scraping the floor. Still, she kept Eddie's gaze, waiting for him to say something.

"I've always wondered, Andy, why did our father change his will? Why did he change the document I'd helped him prepare? The one where the three of us got equal share, the one where he acknowledged all his surviving children...not just you?" His words were like knives.

Andy's eyes grew wide, and she felt heat rising in her chest and into her cheeks. She felt like her throat was constricting, like she couldn't get enough air. Tears threatened to spill from her eyes. Before she could register what was happening, Eric stepped closer to Eddie.

"It's time for you to leave now Eddie," he said in a low, but very serious tone.

"I haven't seen my sister in some time. I'm trying to discuss some family matters with her," Eddie replied, undisturbed and undeterred.

He turned his attention back to Andy. "So, how did you do it? Did you whisper in his ear at night? Did you call the attorney yourself and lay out the details? Did you have a dying man put pen to paper to give you the whole damn thing?" His voice turned into a venom that stung her to her core.

She opened her mouth to speak, but her mind swirled. Her last surviving family member stood before her accusing her of something so disgusting her brain couldn't string together a coherent thought. Eric took another step toward Eddie, but she found the words.

"I was here," she hissed. "When he called, I came. I took care of him, feeding him, bathing him...me Eddie. Where. The fuck. Were you?

"I didn't want this. I wanted to be in New York! I wanted to live my life. But neither you nor Braxton took a goddamn minute to think about that. You decided I was the villain in all of this, that somehow I manipulated him? Fuck you. Do you know how much he hurt in his last days, knowing his sons had abandoned him?

"I am not the villain here, Eddie. You are. You and Braxton made your choice. At least I can understand why Brax couldn't come home, but what's your fucking excuse?" She was panting as she spat the last sentence and willed herself not to cry. She didn't want this asshole to get the satisfaction of seeing that.

Eddie's lips turned into a sneer. "I have a life, Andy. I have obligations—"

"And you think I didn't?" she interrupted. He chuckled once and then his lips turned up farther. He took a step forward, putting both hands on the rail at the end of her bed.

"I'm thinking it's quite a shame that Braxton wasn't more successful in his recent endeavors," he said quietly.

As soon as the words left his mouth and before Andy could register what was happening, Eric grabbed Eddie and slammed him up against the nearest wall. He had bunches of Eddie's expensive coat in each of his hands. She could see a vein in Eric's neck bulging and Eddie's face went white.

"You need to get the fuck out of here. Now. Stay away from her. If I see you near her again, I will kill you," Eric growled into Eddie's face.

They stared at each other for a moment before Eddie pushed Eric away and Eric dropped the cloth from his hands. They were squared up to each other, eye to eye, noses nearly touching. She could see Eric's clenched jaw tick. His hands were in fists by his sides. She watched with her heart in her throat, not knowing what was coming next.

Eddie took a small step to the side and smoothed out the front of his coat, then ran a hand over his hair. He took one last look at Andy. "See ya...sis," he said with a vicious smile, and then turned and left the room.

Eric watched him leave and then shut the door to the room and turned to Andy. She felt like a dam burst. Her breath became shallow and her chest heaved as sobs shook her.

Eric was sitting on the bed next to her when her first tears fell, slow at first, but turning into rushing rivers down her cheeks in seconds. Eric pressed his forehead to hers and rested a hand on her cheek.

When her sobs had diminished, he stood and said, "Scooch."

Gingerly, she moved over on the bed as far as she could. He pressed the button that made the back of the bed go down and somehow he squeezed his body in next to her, his chest against her uninjured arm. He pulled her into him and lay with her as she cried herself to sleep.

45

Four and a half years later.

A gentle breeze blew as Andy walked through the tall grass of the field. She stuck a hand out and ran it over the dancing blades. Tilting her head up towards the sky, she felt the sun's warmth kiss her cheeks. The clean air, scented with lilac, filled her lungs.

She smiled at herself, amazed at the peace she felt as she took in her surroundings. There was a time she didn't know if she would survive if she stayed in this place.

After that night in the barn with Braxton, things had been almost impossible. She woke up every night drenched in sweat, the visions of what happened turning into a terrible nightmare. Every night the same thing would happen, Eric would wrap his muscular arms around her and pull her to his chest. He would bury his lips in her hair and whisper to her, "It wasn't real. I'm real. This is real and you are safe."

The nearest trauma therapist had been an hour away, but each week, on one of his days off, Eric would drive her. He would sit in the waiting room and thumb through a boring magazine, or doom scroll on his phone while she unpacked every emotion that lingered when she remembered that night.

It took time, but eventually she was challenged to go into the barn. She had stood outside the door, drenched in sweat but still shivering. She was breathing fast and fighting the nausea that was growing within her. She had nearly turned around when she had felt Eric's warm fingers thread through hers, giving her the strength she needed.

With his hand in hers, she opened the door and walked over the threshold. She had made it a few steps closer to the bloodstains on the concrete floor before she crumpled into a heap of tears, but he was there. He knelt on the floor beside her and pulled her tight against him. The sound of his beating heart and warmth of his body against hers had calmed her.

After her wound healed, she had an ugly, quarter sized scar on her shoulder. A permanent reminder of the attempt on her life. The first time she and Eric had been intimate after her injury, she had been so insecure.

That night, both of them had been hungry for each other, for release. He had pressed her against the wall of the kitchen and kissed her, his tongue exploring her mouth, causing a moan to escape her lips as she pushed her hips against his. She was filled with desire and heat coursed through her. He started to remove her shirt as he moved his mouth down her neck and she stopped.

"Is it too soon?" He asked, pressing his forehead against hers, dragging his knuckles along her jaw as they both breathed hard. "Do you want to stop?"

"No," she said, her breath still coming fast. "I want this, I just...can my shirt stay on?" He had pulled far enough away from her to look into her eyes, and she saw the confused look on his face.

"We can do whatever you are comfortable with, Andy, but why?" he continued stroking her jaw, and she bit her bottom lip, searching for the right words.

"My scar," was all she could mutter in the end.

He took her face in both of his hands. "Andy, do you trust me?" he asked. She nodded in response.

"More than anyone," she whispered. He slid a hand under her shirt, stoking the embers within her. He brought his mouth down to hers again as his fingers traveled up her stomach. His lips found her ear, and he nipped her earlobe.

"I love, and will always love, every single part of you," he whispered into her ear. "Can you let me prove it to you?" They locked eyes again and her heart started beating faster. She nodded once again.

"Trust me," he whispered. She nodded and closed her eyes tight. He unbuttoned the flannel shirt she wore, sliding it down her arms and catching her hands in his when she moved to cover her shoulder with them.

She saw him looking at the spot, worried that he would be disgusted by it. Instead, the corners of his mouth turned up, and he pressed his lips to the scar. His lips almost felt like butterfly wings grazing her skin.

"Nothing can ever make me stop loving you, or wanting you, or make me stop believing you are the most beautiful thing that has ever happened to me," he said in a voice just above a whisper.

"This," he said, rubbing his thumb over her scar, "Is a reminder of how strong you are Andy. It is a testament to how brave you are, of how lucky I am to still hold you in my arms. I love this part of you like I love every other part. Please, don't hide any part of you from me."

Tears spilled down her face, and he wiped them and kissed each of her cheeks before dropping his lips back to her mouth. She put her arms around his neck and held him as tight as she could against her body. She had run a hand up his bare back and into his hair, trying to pull him even closer before he lifted her into the air.

She remembered that night fondly, a smile on her face as the images of him and the feelings of pleasure he had given floating into her consciousness when a small voice broke her thoughts. "Mama!"

She glanced up and saw the owner of the voice, a little girl with bright blond hair and matching, bright blue eyes toddling toward her through the grass. She fell once, her two-year-old legs having a hard time in the tall grass, but she righted herself. Andy laughed and ran toward her, scooping her up in her arms and planting kisses on her round cheeks.

"I told her to wait for you, but since she takes after her mother, she is pretty impatient," Eric said.

When she looked at him, her breath stuck in her throat. He was still as handsome as ever, maybe even more so. His broad shoulders and muscular frame were the same, but there was something extra in his eyes that hadn't been there when they first met. Fatherhood looked good on him.

He approached the two of them and kissed the little girl on the top of her head before pressing his lips against Andy's. He still evoked desire in her, even with a simple kiss. "Productive day?" He asked as his lips brushed her ear.

"Yes, very," she responded, smiling and planting a kiss on his cheek and interlocking her fingers with his.

"Annie and I can visit you in your studio tomorrow to see what you've been up to," he said, as they walked back towards the house together.

Carl, Romeo and Eric had convinced her to take time away from the ranch after she had been shot. To heal, both mentally and physically. What she hadn't known was that Margie had started a website for Andy, posting pictures of her work. Eric had also called in a favor to his mom, who talked to her friend, the owner of an art gallery.

Before she had known it people were asking to buy her paintings. She was getting requests for commissions, too. She started painting so much that they built a small shed behind the house that would be her studio.

Since the day she was hurt, she hadn't worked on the ranch. She still did the behind the scenes, bills, orders, and of course rancher poker nights, but Carl and Romeo took care of the day-to-day responsibilities in her stead.

That night, after they put Annie to bed, Andy poured them each a glass of whiskey. She had found Eric on the chair in the living room looking at his phone. "Are you reading that article about yourself again?" she asked, not able to hide her smile.

"No," he replied. He had recently solved a huge drug trafficking case, the likes of which the tri-county area had never seen. "But I would just to see his smug face in that mugshot again," he added, smiling now.

"I knew Frank Miller was scum, but I never figured he'd be involved in anything like that," Andy said, putting the glasses on the table beside him and settling herself into his lap. She clasped her hands behind his neck as he looped his arm around her waist.

She pulled his face to hers, kissing him. When his lips parted, she slipped her tongue into his mouth and then bit his bottom lip, eliciting an encouraging moan from him.

"Mrs. Grayson," he whispered against her lips, "What am I going to do with you?"

She kissed him again and then smiled. "I have a few ideas..."

ACKNOWLEDGMENTS

Foremost, thank you, the reader, for giving Troubled Summers a chance. If you enjoyed this book, I would be so grateful if you would drop a review on your favorite platforms. It doesn't have to be detailed or long, but these reviews are integral for Indie authors to keep doing what we love!

Second, I want to my best friend Julie for pushing me. Without her support, encouragement and weekly walks, I would have never made it this far.

Last, I want to thank my very first ARC reader, my grandma. She sent me texts every day full of feedback and love that helped keep me going when imposter syndrome was rearing its ugly head.

ABOUT THE AUTHOR

Addison Elizabeth drinks too much coffee and doesn't sleep enough. She grew up with a passion for writing and studied something totally unrelated in college. She worked in the corporate world before deciding to pursue this writing thing. When she's not writing, she has her hands full with two young, active daughters and is fully immersed in soccer mom life. She has spent most of her life in the American Midwest and absolutely uses the term "Ope."

For information on future releases and sneak peeks, follow her on Instagram @addisonelizabethwrites or visit www.addisonelizabethcreates.com